HAKUDA
PHOTO STUDIO

HAKUDA
PHOTO STUDIO

Her Taeyeon

Translated by Shanna Tan

JOHN MURRAY

First published in Great Britain in 2025 by John Murray (Publishers)

4

Originally published in Korea in 2022 by Dasan Books Co., Ltd.
Published by arrangement with Eric Yang Agency

A CIP catalogue record for this title is available from the British Library

Paperback ISBN 9781399823470
ebook ISBN 9781399823487

Typeset in Sabon MT by Hewer Text UK Ltd, Edinburgh
Printed and bound in Great Britain by Clays Ltd, Elcograf S.p.A.

John Murray policy is to use papers that are natural, renewable and
recyclable products and made from wood grown in sustainable forests.
The logging and manufacturing processes are expected to conform
to the environmental regulations of the country of origin.

Carmelite House
50 Victoria Embankment
London EC4Y 0DZ

www.johnmurraypress.co.uk

John Murray Press, part of Hodder & Stoughton Limited
An Hachette UK company

The authorised representative in the EEA is Hachette Ireland,
8 Castlecourt Centre, Dublin 15, D15 XTP3, Ireland (email: info@hbgi.ie)

I

The Holiday Is Almost Over

The cobalt-blue sea stretched out from the sandy beach and fluffy clouds hung high in the sky. Under the midday sun, the water sparkled.

'I don't want to go home.' Jebi sighed, her mood as heavy as the backpack pressing on her shoulders. All around her tourists were posing for photos in colourful beachwear. The air hummed with their happiness. Jebi thought back to when she'd first arrived at Jeju Island: she'd enjoyed herself just the same, then.

Has it been a month already? It feels like yesterday. A surge of sadness welled up in her chest at the thought of bidding goodbye to the summer.

'Come on, hurry up!' a woman carrying a neon-yellow surfboard shouted, as she brushed past Jebi.

'Hold on!' her companion yelled back.

Grinning, the first woman, kitted out in a black wetsuit, headed towards the sea. Dropping the board flat on the water, she positioned herself stomach-down on it, beginning to paddle out over the swell.

Jebi shaded her eyes. As a wave approached, the woman stood up, spreading her arms and crouching a little to lower her centre of gravity.

Those swimming nearby turned to watch her. Someone whistled and, as if on cue, the water surged. The woman rode the curve gracefully and then, before Jebi could blink, she had twisted her body so that she was doing a handstand on the board.

As the wave broke, she fell and its white crest washed over her.

Loud cheers from the watchers on the beach echoed in Jebi's ears.

'So cool. I wish I could do that.'

Jebi looked down at her bare feet. They made a light depression in the wet sand as the clear water sloshed gently around her ankles.

The trainers dangling from her hand felt extra cumbersome that morning. Just then her phone buzzed. *Who's texting me?* she wondered, fishing out the phone from her pocket with difficulty.

It was Bora, her colleague from the photo studio in Seoul.

—About staying at my place . . . I don't think I can put you up anymore :(Sorry, Eonnie!

Like an anemone in shock, Jebi felt her insides shrivel. *Wait, what? At least tell me why.* Flustered by this sudden change in her plans, she felt heat rising to her face.

Her phone buzzed again.

—My boyfriend hates it when he can't come over anytime he wants >_<

2

'Since when did she have a boyfriend?' Jebi murmured under her breath. *Ah . . . The arrogant prick.*

Right before the trip, she'd noticed something going on between Bora and the new photographer at their studio. Sensing that he was pretty full of himself, Jebi had warned her friend not to get too close to him, but it looked like she'd gone ahead anyway.

'As usual, falling way too hard, way too fast.' Jebi chuckled drily.

She was about to start grilling Bora about it by text when something hard slammed into her suddenly, hitting her right in the eye. 'Ow!' she cried out as, knocked off balance, the weight of her bag pulled her backwards in the shallow water.

Gasping with shock, Jebi half rolled, half crawled back onto the sand. She'd once almost drowned in kindergarten while playing in water. The incident left her traumatised and she had not swum in the sea since then. While she loved the beach, it had taken her a good few days on this trip even to work up the courage to paddle.

'What the—!' A man in swimming trunks was massaging his forehead angrily as he glared down at Jebi.

Dazed, she blinked. What was happening? The man, and everything else around her, was black and white. 'Oh my god, my eyes!' Slumped on the sand, Jebi pressed the heels of her hands into her eyes. 'What were you *doing?*' she yelled at him.

'Aren't you going to apologise?' snarled the man.

'Me, apologise! What about you?' Her vision was still monochrome. Beginning to panic now, Jebi continued

3

rubbing her eyes with one hand as she felt for her phone in her pocket and pulled it out.

It wouldn't switch on.

'My cards! My plane ticket!' She shook the phone desperately, praying that it would come back to life.

The black screen stared back at her.

'Oh no, no, *no*. This can't be happening!'

The man continued to stare down at her. 'How about looking where you're going? Bloody backpackers!'

'Hey, your forehead's all red!' The man's companion said to him. She looked to be the same age as him – in her mid-twenties – her pink ponytail swishing around her shoulders. She turned to Jebi: 'We should sue you!'

Pink?

Phew, she could see colours again.

'You should look where *you*'re going!' Jebi retorted as she tried to stand up, the soaking-wet weight of her backpack making it nearly impossible.

'It's not like *you* did.'

Jebi couldn't think of a retort.

The pink-haired woman tugged on the man's arm. 'Come on, babe. Let's not spoil our day.'

'You're right.' Turning angrily on his heel, the man stalked away, his girlfriend stumbling after him.

Jebi could feel several pairs of eyes watching her from under beach umbrellas. Mortified, she scrambled up. Seawater streamed from her backpack down her legs.

Keeping her head down, she walked a few paces before breaking into a run, her uneven breathing and pounding heart loud in her ears.

Wanting to put as much distance as she could between herself and the humiliating scene, she turned a corner flanked by tangled weeds, not looking back until she reached a deserted spot. She'd left the sand behind entirely.

After making sure no one was around, she slumped down on some large basalt rocks. Her waterlogged backpack was heavier than ever. She set it down, and finally let the tears burst out of her.

2

The Photo Studio on the Cliff

'I'm starving.'

Jebi took out her phone to search for a café nearby, only to remember that it was dead. She wasn't even sure if it could be repaired.

'*I* should've insisted he pay to replace it,' she murmured, touching the black screen.

Wondering what the time was, Jebi looked around, but there was not a soul in sight.

Sighing, she stood up. Her hair and shirt had dried in the wind, but she could feel the moisture from the backpack soaking through as soon as she slung it back on. Recalling that there was a bus stop in front of the guesthouse, she was about to head back the way she'd come when she stopped in her tracks. Those people at the beach would still remember her. And what if she ran into that man again?

Instead, Jebi turned and headed in a different direction, along a road leading inland. As she went, she reached an arm behind her, unzipping a pocket of her backpack and fishing out her wallet. Since her phone was dead, she'd need some cash for the bus fare.

Carefully, she peeled apart the wet notes. 'No! Only seven thousand won—?' *Never mind.* As long as she made it to the airport, things should work out. She could get her phone fixed there, and then pay the repair fees with her digital wallet and access her plane ticket.

Leaving the coastal area behind, she walked up the asphalt road, her wet shoes squeaking. She slowed down a little. *Hmm . . . but where should I go back to? I don't even have a place to stay in Seoul anymore.*

The image of Bora's face floated across her mind, all dewy-eyed over her new boyfriend.

'Urgh, seriously? Putting a man before her friends!' Jebi shook her head.

I'm sick of watching other people be happy.

On the day she'd written that in her diary, Jebi had quit her job at the photo studio.

Seeing young couples and their adorable babies depressed her, and she hated the way the photographers ordered her around.

When will I get to be the main character in my own life?

The thought had hung over Jebi on the train ride home every evening. Until one day, she had chanced upon a billboard featuring beautiful Jeju Island. Jebi had made up her mind in that moment. Life and work had been so draining; she deserved to pamper herself a bit. *Jeju Island, here I come.* And not just a weekend getaway – she would spend the summer there.

Jebi had gone ahead and cancelled the lease for her studio flat straight away. It had come fully furnished, so there wasn't much packing to do. It was time to travel and explore all the exciting possibilities that the future held. She imagined returning to Seoul, refreshed and ready to find a new job and start a new chapter in life. And until her first pay cheque came in, she could sleep on Bora's couch.

Initially, Bora had been reluctant, but after much wheedling from Jebi – who promised to bring lots of presents from Jeju and contribute generously to the daily expenses on top of rent – she had given in.

And that was how Jebi had come to spend a month in Jeju.

As she followed the winding path along the coastline, Jebi thought back over her time on the island.

Her trip had begun perfectly. She visited the local library religiously every day. Sitting in the reading room, overlooking the beautiful library's gardens and the sea, she had pored over books like *Welcome to Your Twenties* or *A Guide to Personal Finances for the Twenty-Something Woman*, and *101 Habits to Boost Your Self-Esteem*, diligently copying out lines of wisdom and nuggets of advice.

But the beauty of the island soon distracted her, and instead of reading, she found herself posing for selfies with the books against the gorgeous landscape and posting them on Instagram.

Her bucket list had included learning to swim and surf, but in the end, she had chickened out. She'd imagined herself trying all kinds of new things, but instead all she'd done was to watch from the beach as others took to the waves. Her grand plan of hiking up to the Baengnokdam Lake on Hallasan Mountain also fell through: she'd been overly confident, picking the notoriously difficult Gwaneumsa Trail. A third of the way into the hike she had given up, and the climb back down was so vertiginous that she had had to crawl on all fours. When she'd finally made it to the foot of the mountain, her legs had been shaking uncontrollably.

Neither did she complete the Olle Trail that circumnavigated the whole of Jeju Island. Her trainers hadn't survived the rough hike on Hallasan, so she'd had to visit the city centre for a new pair. There, she'd been distracted by the beautiful shops and cafés. Jebi found herself going back again and again to enjoy afternoon teas and to sample mouth-watering local specialities at the famous restaurants.

Her posts on Instagram had got hundreds of likes, which spurred her on to keep up the café and restaurant hopping. Before she knew it, she'd blown her budget for the trip and even dipped into the living expenses that she'd set aside for the coming months.

Even if she could stay at Bora's place, Jebi wouldn't be able to keep her promise to share the expenses.

I suppose I can use my credit card. But whatever I earn will have to go straight to clearing the debt. I'll be falling right into that vicious cycle that finance books warn of. But what choice do I have? The first thing I'll have to do back in Seoul will be to rent a tiny room at the gosiwon and get a job. Work hard, scrimp for a couple of months, pay off the debt . . . But will anyone hire me?

Jebi felt a chill running down her spine. Her month on the island had passed by in a flash, and she was still the same old her. Nothing had changed for the better. She hadn't improved her English, nor had she picked up any new skills.

I'm stuck in a rut.

No employer would ever count a month-long getaway as 'career experience'. In the end, it would be back to kindergartens or studios specialising in baby photos for her.

Having studied early childhood education at a community college, the only thing Jebi was remotely good at was handling children.

If only I'd taken some classes from other faculties.

And getting a job wasn't even the most pressing issue: she didn't have a place to stay. There was no one she could depend on. Her parents had divorced when she was a child and that was the last that she'd seen of them. And last winter, her grandmother, who had brought her up, had passed away. Though she was never the most affectionate person, at least she had provided for Jebi. Jebi would have loved to stay on in her grandmother's rented apartment but it had been subsidised housing, the kind that had to be given up once the original tenant died.

Thankfully, Jebi had been earning her own income by then, so she'd been able move into a small, one-room studio. But now she'd rashly cancelled the lease.

Maybe there's a job somewhere that comes with bed and board . . . That way, she'd be able to save on some rent. But would she even qualify for that kind of job?

Lost in thought, Jebi had no idea how long she'd been walking. The asphalt road had petered out to concrete ground. She stopped in front of a banner.

WELCOME TO GIANT OCTOPUS VILLAGE!

Raising a hand to shade her eyes, Jebi squinted at the words. They were written in the island dialect. After a month in Jeju, Jebi was beginning to pick up some words and phrases. The sign must've been there for some time as it was torn in several places – likely weathered by the dry, gusty wind – the letters barely discernible.

Her gaze landed on the jangseung – a village guardian – next to it. The totem seemed to be carved out of the dark basalt common to the island. Staring back at her was a round head with fierce eyes, and hair that stuck out like a sea urchin's prickles. It had a thick neck that was also long, like a giraffe's, from which hung some kind of ornament – was it the fin of a cutlassfish? And instead of legs, eight thick arms were rooted in the ground.

Jebi read the sign next to it.

Mulkkureok is Jeju dialect for 'octopus'. Daewang Mulkkureok village – Giant Octopus village – boasts of the best catches of octopuses on the entire island. Since the Joseon dynasty, we've been famed for producing the best quality gifts, fit for a king. According to Gyuhap

Cheongseo – *the encyclopaedia detailing advice and knowledge for women – the egg of the giant octopus is a rare and precious medicine. The octopus is known to be a highly intelligent animal. According to fables passed down for generations, a giant octopus once saved a haenyeo – the female divers of the island – from drowning, while the gaps in the coastal sand dunes are believed to be tracks left behind by the giant octopus. Every year, the village observes a closed season when the hunting of octopuses is forbidden. To pray for a bountiful harvest during open season, a mulkkureok festival is held . . .*

'Giant Octopus village?' Jebi scanned the rest of the text, cocking her head at the last sentence.

Put your hand into the octopus's mouth and make a wish. It'll come true.

'Mouth? This thing has a mouth?' She studied the stone statue. Seeing nothing that remotely resembled a mouth, she shrugged and walked away. A few steps later, she paused and turned back. Running her hands over the jangseung, she found a narrow slit hidden among its arms. She slipped her hand into the crevice and closed her eyes.

The stone had been warmed by the sun and Jebi could feel the heat spread to her body. And in that instant, a curious feeling enveloped her, as if she were being lifted into the air.

Her eyes flew open. 'Weird,' she muttered to herself.

Even as she walked away, she couldn't help but steal more glances at it.

Turning at a hairpin bend in the road, Jebi found herself at the foot of a slope that seemed to end at a sharp precipice. On the cliff edge sat a white, two-storey shop-house.

'Hakuda Photo Studio? I was hoping for a café . . .'

Jebi had huffed and puffed her way up the hill to the building. Panting, she wiped the sweat off her forehead and looked around. Two palm trees stood tall in the garden. Climbing the stone wall were sky-blue hydrangeas in full bloom. In the distance, she could see the brilliant blue sea.

Jebi tugged at her sweaty shirt and fanned herself. Cautiously, she walked through the gate. Through the window, the interior looked like a typical café. A clock on the wall pointed to half past two.

If I set off soon, I should still make my 4 p.m. flight.

Written on the glass door was a drinks menu: coffee, craft beer, homemade tangerineade. Feeling even thirstier than before, Jebi grabbed the handle and pushed open the door.

Inside, the shop was completely deserted, yet there was music playing and she smelt coffee. Was she right that there was no one here?

Jebi walked towards a table with a view of the ocean. She'd wait for the owner to return; they must have simply stepped out for a while.

The moment she put down her backpack, she heard a baby crying. Jebi looked up, her back stiffening as she glanced around cautiously. Still no one.

But, as she began rooting around in her bag to find her wallet, she heard a voice.

'Ooh, cutie-poo, peek-a-boo!'

Jebi turned her head sharply. For the first time, she noticed the stairs in the corner of the room. The voice had seemed to drift down them. Slinging her backpack over her shoulder, Jebi found herself walking towards the stairs if they were exerting a magnetic pull on her.

When she emerged onto the first floor, she saw a tall, broad-shouldered man. He was bending over, perspiration soaking through his blue shirt. A spotted puppy was sniffing around his feet.

The man was smiling awkwardly as he tried to soothe a crying baby cradled in a young couple's arms.

At the sight of an intruder, the puppy barked. The man turned, his eyes widening in surprise.

Wow, he's cute. Totally my type . . . No, Jebi. Now's not the time.

'I'm so sorry. We're in the middle of a shoot. Could you give me a moment, please?' The man nodded towards the couple and then, seeing she hadn't moved, spoke again: 'Ah, no, don't wait here. Please go downstairs and enjoy a cold drink from the fridge. Take anything you want. Sorry, I'm a little understaffed right now. My apologies. I'll be with you in a moment.'

'Erm, I . . .' Not knowing what to say, Jebi quietly went back down the stairs.

Anything I want? Jebi looked around the café. On a small corner table was a jug of iced water with slices of lemon floating in it. She poured herself a glass to quench her thirst before looking at the price list stuck to the drinks cooler. The tangerineade was the most expensive, and she was about to choose that when she hesitated. Pursing her lips, she ended up reaching for a can of coke.

With the cold drink in hand, she slowly walked around the café – or should she call it the photo studio? The shopfront boasted a large window facing the ocean. On the other side of the room was a much smaller window with a partial view of the palm trees and the hydrangeas. Photo frames decorated the walls of the café, so that even though it was small, the space didn't feel stuffy at all.

Jebi took a closer look at the photos. Having worked for eleven months in a photography studio, she was quite proud of her artistic eye. *Well, when it came to baby photos, at the very least.* On the left of the door was a photo that appeared to have been taken at the village entrance: Jebi recognised the octopus totem statue. Her gaze slid over to the next photo, which was of a group of women in white looking out to sea. Against the dark coastline, the white sand dunes they were standing on looked like fresh snow; the scene was solemn, peaceful, as if the women were sending off someone – or something. In the next frame was a photo of a bunch of freshly dug peanuts. The dark soil was still damp, but from the carefully focused details of the image, Jebi could almost feel the heat radiating from the ground. She glanced next at a photo of freshly caught sea urchins, and a man with a big armful of carrots. Captured in the last frame was the spotted puppy she'd met upstairs, snuggling next to its mother. The photo looked like it had been taken some time back. Unlike her newborn, the older dog had a black glossy coat, and she was curled up protectively over the puppy, nuzzling it with her nose.

These are pretty good. Jebi could tell that the photos had barely been edited.

She sipped her coke. Upstairs, the baby was still crying.

Just as Jebi was getting worried, she heard a scampering of paws. The puppy had come downstairs and was now barking at her feet. '*Woof!*'

'Would you like some too?'

Jebi crouched down and was about to dribble some drink onto the floor when a thought stopped her. Was it okay to be offering a carbonated drink to a dog?

'Never do anything you are unsure of. Rule number one of surviving in society.' Remembering the tone of the photographer she'd worked with when she first started out, a man who'd yelled at her whenever he felt like it, Jebi shuddered.

Pursing her lips, she poured some water into a paper cup instead and held it out to the puppy. '*Woof!*' It came forward and lapped up the water noisily.

Looks like I've gained its trust, Jebi thought. 'Good doggy. Growing up well, even without your mama.' She stroked its fur.

The baby upstairs was now wailing at the top of her lungs.

'For goodness' sake!' Jebi couldn't stand it any longer. She headed towards the stairs, followed by the big-pawed puppy.

Upstairs, Jebi saw that the baby was turning purple in the face while the young couple hovered anxiously, unsure of what to do.

The photographer cast a quick glance at Jebi. The front of his shirt was soaked through, and beads of sweat ran down his cheeks.

Meanwhile, the young puppy, oblivious to what was going on, was zooming around the room.

'Perhaps you could come back another—'

Jebi interrupted the photographer mid-sentence. 'Do you have a muslin?'

'If you need napkins, they're on the counter,' he replied. His tone was polite, but Jebi could tell that he was annoyed.

'Nope, I mean a baby's muslin cloth.' Jebi turned to the baby's mother. 'You have one, right?'

Taken aback at being spoken to, the mother cast a quick glance at the photographer before rummaging in her bag.

Jebi took it. 'May I?' She held out her arms.

The young couple hesitated for a moment before passing their child to Jebi. With a bright smile, she gathered the baby to her and gently lay her down on the rug. The baby screamed and struggled. Jebi quickly checked her diaper before picking her up again to pat her back.

'When was the last time she was fed?'

'An hour ago. I breastfed her before coming here.'

'So she's not hungry.' Jebi took a closer look at the baby's clothes. She was dressed in beautiful summer knitwear, but the material was rather rough, and Jebi could see that the skin around her armpits was red.

Jebi folded the thin material of the muslin and slipped it through the armhole of the baby's top. She did the same for the other armpit, and with the baby in her arms, she slowly crossed the studio to the standing air conditioner, lowered the temperature and increased the fan speed. 'Ohhh, you must be hot,' she cooed, rocking the baby gently. 'Your armpits are hurting, right? Poor baby. Is that why you're cross?'

Gradually, the baby's cries subsided. Sensing that she was still upset, Jebi hugged her close, patting her gently. Then she looked up, nodding a smile at the young couple, who returned it.

The photographer was sitting down and mopping his sweat with a handkerchief, his eyes wide with gratitude.

When the baby had calmed down, Jebi returned her to her parents. Back in her mother's arms, the baby didn't cry, but her tiny features were still scrunched up.

Jebi turned to the photographer. 'I think you can start now. She's a little tired. Best to work quickly!'

The couple hugged the child and got into position as the photographer picked up his camera.

'What's her name?' Jebi asked.

'Yoona,' said her mother.

'Yoona! What a pretty little thing you are!' Jebi tickled the baby's cheeks with a corner of the muslin.

Yoona gave a gurgle of laughter and, immediately, her parents broke into wide smiles. *Click, click.* The photographer pressed the shutter.

'I'll deliver the images to the bakery when they're ready,' the photographer told the couple when the shoot ended. He bowed his head again, looking apologetic.

'Thank you,' the woman replied. Yoona was fast asleep in her dad's arms.

The photographer went with the couple to the door and, when he returned, dipped his head in Jebi's direction. 'Thank you so much. You've done me a huge favour.'

'If you'd like to return the favour,' Jebi said, smiling, 'you can tell me where to catch the airport bus from.'

His smile faltered. 'Oh . . . you aren't here for a photo?'

'Ah, no . . . the thing is . . . I dropped my phone in the sea . . .' Jebi replied vaguely.

'What time is your flight?'

'It's—'

'—wait! What time is it?' The photographer frantically checked his watch. 'No! I need to be somewhere, now!'

'Oh, if you could just tell me how to get to the—'

'We'll sort that out. Let's go!' He threw open the door.

'Wait! I have a flight to catch—'

'I'll book you on another one!' With that, the man grabbed Jebi's wrist and pulled her through the door.

The puppy wagged its tail and attempted to follow.

'No. Bell, stay. Oppa will come back in a jiffy.'

Bell whined and tried to nudge her nose through the door crack, but the photographer pushed her back firmly, closed the door and turned the key.

Parked behind the palm trees was a motorcycle. Before Jebi knew what was happening, she had a helmet jammed on her head, the strap tightened, and then she was sitting behind the man, gripping his shoulders.

It was her first time riding pillion. The strong winds whipped her face as he sped down the road, and she screamed as the low stone walls, different-coloured roof-tops, plants and trees flashed past in a blur. Villagers who were out tending to fields and gardens looked up as they zoomed by.

In no time, they were at the coast. The motorcycle screeched to a halt by a breakwater, and the photographer got down quickly. Jebi put a tentative foot on the ground and dismounted unsteadily.

In the distance, a group of haenyeos had just surfaced from their dives and were wading back to the shore.

The photographer made a beeline for one of them and tried to take the net from her hands. 'Yanghee-ssi. That looks heavy, let me help,' the photographer said, switching effortlessly to the Jeju dialect.

Is that his wife? I knew it. Of course he's not single. Jebi felt ashamed for having felt butterflies.

The woman shoved him aside. 'Don't you use my dialect with me!' she snapped, grabbing her net back and slinging it over her shoulder.

One of the older haenyeos piped up. 'Yanghee-ya, don't be like that. It's okay to let a man help.' She gratefully handed her full net to him.

'Hear, hear! Don't put him down just because he's a mainlander,' another one said, giggling.

'You're only saying that because it's got nothing to do with you,' Yanghee retorted as she walked away.

Pulling her rubber swimming cap off, she shook her head and her long, beautiful hair tumbled down. The wetsuit clung to her, showing off her curving figure.

She stopped abruptly in front of Jebi. 'You're in my way.'

'Excuse me?'

'You're blocking the door.'

Jebi turned around, only to see that she was standing right in front of a changing room. She quickly moved to the side.

'Thank you so much!' the older haenyeos gushed as the man set their nets down gently. The fresh catch of urchins, abalones and octopuses glistened in the sunlight. In the hundred-metre walk from the shoreline to the changing room, his sky-blue shirt had become a dark ocean-blue from the nets' drips.

The haenyeos thrust a few giant clams into his hands. 'Take these. They'll be delicious steamed.'

Grinning, the man walked back to his motorbike and put them into his top box before turning to Jebi. 'Come on, let's go.'

On the ride back, she gingerly held his waist. Now that he was going more slowly, she could appreciate the scenery: the colourful flowers on the trees, the glowing tangerines, the mix of yellow and blue rooftops, even the weeds in the cracks of the stone walls; everything was beautiful in her eyes. Whenever they passed someone on the street or in their front gardens, he'd nod in greeting. Some returned his gesture, while most ignored him. The wind blew, carrying the smell of the sea from his sweat-soaked shoulders.

Suddenly a thought hit her. *We've only just met but that haenyeo dropped straight into speaking casually with me!* Jebi frowned. By rights, Yanghee should have spoken to her in formal Korean. *How rude*, she thought, with a sniff.

*

'Bell! Sorry we left you behind. Have you been a good girl?' The moment he opened the door, the man scooped the puppy in his arms. He turned to Jebi. 'I'm sorry. You must've missed your flight.'

Jebi's thoughts jolted back to reality as she glanced at the wall clock. 'Um. Not yet . . . but it's too late to head to the airport now.'

'Here, take my laptop and book the next flight. I'll take you to the airport,' he said, putting his laptop on the table by the window.

Jebi clicked into the airline website. Mulling over the options, she sighed. Her trip really was finally ending.

The man came back into the room, having changed into dry clothes.

Jebi watched him scribble something on a blank piece of paper and tape it to the glass door. Pretending to get a refill of water, Jebi glanced at the sign.

NOW HIRING:
ONE PHOTOGRAPHY AND CAFÉ ASSISTANT

Oh yeah. He said something about being understaffed earlier. Jebi's heart suddenly raced, but she reminded herself sternly: *You said no more photo studios!*

She refilled her paper cup and returned to the table. Outside the window, the ocean stretched out to the horizon.

'Um . . . do you do a lot of newborn photography here?' Jebi ventured tentatively. Her heart was still pounding.

'Nope, not really.'

From the fridge, he took out the bottle of tangerine-ade and poured some into a glass of filled with ice. He placed a peppermint leaf on top, stuck in a straw and held it out to Jebi. 'Try it. I made this from tangerines grown in the village.' She took the glass from him as he continued: 'The couple you saw live nearby too. They just moved here and are in the process of opening a bakery. It's been a whirlwind for them trying to settle down, especially with a newborn. They're the only young family here.'

Jebi nodded. Then: 'So . . . I saw your hiring notice.'

His eyes lit up. 'Aren't you here on holiday?'

'Yes, but I've come to the end of my trip.'

He deflated a bit. 'I'm not looking for short-term help, though. I need someone who can commit.'

Jebi shook her head. She liked Jeju, but she wasn't sure how long she could stay. She'd never kept a job for more than a year.

'But it's proving to be next to impossible to hire some-one here. So, if you can help out, even if it's for a while, I'll be grateful. How long do you think you could stay?'

Jebi tried to contain her excitement. 'I haven't decided. Maybe . . . three months?'

'Alright, send me your resumé. You can create one on my laptop.'

Please, everyone has one on hand these days.

Jebi logged on to her email, clicked on one of the many job application threads there and printed out the attachment.

'Your name is . . . Jebi?' He looked surprised.

'Mm-hmm.' She scratched her cheek awkwardly. She wondered what had surprised him. Perhaps he had never heard the name before, which could also mean swallow.

'And you were born in 1997 . . . a 97-liner?'

'Yep, I turned twenty-five this year.'

For a moment, the photographer looked deep in thought.

Is he having doubts? Jebi felt a stab of fear. Was she now past the age of jumping from one casual job to another?

'Where's your hometown?'

'Seoul.'

'Have you ever lived in Jeju?'

Jebi shook her head.

'Nor your parents?'

'No, not that I'm aware of.'

'I see.'

For a moment, there was silence.

Guess I'm flying back to Seoul.

Just as she had convinced herself that the job was a no-go, he spoke. 'I'm Lee Seokyeong.' He gave his family name first, as was customary. 'An 88-liner. I look forward to working with you.' He paused. 'You'll need a place to stay, I presume?'

'Yes . . .' Jebi's hands paused on the keyboard, and she averted her gaze. 'I—I'm really sorry, but the thing is . . . Can I ask for an advance on my pay? This is embarrassing, but I'm broke right now. I've spent all my money during my trip. My only credit card is in my mobile wallet, and when I tripped at the beach earlier today, my phone fell into the water and it's dead . . .' Mortified, she buried her face in her hands. *Why am I like this. He must think I'm pathetic.*

'I can cover the first month's rent for you . . . but on one condition.'

Jebi gulped and waited for him to continue.

'I know an old woman living nearby who has an extra room. I hope you can stay there. She may seem grumpy, but she's a real softie at heart. Because her house is old, she barely gets any bookings for her annex room. Please do me this favour.'

Jebi nodded, but anxiety gnawed at her. *Grumpy but a softie?* The principal at a daycare centre she had worked at had described herself as having a 'fiery temper but truly caring for her staff.' Jebi had rarely got to experience the care; as for the fiery temper, she'd borne the brunt of it every day. Would this woman be just as bad, or even worse?

Recalling her grandmother's sharp words and cold eyes, Jebi shivered. *But beggars can't be choosers.*

It was at this point that Bell came trotting up to her, and, with a wag of her tail, settled down next to her feet.

Seeing the puppy looking quietly up at her was all Jebi needed to make her decision. 'As you please.' She reached out to pick Bell up. The little dog curled up docilely in her lap, pricking up her ears as she looked out of the window.

Over the green-blue sea, the sky was painted a pastel pink.

3

A Discount for People Who Live Here

With the employment contract signed, Seokyeong gave Jebi a tour of the photo studio. She followed closely behind, cradling Bell in her arms.

The ground floor was the café that also functioned as a gallery and shopfront, with a small workroom at the back where Seokyeong worked on his images; upstairs was where he did the photoshoots. Out of the four rooms on the first floor, three were used for shoots with different backdrop set-ups, while the last one was Seokyeong's bedroom. At the end of the corridor was a toilet and shower. Everything was kept clean and tidy.

'This used to be a bed and breakfast. But the owners couldn't manage it any longer, so they had to sell.'

'Wow! Sajangnim' – now that he was her boss, Jebi had naturally switched to addressing him as such – 'How did you afford this place? Were you born with a silver spoon in your mouth?'

'Not at all.' Seokyeong scratched his head awkwardly. 'The building was put up for auction, and I got it cheap. A stroke of luck. But the first floor technically still belongs to the bank,' he finished, with a sigh.

The two of them took a quick tour of the rooftop, which boasted an open view of the sea.

Back in the café area, Jebi looked around her. 'If this was a Bed and Breakfast, how come it's all open-plan down here?'

He followed her gaze. 'Oh. Because I knocked the walls down, keeping only the key beams of the structure. I did the work myself – over ten months.' Seokyeong clasped his fingers together and mimicked swinging a hammer.

'Seriously? That's impressive.' Just then, Jebi's stomach rumbled loudly.

Seokyeong chuckled.

Thoroughly embarrassed, Jebi lowered her head.

Bell looked up and gave her chin a good lick.

Seokyeong cooked ramyeon, adding the three big clams that the haenyeo women had given him. A mouth-watering aroma filled the photo studio, and Jebi could barely keep still as she waited for Seokyeong to serve the noodles.

Bell, too, flopped on the floor, her tail wagging in anticipation. Sure enough, Seokyeong poured out kibbles onto a shallow dish, and topped it with thinly sliced clam meat. The moment he put it down on the floor, Bell buried her nose in it.

Likewise, Jebi pounced on the noodles as soon as Seokyeong picked up his chopsticks. It was the most delicious meal she'd had on the island.

Chewing the thick slices of clam meat, she glanced at the entrance. 'Is it okay to cook at the photo studio? Won't the customers mind the smell?'

Earlier, with a remote control, Seokyeong had turned off the main lights on the ground floor and switched on a smaller light next to the window. Now, he pressed a small, round switch below the window and a panel slowly opened with a *znnng*, inviting the cool sea breeze in.

Outside, purple waves gently pulled ashore before receding, and a silvery orb hung high above the sea.

'I'm actually going to turn this place into an integrated culture space.' Seokyeong dropped the last of his noodles and clam meat into his mouth before holding up the bowl and gulping down the soup.

'I'm sorry? An integrated what?'

'These days, you can't survive doing just one thing. That's why bookshops all double up as cafés now, and cafés also sell full meals and in-house merchandise.'

Jebi nodded. She remembered queuing up to get a recyclable tote from Starbucks.

'I want to make a living from photography. But it's hard to rely on shoots alone. I've thought hard about it and I'm going to turn this place into a photo studio, a café and a party venue.'

'A party venue?' Jebi asked as she swallowed her last piece of clam meat, savouring the burst of flavour in her mouth.

'Yup. So the clients can enjoy a photography exhibition at the gallery, do a shoot, and later, they can sit around in the café to chat as they view the photos. A party of delicious food, good alcohol and great conversations. I can take even photos of the party and give them to the guests as a free memento. What do you reckon?'

His slight faltering at the end of the sentence gave Jebi pause. He didn't seem very confident, but she knew how hard it was to make money with photography. The studio she'd worked at for the past eleven months was touted as one of the bigger players in Seoul, but even they struggled to make ends meet every month. Unless they managed to sell photoshoot packages worth millions of won, or expensive frames, they rarely turned a decent profit. But of course, customers had no idea how difficult things were.

Jebi also suspected that the studio she had worked for had got its marketing strategy all wrong in the first place. Most of the customers at the baby photo studio were new parents who'd come to redeem a free album of twelve photos: part of the partnership the studio had with gynae clinics and postnatal care centres. The idea was to attract the customers with a freebie and after the free shoot was done, the studio would show them how beautifully many of the photos had turned out and cajole them into buying the expensive packages. And if the customers stood firm, they'd push for them to buy at least the unedited photos, worth a few hundred thousand won.

But this hard-sell tactic had led to many disgruntled customers.

'Didn't you guys say it would be free?'

In her time there, Jebi had seen hundreds of angry couples. They'd come with their precious bundle of joy, expecting to make good memories, but ended up leaving, flushed with anger, after a shouting match with the manager.

Jebi had been sure they were approaching the customers in entirely the wrong way 'We shouldn't be offering these albums for free. Why can't we let the customers see how expensive it is to take a set of photos, and then they'll understand why we charge the way we do—?'

But whenever she made this point, Bora would only shrug and say, 'Yeah, I know, right?'

Jebi looked down at her bowl. She'd finished her noodles; only the soup was left. *Come to think of it, aren't photos similar to food?* If this porcelain bowl of noodles was priced at 7,000 won, it didn't just include the cost of the noodles and the seafood. To cook the dish in the first place, they'd need a kitchen, and a dining space to serve the noodles. Not to mention the water and gas bills. They'd also need other fresh ingredients, condiments, and a chef to cook it. It was the same with photos. A photo that cost 7,000 won didn't just include the price of photo paper. There was the rent of the studio, the expensive equipment and lighting, the occasional maintenance fees, and because their industry was sensitive to trends, the backdrops for the shoots needed to be updated regularly. Hiring a good photographer was also costly, not to mention the need for at least one employee to greet the customers. Of course, no customer would recognise that. They'd think that they could take the same picture with a phone camera – why bother spending that money? But it wasn't the same at all. Just like how she'd never be able to replicate this delicious ramyeon on her own.

'How long have you been running the studio? Is business good?' Jebi asked.

Seokyeong got up and began clearing the table. Jebi quickly followed him into the kitchen area but when she reached for the apron, he stopped her.

'I'll do the dishes. When you start work, we can take turns.'

Jebi nodded and stepped back.

Seokyeong put on some washing-up gloves and spoke over the sound of the water as he turned on the tap. 'About a month. Customers are few and far between – and they're all from the neighbourhood.'

Jebi's jaw dropped. Would he even be able to pay her a salary? He must be racking up a debt of at least two million won every month.

She pointed to the frames on display. 'Then where did those photos come from?'

Seokyeong looked over to where she was pointing. 'Those? Some of them I took for myself – like the statue of the octopus, and the photos from the mulkkureok festival. The rest I plan to sell online.'

'A festival . . . of octopuses?'

'Yeah. It's an annual festival in spring. It's fun. Jebi-ya, if you stay until then, you'll be able to experience it for yourself.'

That seems a bit presumptuous. She decided to change the subject. 'But those photos of the carrots and the peanuts . . . Product photos are hard to shoot, and expensive. Did you get properly paid for them?'

As he rinsed the bowls, he shrugged. 'Can't be too picky. I needed that work. In fact, I had to beg for it.'

'That's not the way to go!' Jebi's voice rose without her realising it. 'If you keep taking photos for free . . . I mean, you just can't!'

Seokyeong nodded. 'I know. But when you start something new, you basically have to pour money into it, right? It's the same in any industry, like how YouTubers start off by making free content. I'm just grateful that they trust an outsider like me with the work. I've been thinking about offering a permanent 30 per cent discount for people who live here.'

Jebi blinked. 'Sajangnim, you're not local?'

Putting the dishes on the drying rack, he shook his head.

'But you speak the Jeju dialect so well . . .'

'I learnt it. And, way back, I lived here for a bit with my parents.'

Seokyeong let his sentence hang in the air. Sensing the change in mood, Jebi quickly moved on to a new subject.

'There's something I've been wondering. What does "Hakuda" mean? Is it a Japanese word?'

'Aha!' Seokyeong smiled as he untied his apron. 'It's a Jeju Island word – from their dialect here. It means something like "I'll do it".'

'So . . . the "I'll Do It" Photo Studio?' Jebi frowned slightly.

Seokyeong laughed. He stood upright and gave her a little bow. 'I'll do my best for any shoot. That's what I hope the name tells people.'

After closing for the day, Seokyeong suggested that they take a stroll to look at the room Jebi would be renting, and take Bella out for a walk, too.

Under the full moon, the alleyways of the village were bright; Jebi could even make out the shapes of the waves in the distance. Feeling the sea breeze against her cheek, her heart thumped with anticipation. While she was a little anxious about meeting the grumpy old woman, worst-case scenario, she could move out after a month. Finally, she would have a roof over her head, and a job. She didn't have to leave beautiful Jeju Island, at least not any time soon. And right then, she was walking this countryside road with a cute guy!

Jebi remembered the motorbike ride back to the photo studio. His warm, muscled back . . . Suddenly, Bell skittered at her feet, as if to snap her back to reality.

'Bell, no.' Seokyeong held firmly to her lead.

Casting around for conversation, Jebi asked now: 'By the way, what breed is Bell?'

Seokyeong chuckled. As if not wanting Bell to overhear, he cupped his hand around his mouth and whispered, 'She's a countryside mix.'

'How do you mean?'

He laughed. 'Well, she's a St Bernard and Jeju dog mix.'

'Jeju dog?'

'Yeah, appearance-wise, they're quite similar to a Jindo dog, but Jeju dogs are native to the island. Purebreds are on the verge of extinction. The village head is a huge Jeju dog lover. He breeds them, and among his pure-breds, he's particularly fond of one named Soondeok – treats her practically like a daughter. But despite everything he tried, she wouldn't get pregnant. The vet couldn't find any issues with her health, either.' He chuckled again. 'The village head takes her out on daily walks and, one day, he took his eyes off her for a moment while he answered a phone call. When he discovered she was pregnant, he was ecstatic, thinking the mating with a Jeju purebred had been a success. Only when the puppies arrived did he realise something was amiss – they were all spotted. That was when he remembered seeing a St Bernard on the walk that day. You can imagine his disappointment.'

'Because the pups weren't purebred?'

'Yeah. Still, Soondeok is like his daughter, so of course he took care of her, even cooking her seaweed soup. With a good supply of milk, the pups grew up big and strong.'

'And then?'

'Hmm?'

'What happened to the pups?'

'Oh, the village head gave them away. They weren't purebred, so he didn't want to keep any.'

'And Bell?'

'I took some carrot photos for him, and he gave her to me.'

'Carrots? Oh, the photo on the wall.'

'Yeah, that's the village head . . .' Seokyeong paused. They had arrived at a house with a low blue roof. It was encircled by a stone wall, but there was no gate. In the garden stood a few tangerine trees. 'Mokpo Samchon, are you there?' Stepping into the front garden, Seokyeong called out respectfully.

Uncle Mokpo? Didn't Seokyeong say that it was an old woman living here? Jebi wondered.

'Who's there ?' came an answering voice.

'It's Seokyeong. From the photo studio,' he replied.

'What brings you here at this hour?'

The door to the stone house opened and an elderly woman stepped out. She had broad shoulders, and her voice carried a long way. Noticing Jebi, she gave her the once-over.

After Seokyeong explained Jebi's circumstances, the woman took the credit card he held out and, with a practised hand, completed the transaction on an app on her phone.

'Until the next full moon, that room is jibi's.' She pointed a finger at the annex.

'Jebi? Granny, how do you know my name?'

'Jebi what? I said "jibi"!' With that, she turned and went back inside.

'It means "you",' Seokyeong explained.

'Looks like it'll take me a while longer to really get used to the Jeju dialect,' Jebi said, as she and Seokyeong made their way over to the annex. As the old woman had gone back inside, the task of showing her around was left to Seokyeong.

'Oh. That's actually Jeolla Province dialect. Granny moved here from Mokpo after she married her husband. He was from here,' he said, as he inserted the key into the keyhole.

Jebi felt her stomach sink. It was already hard enough following the Jeju dialect – now she'd have to deal with someone who mixed it with Jeolla dialect too. Her head spun.

'The room's quite bare, but it's clean. And you can shower properly. I installed it myself.' Seokyeong smiled as he pointed at the rainfall shower in the bathroom.

Jebi didn't like the look of the bare stone walls in the shower – it was probably going to be a sauna in summer – but she didn't have much choice.

'Rest, and I'll see you at nine tomorrow.'

'Good night.' Jebi lugged her rucksack into the room.

Suddenly, a thought occurred to her, and she went back outside quickly. 'By the way, why did you call Granny "samchon"? Isn't that "Uncle"?'

'Oh, in Jeju, we use it to address our elders, it's an endearment.' He grinned. 'Gender doesn't matter.' Seokyeong waved, saying that he'd wait for her to go back into her room before he left.

Meanwhile, Bell was chasing her tail in the garden.

The next day, Jebi woke up early. Or rather, she was startled awake when something fell with a plop on her forehead. Feeling groggy, she raised a hand to feel what it was

The thing wriggled.

Screaming, she quickly pushed herself up, only to see a huge centipede on her pillow, its many legs squirming as it struggled to right itself.

Jebi jumped out of bed, shrieking and stamping her feet.

'Oh my! Goodness gracious! What on earth's going on?' Mokpo Granny dashed in, the master key in her hand.

'C-cen-cen . . .!' Unable to speak, Jebi pointed a shaky finger in the direction of her pillow.

Upon seeing what it was, Granny let out a sigh – clearly one of relief. Using a dustpan and brush, she quickly swept up the centipede and threw it out into the vegetable patch.

When she returned, she took out a roll of green adhesive tape from the drawer and began to examine the wall. 'Confounded creatures! They found a way in again,' she grumbled as she pulled out a length of tape and started plastering it over a hole in the wall that was already layered with old tape running across it in different directions.

Without bothering to apologise or to ask how Jebi had slept, Mokpo Granny looked at her askance and exclaimed, 'What's that smell?'

Emanating from Jebi's clothes and her backpack was a pungent, musty smell of damp. *Oh, right.* Jebi had been so exhausted the night before that she had only brushed her teeth before collapsing into bed.

Jebi jolted back to her senses. 'Granny, what time is it?'

The elderly woman jabbed a finger at the clock above the TV. 7:30 a.m.

'Phew. Enough time for a shower, and maybe I can do my laundry. Granny, is there a keonjogi here?' She remembered seeing a washing machine in the shower room yesterday.

'Dried jogi fish? We've got dried octopus, if you want.'

'I mean, a drying machine for laundry . . .' Jebi faltered as she slumped onto her bed again. With pitiful eyes, she looked up at her landlady. 'Um, I'm really sorry . . . but can I borrow some clothes?'

And that was how Jebi ended up in a white blouse and a long dark navy skirt, on the first day of her new job.

*

37

Looking at herself in the mirror after her shower, Jebi's eyes widened in horror. Overnight, a dark bruise had spread over her eye socket.

'Damn. I didn't know it was that bad . . .'

She had no choice but to also borrow one of the wide-brimmed sun hats that the villagers used when working in their gardens.

Lurid flower patterns decorating her head and, she hoped, hiding her black eye, she stepped outside. The night before, the alleyway had been dark, but now the sun shone so brightly that she had to squint. It was a clear day, with not a wisp of cloud in the sky.

Jebi stuck close to the stretch of stone wall, as if it might offer some camouflage. She flinched to the side each time she saw someone, earning her suspicious glances from them.

Seokyeong was writing at the counter when she pushed open the door of the studio. He put down his pen, looked up, and blinked. The next second, he broke out in uncontrollable laughter. 'Ha! Oh my, I'm sorry. Haha! Sorry, sorry . . .'

He was still laughing as he headed upstairs, returning a moment later with something that he held out to her.

He chuckled. 'Take off that ridiculous hat and wear these instead. What happened to your eye?.'

'I don't want to talk about it,' Jebi replied firmly.

With the oversized shades perched on her nose, Jebi started her cleaning duties. Carefully, she wiped the shelves where the equipment sat, and the café tables. Keeping the door wide open, she enjoyed the fresh breeze from the sea.

Meanwhile, Seokyeong was deep in concentration in front of his laptop.

'What are you looking at?' Jebi asked.

'The reservations. No customers today, I'm afraid.'

'May I take a look?' Jebi pulled off her apron and came to the table.

'Sure.' Seokyeong turned the laptop towards her.

Jebi quickly checked the website, the blog, and Instagram. Indeed, there were no enquiries. But there was also barely anything on the platforms – just a few photos, the same ones she'd seen in the shop.

Jebi let out a sigh. 'Why is the website so . . . basic?'

'Well, I only share the photos I'm happy with and so far, these are the only ones.' Seokyeong scratched his head.

'This won't do. You need to post every day, and multiple photos each time.' Surprised at how firm she sounded, Jebi cast a worried glance at her boss, afraid that he might take offense.

'Mm, is that so?'

Jebi couldn't tell if he was dismissing her suggestion or considering it.

She felt in her pocket but realised she'd left her phone in the annex. She needed to get it repaired, but it looked like she would only be able to go when the photo studio closed on Wednesdays.

Instead, she logged in to her personal Instagram account on the laptop.

'A thousand followers? Amazing!' Seokyeong exclaimed.

Jebi, despite wearing the oversized shades and her landlady's clothes, allowed herself a small smile of satisfaction.

It wasn't much, but compared to the photo studio's thirty followers, it was a lot.

'Leave it to me. Sajangnim, you focus on your photography; I'll handle the marketing side of things.'

Seokyeong's eyes widened, as if he wasn't sure whether to say yes or to refuse

Jebi went on the offensive. 'At this rate, you won't be able to afford my salary. And I don't suppose you want to stack up more debt!'

His face reddened. Then finally, he nodded. Jebi's heart pounded in her chest. She'd never done sales or promotion before, but she was not going to let that deter her. She felt energy course through her, and she sat up a little straighter.

Confidence . . . I've only read about it in books. Is this what it feels like? Jebi smiled to herself.

'By the way . . . you shot this?' Seokyeong asked, pointing at her feed.

'Hmm? Yep.' Jebi waved her hand. 'I know it isn't any good. I just snap photos for fun. I don't have any artistic sense, or anything—'

'No, no. I like the atmosphere of it, that's why I asked,' he explained. 'Do you enjoy photography?'

Jebi nodded.

'Then keep going. If you take a good one, I'll display it in the shop.'

Jebi stared at him in surprise, feeling her heart flutter. And this time, it wasn't because of his looks.

4

Seokyeong's Dream

'A phone that has been submerged in saltwater is unlikely to last long, even if we manage to revive it.' The technician spoke carefully. 'Since you've had it for four years, perhaps you might consider getting a new one.'

Jebi nodded and bought a basic smartphone on instalment.

Today was her first day off from the Hakuda Photo Studio and Seokyeong had kindly given her a ride to the repair shop.

The village head had agreed to watch Bell for the morning, and when, later, they had gone to fetch her, the puppy had been joyfully clambering all over her long-suffering mum.

Out in the carrot fields, the farmers, having spent the entire morning planting seedlings, were eating an early lunch in the shade.

After fetching Bell, the three of them headed back to Jebi's lodgings.

'That black dog was Soondeok, right?' Jebi asked, as she got off the motorbike.

'Yep.'

Seokyeong unzipped the dog carrier, and Bell immediately poked her head out, then jumped down and made a beeline for the garden.

'With all her pups gone, Soondeok had postnatal depression, so for a while, I brought Bell for a visit quite regularly. She's okay now, though.'

Jebi watched Bell bark and then, to her horror, begin digging at the lettuces in the vegetable patch. Before she could shoo the little dog away, Mokpo Granny had burst through the door and yelled, 'Cursed creature! Get away from my lettuces!'

Bell, unfazed, scampered away, tongue lolling.

Granny had prepared a delicious seaweed bibimbap, with top shell meat, a type of conch. After lunch, by way of thanks, Seokyeong helped to fix the hole in the wall.

The moment he pulled off the mess of tape, loose sediment fell out, along with a centipede.

Jebi, who'd been hovering at the door, screamed and ran out to the garden again.

Seokyeong reached out a gloved hand, picked up the wriggling creature and released it outside, Bell casting a wary eye at the multi-legged intruder and growling.

He bent down and patted the dog, reassuring both her and Jebi: 'It's because there is lots of fertile land in the area . . . And on the bright side, it means you don't get cockroaches in the house. The centipedes catch them all.'

'Ew! Does that mean I'll be seeing cockroaches next?'

'That's not the point . . .' He chuckled as he walked back into the room.

He applied a layer of silicone sealant, waiting for it to dry before pasting wallpaper over the hole. Granny had kept leftover pieces for this purpose.

'Centipedes love damp environments. Here, use this,' he said, taking a dehumidifier from a cupboard in the kitchen. 'Remember to empty the water out each time it fills up . . .' He smiled. 'And if you see a centipede again, don't panic. They rarely bite.' *But those legs! Who wouldn't freak out?*

Jebi smiled weakly back at him.

After Seokyeong left, Jebi logged into her Google Drive to download all her photos to her new phone.

A few months before, she had been scrolling on her phone when it had slipped out of her hand and bounced off the pavement. Clutching it tearfully, she had rushed to the nearest repair shop. No matter what, she knew she had to recover the photos saved in it; the thought of losing them forever too much to bear.

'The screen is beyond repair, but you're lucky – the memory chip is intact.' The technician's words had been music to her ears. 'Best to make a habit of backing up important photos regularly.'

Gripping her phone, Jebi had nodded her head vigorously.

Now, Jebi lay on the rough bedsheets, staring at the photos on her phone. Tears trickled from the corners of her eyes and wet the hair at her temples as she wept in silence. Sniffing, she opened Instagram instead.

In just four days, she'd grown the follower count for the photo studio tenfold. Seokyeong's look of surprise and delight when she'd told him this would be etched forever in her memory.

'Amazing! Time to celebrate!'

Jebi had shaken her head. 'Let's celebrate when we get our first booking from Instagram.'

Seokyeong had agreed, grinning.

What can we do to attract customers?

With the shop empty for days on end, Jebi spent the entire time mulling over that question. Sitting around idly wasn't an option. Only if the photo studio was doing well would she be able to stay there. She had to protect her job. Where else would she find a role where she liked the place, the work, and even the boss?

Of course, it wasn't like she didn't have any complaints about him: on the days the haenyeos went out to sea, he'd drop everything in a heartbeat, head for the coast and return whistling. Jebi found that behaviour unbecoming. Clearly, he went to help the haenyeo Yanghee with her nets.

Meanwhile, Jebi spent her time doing market research, scrolling through the websites of established photo studios. Because Seokyeong wanted the café to serve as a gallery, she also read up on photography exhibitions.

One day, on a whim, she decided to google his name, and her jaw dropped.

Jebi tackled Seokyeong the moment he walked in: 'Sajangnim! You won a photography award?'

Seokyeong, who had begun wiping a table, looked up in shock. 'H-how . . .'

'So it really was you! And first prize, no less!'

'Um . . . I mean—'

'We must put that up! And you bet I'm going to plaster it all over our social media!' Jebi grinned.

'Put *what* up?' Seokyeong stood up straight, dishcloth in hand.

'The certificate, of course! And a photo of you receiving the prize. Wait, we also need to display the award-winning work.'

'Um . . .'

'What's wrong?'

'I'm not sure the customers will like it? That photo is quite abstract.'

Jebi snorted through her nose. 'What they care about is whether you have credentials. They want to know if the person is a professional that's worth paying for. We're giving them the info they need.'

Wow, did that just come from me? Jebi was secretly rather pleased by her analysis. She pointed at the photos on display. 'And don't worry about it being abstract! You have other photos like these – the village head, Bell, Soondeok – that they can appreciate.'

'Really?' Nonplussed, Seokyeong started to mop his forehead with the dirty dishcloth.

Jebi opened the laptop and screenshotted the articles about the prize, as well as a photo of his award-winning work, immediately posting them on Instagram.

'And since we have an award-winning photographer in the house, we should bump up the prices . . .'

'Are you sure? The customers . . .' Seokyeong bit distractedly on the dishcloth.

Grimacing, Jebi plucked it from him. 'I'm sure you know the market rate.'

'But the customers we get are only here to take keepsake photos . . .'

'It's probably going to be hard at the start. But, Sajangnim, you take great photos. I'm sure the clients will come to appreciate your skills. Would you fetch me the certificate? It's upstairs, right?'

Seokyeong took a step backwards. 'Why?'

'I told you just now. We need to display it.'

'About that . . . umm. Bell! Where are you?' Seokyeong turned to look for the puppy, using the excuse to move towards the garden.

Jebi was not letting him get away with that, however, and moved quickly to block his way. 'Sajangnim, don't forget you need to pay my salary. Are you going to give it to the bank instead?'

With a sigh, he turned and slowly trudged up the stairs, returning with the certificate.

'You won a major award. What was the point in moving here to open this place, if you're going to be like this?' Jebi said absent-mindedly as she brushed dust from the frame.

'Be like this?' Seokyeong answered stiffly.

Jebi looked up. *Damn. I shouldn't have said it like that.* 'Um. What I mean is . . .'

'This kind of award is meaningless,' he snapped. 'I did have my days of being obsessed over accolades, of course . . . but it was just the lack of confidence of a fool.'

The lack of confidence of a fool. Chastened, Jebi turned the phrase over in her mind.

'I've chosen to be here in Mulkkureok village because I want to start a family and settle down. That's my dream. Does that satisfy your curiosity?'

Seokyeong turned and stalked upstairs.

5

Wild Bikers

Seokyeong and Jebi were arguing over where to display his certificate and the award-winning photo.

'I'm telling you, not the entrance. You're shoving it in people's faces.' Seokyeong tugged at the frame.

Jebi held on to it tightly. 'It's perfectly fine. They aren't going to be staring at it. Have you ever seen anyone actually pay attention to the PULL sign on the door?'

'Even less of a reason to hang it there, then! Since people aren't going to look at it.'

Exasperated, Seokyeong finally freed it from her grip.

'The point is to make it easy to find!' Jebi glared at him, frustrated. 'There's no better spot for it.'

Bell yawned from her corner, scratching her neck with her hind leg.

Leaning against the counter by the entrance a few hours later, Jebi opened the laptop. She'd improved the follower count by another hundred. She scrolled through several comments about wanting to take photos at the studio if they ever visited Jeju, but, so far, no one had made a booking.

Seokyeong, meanwhile, was wiping dust off his cameras with a microfibre cloth, refusing to catch Jebi's eye.

Behind the counter, the certificate and the award-winning photo hung on the wall.

At each tinkle of the octopus wind chime Jebi had hung over the door, they'd look up eagerly. But it was only the wind playing tricks. A fortnight had passed since she had started working there, but she had yet to see a single customer.

Jebi was getting anxious. She had even designed a brochure that could be printed and distributed at the airport, as a last resort for drumming up custom. Beside a beautiful panoramic view of the studio she'd taken on her phone, she had listed Seokyeong's impressive accolades.

Of course, he had no idea.

'Hello!'

The door opened suddenly and Seokyeong and Jebi jumped up, flashing bright smiles.

'Er, oops. Sorry to disappoint.' It was Yoona's dad – from the young couple Jebi had met on her first day there. He waved a paper bag in his hand. 'We're planning to launch a new item at the bakery – we've even designed special packaging for it. I'd love some feedback.'

He pulled out a box from the paper bag he was carrying. Given its rather dog-eared appearance, it looked like he'd been going around the village the whole morning.

'This yellow one here is the kumquat bun, the darker one is the octopus bun. We used octopus ink to get the colour, and there are slices of octopus meat in the filling.'

Jebi picked up a kumquat bun and bit into it. 'Mmm, this is delicious! So soft and sweet – I don't taste any of the bitterness of the seeds and skin.' She gave a thumbs up.

'We only use the flesh when making the jam. And the colour is from the gardenia fruit,' Yoona's dad explained.

Seokyeong put down the octopus bun after a bite. 'This tastes exactly like takoyaki. It's nothing special.'

Jebi glanced at Yoona's dad, who looked stricken.

'Haha.' He gave an awkward laugh. 'Is that so?'

'Maybe make it flatter and crispier? Or get creative with the shape. An octopus design would be nice.'

'Ah. I should, haha.'

'Oooh, what's this?' Jebi quickly jumped in. 'Looks like a snack.'

'Octopus crackers. Like prawn crackers, except we use octopus . . .' Yoona's dad cast an awkward glance at Seokyeong. 'Well, you could call it plagiarism again, I guess.'

Seokyeong, who'd taken one, nodded. 'Yeah, tastes just like the Jagalchi octopus snack you can get everywhere.'

'But the kumquat bun is truly delicious,' Jebi added hurriedly. 'An amazing creation!'

She grinned and gave two thumbs up this time. *I might be overdoing this.*

'Thank you.' Yoona's dad pulled his earlobe shyly. 'I heard you were working here. Yoona's mum wants me to tell you that anytime you're bored, feel free to drop by our place. She'd love to see you again.'

Jebi's shoulders drooped slightly. 'Oh, sure . . .'

'You should've heard my wife! She was singing your praises. How are you so good with babies?'

'She studied early childhood education, and she used to work at a photo studio specialising in newborn photography.' Seokyeong answered on her behalf.

'No wonder!' This time, it was Yoona's dad giving the thumbs up.

After he left, Jebi put the rest of the buns in the fridge. Yoona's dad had been generous: after making his rounds in the neighbourhood, he had still had two boxes left.

Jebi watched Seokyeong test the cameras that hadn't been in use for some time. He was always kind to Yanghee, to Bell, and even to her. Why was it that he'd been so rude to Yoona's dad?

'It must have taken courage to go around the village asking for feedback on his food. Why did you have to be like that?'

Seokyeong looked confused. A beat later, he let out a soft, 'Ah,' and nodded. 'Because Hajun Hyung is a dad. And that's his livelihood, his work.' Seokyeong suddenly turned the camera towards Jebi and pressed the shutter.

'What do you mean?' Surprised, Jebi belatedly raised a hand to hide her face.

'Just as these cameras have to function well for us to make a living, Hajun's bread must be excellent so that Yoona will grow up well and be able to do anything she wants . . . don't you agree?'

'Yes, I get it. Now, delete that photo!'

Seokyeong blinked. 'But this is a film camera.'

The wind chime tinkled again and they both turned at the same time. In the garden, the hydrangeas were still in full bloom but there was no one in sight. However, there was a faint noise, as if the ground were vibrating.

Seokyeong and Jebi exchanged glances.

'Bikers!'

Seokyeong ran out, still holding the camera. Jebi hurried behind.

It was a striking sight. A dozen motorbikes were cruising along the coast road, and in no time at all the pack was riding uphill, stopping in formation outside the garden. Among the bikes Jebi recognised a Harley-Davidson, a BMW, a Benelli and a Suzuki Hayabusa.

Seokyeong quickly put the viewfinder to his eye and pressed the shutter.

'A photo studio?' A petite, fifty-something woman exclaimed as she took off her silver goggles and helmet.

'Yep. But we checked, remember? They sell drinks here. You've got the memory of a goldfish!' a broad-shouldered woman of around the same age retorted. She removed her helmet and whacked down the kickstand of her motorbike with her sturdy red boots.

The first woman chuckled in embarrassment. 'Oh yeah, we looked it up on the map.'

'I'm dying of thirst.'

'I could eat a horse.'

The group of middle-aged women parked their bikes and made their way inside the photo studio. There was someone in a jumper with an embroidered tiger on the back, and another in a studded leather jacket.

A second later, a yellow Honda Super Cub sputtered up the hill. Parking her bike at the back, a woman in a plain windbreaker and cheap-looking hiking shoes took off her helmet and followed the others inside.

Recovering from their initial shock, Seokyeong and Jebi hurried after them. A couple of them leant casually against the counter, while the rest crowded around the drinks fridge.

Jebi had put a few glasses into the freezer, but they hadn't expected this sudden crowd. Luckily, there was enough ice to cool the drinks.

'The Tangerineade looks good. Hyeyeon-ah, can I have one of these?' This woman, and all the others, spoke in a dialect that Jebi didn't recognise. It certainly wasn't local to the island.

At that, everyone turned eagerly to look at Hyeyeon. 'Sure, sure. But mind you, that'll mean we can only afford cutlassfish head for dinner!'

'What? It's just a drink!'

'I mean, if we're so short of funds, you could at least suggest a cheaper fish – mackerel or something? Cutlassfish head sounds so pathetic,' someone else retorted.

'Okay, okay, stop it, you girls.' The Harley-Davidson owner sat down and took off her sunglasses. She was the one who had been riding at the front of the pack, and from the tone of her voice, it seemed she was the leader.

'Since this is an unexpected stop, let's do it ppumppai. Splitting the bill will solve the problem, no?'

'How many times do I have to tell you that ppumppai comes from Japanese? Use the native Korean word

– noneumaegi,' said the woman standing next to the leader, an intellectual, sophisticated air about her.

'Fine, fine. Kim Yoonja isn't the Korean literature professor for nothing. Everyone, listen to her. Take what you want but let's noneumaegi and split the bill.'

There was a flurry of orders for tangerineade, carrot smoothies and Jeju iced coffee.

Jebi glanced at the clock. It was three in the afternoon. Thinking on her feet, she began to heat up the kumquat and octopus buns from Yoona's dad. As the mouth-watering aroma wafted in the air, the ladies ordered some of the buns for themselves and polished them off to the last crumb within minutes.

Feeling refreshed, the women took their time to explore the photo studio. One woman posed for a snap with the palm trees and hydrangeas outside, while two others cooed over Bell. Most remained inside the café gallery, however, looking at the photographs. The most popular ones appeared to be the ones of Bell and Soondeok, as well as the photo of the haenyeos taken during the last mulkkureok festival.

'Sajangnim, who are these people?' the leader asked.

'Haenyeos. They live in the village.'

'I thought haenyeos wore rubber wetsuits?'

'Right. I've seen them on TV,' the biker ladies chorused.

'True,' said Seokyeong. 'That's what they usually wear on their dives. But during the mulkkureok festival – the giant octopus festival – the village holds a special ceremony to send the octopuses that've come onto the land back to the sea. For the ceremony, the haenyeos dress in traditional white costumes made of cotton. Like in that photo.'

'I see.'

'How elegant.'

'Indeed.'

There was a smattering of nods, and the group fell silent so that only the gently lapping waves could be heard.

Maybe they'll want to have their photos taken.

Jebi stared at Seokyeong with wide eyes. He chewed his lip nervously.

The leader was the one to speak. 'Shall we have some photos taken?'

Yes! Jebi had to stop herself from doing a fist pump. Seokyeong still said nothing.

'But we've taken loads of photos, haven't we? Just yesterday and earlier today, too. What are those if not photos?' the woman called Hyeyeon retorted.

Looks like she's the one in charge of finances for the trip.

'Sure, we did. But not when we were actually on our bikes,' said the leader. There was a murmur of agreement. 'We've been doing a motorcycling trip for every one of our high-school reunions, for years now, but don't have a single photo of us riding.'

'Was it Miran? Someone tried to take a photo on their bike a few years ago and almost drove into a ditch!'

'Oh yeah. I remember how my husband teased us, saying we weren't riding our bikes, but getting dragged around by them instead.'

'That's another Japanese word – yaji. The word for "tease" is nollida,' said Yoonja. In their excitement, however, no one paid her any attention.

Hyeyeon pursed her lips. 'Okay, but we'll split the bill for it.'

'Fine. Hey, Mr Photographer, are you up for taking some photos of us?' the leader asked.

'He'd love to!' Jebi was delighted.

But the leader wasn't looking at her at all. With legs casually crossed, she fixed a piercing gaze on Seokyeong. 'What I mean is . . . can you take photos of us while we're riding? Or rather, can you ride with us and take photos along the way?'

Jebi swallowed.

After a moment of silence, Seokyeong replied, 'Yes, sure.'

'Think carefully, young man. I don't want anyone to get injured.' Her tone was sharp.

Jebi flashed Seokyeong a worried glance.

'Come on, he has a motorbike behind those palm trees. He's one of us!' someone said. Behind her, Jebi noticed, was the woman in the cheap hiking shoes. She was holding a small can of coke and staring out to sea.

'Is that so?' The leader looked pleased. 'Fine, then he should know what flavour of photograph we're looking for.' She smiled.

' "Flavour"?' Jebi asked.

The leader flipped back her short hair. 'The taste of the wind. The sweetness of speed.'

While the group went off for a stroll down the hill to the beach, Seokyeong quickly got ready.

Jebi's heart raced. At her previous workplace, she'd never been involved in an outdoor shoot, much less gone racing around with a pack of motorcyclists. 'Sajangnim, are you sure about this?' She looked on worriedly as Seokyeong tucked a spare battery and a light meter into his bag.

'Hm?' replied Seokyeong, as he fixed a wide-angle lens onto his camera. 'By the way, do you know how to ride a bike, Jebi-ya?'

Jebi, busily packing a gimbal and a tripod, frowned. 'Of course not. Remember how I screamed the whole town down the first time you gave me a lift?'

'Oh, that's right. Then what about a driver's licence?' Seokyeong looked at her eagerly.

Jebi lowered her gaze. 'I do have one . . . but I haven't driven—'

'Excellent!' Before Jebi could finish, Seokyeong had headed out.

A while later, Seokyeong returned, driving a black pickup truck up the hill, and parking outside the café.

'Jebi-ya, you drive. I'll sit behind and shoot,' he said, as he held out the key to Jebi.

Jebi's jaw dropped. 'Sajangnim, we'll be flouting every traffic law . . .'

Seokyeong put a finger to his lips. 'Who was the one telling me I needed to earn enough money to pay your salary?' Casting a glance at the bikers, who were slowly making their way back up the hill, Seokyeong disappeared upstairs.

He quickly changed out of his white button-up shirt into a black, round-necked T-shirt with a print of a European-looking man staring into the distance, a Leica camera held to his eye.

At the entrance to the café, he paused and closed his eyes. For a few seconds, he pressed a hand over the T-shirt and remained silent.

'What are you doing?' Jebi whispered urgently.

'Praying. To the great Stephen Gertz.'

'As in, he's dead?'

Seokyeong's eyes flew open. 'What! Of course he's not – he's in Africa exposing the horrors of civil war. I'm going to take a leaf out of his book today. He's famous for riding a motorbike close to a guerrilla camp and getting an iconic photo of the leaders deep in discussion, his shot carefully timed for when there was a clear view between the shoulders of the sentry guards.'

'Oh, wow, to go to that extent . . .'

Sensing the risks involved, Jebi wondered if she should try to stop her boss, but the next thing she knew, she was strapped into the driver's seat of the pickup. Luckily, it wasn't a manual drive.

Seokyeong confirmed with the pack on the route to take before climbing into the cargo bed. Feeling the slight dip of the truck as he did so, Jebi was reminded of the heavy responsibility on her shoulders, as if his life was in her hands.

She started the engine and drove down the hill. Behind, the bikes followed. Leading the pack was the Harley-Davidson, followed by the BMW, Benelli, Suzuki and the rest.

Balancing himself precariously at the back, Seokyeong eased into work mode. Jebi gripped the steering wheel with trembling hands: it'd been a long time since she had last driven. It was just past four, and the sun still shone brightly as it gradually moved westward.

For Seokyeong's safety, Jebi drove slowly along the narrow, winding road. But soon the bikers were sounding their horns. Jebi glanced at the side mirror; the leader was gesturing at her to speed up. Jebi shuddered to see her riding with just one hand, but she obliged and stepped on the accelerator.

Strong winds blew in from the sea, making the bikers' jackets billow behind them. As the leader turned at a sharp bend, the waves broke against the breakwater and drops of water sprayed across her. Seokyeong quickly pressed the shutter. Surprised, the leader leant further into the bend – as did everyone behind her. Jebi glanced in the side mirror, her heart in her throat. Luckily, no one skidded.

Jebi drove past the wind turbines lining the coast. She knew that Seokyeong planned to angle the shots so that the turbines would appear in the background. He clicked away as the haenyeos came ashore in the distance.

The pack pulled over onto the hard shoulder and gathered around Seokyeong to check the photos. The leader, who'd taken off her sunglasses, looked satisfied. Not the rest of the bikers, though.

'Is this all you've got?' Sitting on her BMW R nineT, Hyeyeon tapped her thighs impatiently.

'My thoughts exactly. Not quite gaegal. I'm not paying for this!' Yoonja grumbled as she sat back down on the smooth leather of the Benelli Leoncino and took off her helmet.

'What do you mean?' asked the leader.

'Oh, please. These are basically solo shots of you, Jeongsoon? We're like ants behind you,' Yoonja grumbled.

It was decided that everyone would take turns to ride in front.

Two hours had passed in a flash, the sun ripening to a fiery red as it tilted towards the horizon.

On the second rest stop to check the photos, everyone appeared pleased with the individual shots. Not the group photos, though.

'It's not that they're bad . . .'

'Yeah, they're not bad.'

Seokyeong looked at the women. 'Feel free to speak up . . . what can I do better?'

'Alright, young man. Don't misunderstand us—' the leader began, pressing a hand on Seokyeong's shoulder. 'We do like the photos. But they don't quite . . . scratch the itch.'

There was a murmur of agreement from the assembled bikers.

'So, what you're looking for is—'

The leader looked him square in the face. 'Young man, how about riding pillion with me?'

There was a pregnant pause. The only sound was the rough waves crashing on the rocks near them.

'What I'm saying is that it's an issue of the angle, the point of view.' Lifting an index finger, the leader pointed at Seokyeong's and her eyes in turn. 'Because you're always taking the photos from the front, the gaegal's not quite there. You need to be *among* us . . .'

Frustrated, Jebi interjected: 'Wait. I've been hearing "gaegal" this and "gaegal" that, but what does it even mean?'

'Basically, it means it doesn't quite hit the spot, young lady,' Yoonja relied – and immediately covered her mouth, horrified.

'Aha! Caught you! You just spoke standard Korean!'

At Jeongsoon's exclamation, the ladies all exploded in wild laughter, clapping and smacking the arm of the person next to them her.

Yoonja huffed and stamped her feet, cursing herself for having forgotten to speak in their dialect.

'You owe us a meal, ha! But let's settle that later.' When the leader turned back to Seokyeong, the laughter on her face had been replaced by a serious expression. 'What do you say? Can you do it? Or not?'

'Come on, it's too dangerous,' one of the bikers piped up, looking worried.

'Yeah, it's risky! Don't endanger someone's precious son!' Hyeyeon, too, wasn't keen on the idea.

The other bikers nodded.

'It was just a suggestion! Of course I don't want anyone risking their life.' The leader was about to lift her hand off his shoulders when Seokyeong quickly grabbed her wrist.

'I'll do it. I'll try my best.'

'S-Sajangnim . . . what if you get seriously hurt!' Jebi whispered urgently.

'Excuse me . . .?'

Jebi turned around. It was the lady who had arrived late on the Honda Super Cub who was speaking. Jebi had noticed that she hadn't taken a turn getting a solo shot.

'President, if it's okay, how about letting him ride with me? My pillion seat is much wider than yours.'

Seokyeong and Jebi turned to look at the Honda. The pillion seat had quite a few scratches, as if something was regularly attached on top of it and then taken off.

The other bikers nodded.

'Good idea. There's more space.'

'Yeah, young man. If you're really okay to do this . . .'

But the leader looked doubtful. 'Really? With all the winding roads, and you need good speed . . .'

'I've been doing deliveries in a hilly neighbourhood for over twenty years,' said the Honda owner, mildly.

The bikers' eyes darted nervously to and fro between the two.

'Yeah, Jungmi has been riding well, hasn't she?'

'She hasn't had the chance to ride in front, either.'

'Let her lead.'

'Yeah, let her do it.'

In the midst of all these murmurings, Seokyeong raised his hand. 'But . . . this means she won't be in the group photos too. She'll be behind the camera.'

At that, everyone looked at each other.

'I don't mind.' The Honda owner smiled as she put on her helmet. 'My eyes are my camera. The photos will be etched on my mind.'

Seokyeong climbed calmly onto the pillion seat of the delivery motorbike – facing backwards– to check if the pillion rider's handle was firm. Satisfied, he dismounted and went over to take his camera bag from the back of the pickup truck. Move it to the front passenger seat, he took out a small camera the size of a biscuit from one of the pockets.

As he climbed back onto the Honda, sitting back-to-back with Jungmi, the rest of the women slowly got onto their bikes.

'I don't think this is going to work.' Yoonja stared apprehensively at Seokyeong.

'It's too dangerous. It's not worth it, not for a few photos,' Hyeyeon agreed.

Seokyeong smiled. 'It's okay. I'll shout if I'm falling.'

'I'll go slow. As if I have a baby on board.' Jungmi smiled over her shoulder at him.

'I have faith in you.' Seokyeong nodded his head firmly.

'Everyone, on your bikes! Let's not waste Sajangnim's time!' the leader shouted as she put on her shades and straddled her Harley-Davidson.

The rest of them still looked slightly doubtful.

Jebi went over to Seokyeong and wordlessly helped him to secure his helmet strap.

The yellow Honda Super Cub moved off first, followed by the Harley-Davidson, BMW, Benelli and the rest of the pack.

Seokyeong was already starting to shoot. Returning to the pickup truck, Jebi followed on behind.

A while later, she had to step on the accelerator as she realised that the riders ahead were speeding up. *It looks like they've found their momentum.* Some of the bikes pushed ahead of Jungmi, while others fell behind. Someone whistled hard.

As the sun set over the sea, she saw that Seokyeong had closed one eye as he used the other to find the best shots. He was focusing so intently on the shoot that he had begun swaying slightly to the left and then to the right.

'Madness! Putting his life on the line for people he just met!' Jebi sounded the horn, her hands sweating.

'Because it could be their last time.'

Seokyeong's answer when Jebi asked why he'd acceded to such a dangerous request had made her frown.

'But they're only in their fifties. What do you mean *last time?*' Jebi was upset. And confused.

'I'm quoting Stephen Gertz,' Seokyeong replied, as he put his camera bag on the counter. He deepened his voice in imitation. ' "*This evacuation, this shooting, this vigilance – it's their last.*" Sometimes, it just hits you – call it instinct. So, I take my camera, and I follow. Unfortunately, my instinct is almost always right.'

Seokyeong cleared his throat. He was back to himself. Picking up his phone, he made a call and ordered an assortment of seafood. Because the closed season for octopuses had started a week earlier, at the start of August, he ordered frozen ones.

The riders were planning to have dinner at a grilled cutlassfish restaurant which they'd made a reservation at. Afterwards, they'd return to the photo studio for a photo viewing party.

It was all thanks to Jebi.

Right after the shoot, just when the riders were complaining about being thirsty and hungry, she'd announced: 'We offer a photo viewing party at the studio, where we serve fresh abalone, chewy octopus . . . and drinks, of course. Would you be interested?'

Everyone was famished, and despite knowing that they were heading for grilled cutlassfish, they hadn't been able to resist the appeal of the seafood feast Jebi described.

'Of course, if you aren't keen to take up this option, we can send you the photos by email or the post. But then you'd miss out on the opportunity to enjoy viewing them for the first time together. We'll be doing a slideshow using our high-quality projector, and—'

'Sounds amazing! We'll head back to our hotel to freshen up, go and eat, and then come back later for the viewing party.' The leader turned to the rest of the pack.

Everyone nodded.

While Seokyeong was selecting the best photographs and printing them, Jebi drove off to collect the seafood.

'By the way, where did you get this truck? It's such a smooth drive,' Jeju commented on her return, as she placed the trays of seafood in the kitchen.

'Borrowed it from the village head.' After setting the printer going, Seokyeong put on an apron.

'Wow, I love the community spirit here. He let you borrow the truck just like that?'

'Not *just*. I promised to do a shoot for him – he wants photos of his Jeju dogs to send to the association,' Seokyeong said, as he washed his hands.

Jebi took down the frames from the wall, removed their photos and replaced them with the newly printed ones. As Seokyeong busied himself with the food preparation, he looked up occasionally to decide on the position of each photo.

After she had rehung the frames, Jebi stepped back and looked at the gallery. What a breathtaking sight – bikers speeding along the coast against the sunset. The splashing of the aquamarine waves that threatened to break the formation of the pack, the wind turbines that seemed to fuel their speed, the haenyeos emerging from the sea and wading ashore – each photo held a compelling narrative. In the single shots, the logos of the motorbikes were in clear focus, as if highlighting their individual characteristics.

While Seokyeong was steaming the octopus and the top shells, and preparing the raw abalone hoe by slicing it into thin strips, a honk sounded from down the hill. He quickly washed his hands and turned off the main lights with the remote control, switching on the gallery lights that shone a warm glow on the frames. At his instruction, Jebi turned on the music. The sound of a lively jazz octet filtered through the speakers.

They pushed open the door and stepped out. Tail wagging, Bell trotted out behind them.

Two minivan taxis had stopped at the bottom of the hill. Clad in elegant dresses and evening shoes, the ladies chattered happily as they walked up the hill. Perhaps they had already had a drink at dinner; they were looking a little unsteady on their feet.

'Sajangnim . . . are you sure the guests will order all the food we prepared? We worked so hard to earn the money from the shoot . . . what if we make a loss now?'

'I used to work in the kitchen of a hoe restaurant,' Seokyeong said, rubbing his palms together.

'You? A hoe restaurant?'

'Yep. I wanted to open my own business, and I thought the skill might come in useful. Anyway! Only those truly addicted to alcohol refuse food with their drinks. Jebi, look at those ladies. Don't you get the sense that they are foodies? We're going to sell out of all the dishes we've pre-pared, you wait and see. In fact, we may not have ordered enough.'

'But they just had dinner, remember.'

'Well, we'll see. Anyway, Jebi, can you take the party photos? I'll need to be in the kitchen. You can help with the serving, and in between, take some snaps.' Seokyeong patted her shoulder.

'*Me?* But they'll be so annoyed when the photos turn out bad!'

Seokyeong smiled. 'I don't think so. I've seen your work, remember? And it's an extra freebie we're throwing in. If anything, they'll be ecstatic. You can do this.' From his pocket, he took out his mini camera and pressed it in Jebi's hands. It was the same one he had used on the afternoon's shoot. Jebi looked at the model – it was a Sony RXo.

Oh my god. Did he just pass me a camera? An actual camera?

Jebi couldn't believe it. She was being entrusted with a professional photographer's gear – something she wouldn't have dared dream of in her previous workplace. Once, when she couldn't contain her curiosity and touched a camera, the photographer had lashed out at her as if she'd committed a major crime, yelling, '*Do you know how expensive this is?!*' in front of everyone in the room. Jebi remembered blinking back tears.

'Alright, let's go!'

As Seokyeong went ahead to greet the guests, Jebi trailed behind. In her hands, the camera was warm and light, like a newborn chick.

A buzz spread among the bikers as they noticed the photos hanging on the wall, some clapped while others whooped with excitement. There was jostling, too – everyone eager to take selfies with the frames in the background.

Seokyeong and Jebi were busy setting out the beautifully plated seafood. There was abalone hoe with a tangerine compote on the side, parboiled octopus with roasted seaweed sheets and horseradish and, in a brass bowl, a mountain of boiled top shells. Next to the spread were bottles of takju, a rice wine brewed with volcanic spring water from the island.

'Sajangnim, I thought you were only good with cameras. But you're a dab hand in the kitchen too, eh?' said

Jeongsoon as she picked up two slices of abalone hoe at one go and delivered them into her mouth. As she savoured the crunchiness of the fresh, raw abalone, she let out a sigh through her nose and shook her head in bliss.

Picking up the bottle of takju, she gestured at Yoonja. 'Here, open it!'

'Come on, does she look like she's in the mood for it?' Hyeyeon said, as she took the bottle instead, twisted the cap open, and poured out the liquor for Jeongsoon.

She cast a glance at Yoonja, who was trying hard to smile, but the corners of her mouth wouldn't stay up. Paying for having slipped up and spoken standard Korean earlier was obviously going to be hard for her.

The group laughed teasingly.

'Hey, we have to thank dear Yoonja here for this treat!' Jeongsoon cackled in delight.

Yoonja huffed. 'Sajangnim, turn that music off, will you? I can't hear the waves at all!' she shouted irritably. Then she took a bamboo skewer, jabbed it into a top shell and pulled out the meat. As she chewed, her frown disappeared.

'Want some?' Jeongsoon picked up the liquor bottle.

Yoonja made a show of declining but took a glass in the end. 'Kyaaaa!' She gave a shiver of satisfaction after her first sip.

At the sight, everyone broke out in laughter again.

While the ladies were enjoying themselves, Jebi and Seokyeong weaved in and out swapping dirty plates with clean ones and trying their best to make sure that everyone was taken care of. On top of that, Jebi was busy taking photos of the party, so it was some time before she realised someone was helping them.

'Oh, please leave that to us!' Jebi quickly took the plates from Jungmi's hands.

'Please don't worry. I'm the sort who can't sit still when there's something to do,' said Jungmi.

In between taking the party photos and serving the food, Seokyeong and Jebi chatted with Jungmi and learnt a few things about her. Firstly, her son had been accepted into a top university that year. Secondly, she had spent half her life working as a seamstress in a factory that produced jeans and shirts. Her husband was a tailor.

'Back then, we were doing quite well for ourselves. Times were good, and my husband and I left the factory and set up our own. But one day, we lost it all. The kids were still young, everything we owned was seized, my husband collapsed from the stress . . . my world spun out of control,' Jungmi recounted, as she cleared away the brass bowl of empty top shells. 'Those girls over there, they helped me . . . with the debt, with the school fees for my kids . . . with everything.'

Seokyeong and Jebi looked on in silence as Jungmi dabbed the corner of her eyes with her sleeve, then, pulling several pieces of tissue from a box on the counter, she blew her nose and smiled.

'We went to the same girls' high school. For years, we were busy with our own lives, working, getting married . . . Until about ten years ago, they started up this annual reunion and bought their motorbikes. I heard about it but never thought of joining them. But they kept inviting me along . . . so I came here to pay my debt.'

'Your debt?'

'Yeah. They told me in the four days I spent with them, I should only smile. Then they'd take it that I've paid off what I owed.'

Seokyeong was slicing the parboiled octopus with a practised hand. He paused and glanced up. He now understood why Jungmi had wanted to help with the shoot even if it meant that she would not appear in the photos.

'So that's why you're smiling so brightly – thanks to your friends,' Jebi said, as she looked at Jungmi's face on the camera's LCD panel.

Jungmi nodded lightly. 'Yep, but that's not the entire reason. It's also because of my lucky wisdom teeth.'

Seokyeong looked up curiously. Jebi, who had returned to the kitchen after serving the sliced octopus, also glanced at Jungmi.

'All four of my wisdom teeth came in perfectly straight,' continued Jungmi. 'The dentist said he'd never seen anyone so lucky.'

Almost simultaneously, Seokyeong and Jebi used their tongues to feel their molars. Catching each other's eyes, they chuckled.

'I had to have two of mine taken out. The other two are dormant,' said Jebi.

'I had all four removed. They were impacted.'

Jebi shuddered.

Jungmi nodded. 'Told you. It's not common for wisdom teeth to grow out straight – and all four, too! The dentist told me that wisdom teeth help to support the molars, so that they're less easily worn out. This means that when people are chewing beef short ribs with two molars, I've got three!' She leant in closer. 'When the factory went under, when my husband fell apart, when I had to pull the kids out of cram school . . . I would touch my wisdom teeth with my tongue and tell myself, *Don't be scared. You're a lucky person.*'

Seokyeong washed his hands with soap and dried them with paper towels. He turned to Jungmi. 'If you don't mind, I'd love to take a photo for you. At no cost.'

'A photo? Of what?' Jungmi's eyes widened in surprise.

Seokyeong smiled. 'Your lucky charms.'

Leaving Jebi to keep an eye on the noisy gathering in the gallery, Seokyeong led Jungmi up the stairs. In one of the rooms was a simple shoot set-up, with only a single chair in the centre of the room.

As Seokyeong was setting up the backdrop and the lights, Jungmi brushed her teeth with a travel toothbrush she always carried everywhere.

'It could get a little tiring, holding still for the photo-graph,' Seokyeong said, as he hung a black backdrop behind the chair.

'How hard can it be? I'm sure I've gone through worse,' said Jungmi.

Seokyeong looked up in surprise. It was the first time he had heard her speak standard Korean.

Jungmi flashed him a grin. Glancing at the stairwell as if to check that no one was listening, she explained:

'It's our promise to each other, that when we meet, we'll use our hometown dialect. These days, we're all living in different parts of the country. Every year, three hundred and sixty two days are spent as someone's mother, daughter, boss, employee. Besides me, everyone in our class is successful. Yoonja is a university professor; Hyeyeon owns the largest mart in her neighbourhood; and our leader Jeongsoon was a cycling star back in the day – she even made it to the Olympics. She never won a medal, but later on, she grew interested in motorbikes and now she owns a motorbike shop. This annual meet-up is also her idea. Thanks to her, every year we get to have three days behaving like teenage girls again. We made a pinkie promise that in these few days it will be just like when we were teenagers, so we stick to speaking our hometown dialect, as we did back then.' Jungmi cast another careful glance towards the stairs. 'And if we get caught speaking anything else' – she wrinkled her nose, her eyes twinkling – 'we get fined. And it's expensive.'

'How much?'

'Well, we have to pick up the tab for everyone. That's why tonight's party is on Yoonja.'

Seokyeong chuckled. As if in response, laughter drifted up from below as he looked through the viewfinder and adjusted the aperture. 'Okay, I'm ready.'

'Gosh, I can't do this.' Jungmi ducked her head, her face flushed.

'Nudge those lucky charms with your tongue. Ask them if they're ready.'

Jungmi burst out laughing.

'I'll photograph the lower teeth first, then the upper ones, and I'll combine the photos post-processing. Say *ahh*, like how you would at the dentist. Ready?'

With her eyes shut, Jungmi quietly opened her mouth.

Through the viewfinder, Seokyeong had a clear look at her teeth. *Indeed, a full house.* Not a smear of plaque in sight, her tongue a healthy pink. Seokyeong could see why her dentist had congratulated her. It was hard to believe that this set of teeth belonged to a woman in her fifties: only a few gold fillings gleamed like stars.

Seokyeong did his best to capture the perfect shot but as the seconds passed, Jungmi started to groan with discomfort, her jaw aching. Seokyeong, too, could feel his palms sweat as he held the camera at odd angles.

'I'm sorry. Please bear with me for a moment,' he murmured.

When he finally had the shot that he wanted, they were both exhausted.

Jungmi rubbed her jaw, her pale lips parched. 'Oh god, that was embarrassing. I don't think I can look at the photos,' she said, a flush breaking out on her cheeks.

'They'll turn out beautifully, I'm sure. I'll print them out and display them next to the photos of the motorbikes.'

'Oh, no, no!' Jungmi jumped up and waved her hands in protest, her face turning an even deeper shade.

Seokyeong grinned impishly as he checked through the photos he'd taken. 'Such beautiful and strong wisdom teeth. Everyone will be in awe. Trust me.'

'Will they? Not that I'll know. I don't think I'll ever get to the chance to come back to this island again.' Jungmi sighed.

'I'm sure you will. These are lucky wisdom teeth, aren't they?' Seokyeong smiled again.

Just then, Jebi came upstairs. 'Have you finished? We're all ready for the viewing party.'

'Yep.'

'Oh, you're showing the photos from this afternoon?' Jungmi asked. And before either of them could reply, she had hurried downstairs, Seokyeong and Jebi following behind.

'Jungmi, where've you been?'

Jeongsoon the leader waved her over. Jungmi smiled in place of an answer and sat down with the rest.

The tables and chairs had been rearranged to form a row facing a screen that had been put up on the far side of the room. Jebi sat down with the other women to look at the photos.

Everyone was delighted, oohing and ahhing, occasionally nudging each other and laughing happily.

At the last photo, the bikers gasped in surprise.

'Wait, isn't that Jungmi?'

'Indeed! She got her solo shot after all!'

It was a photo of Jungmi taking off her helmet, her side profile captured against a backdrop of the setting sun. Because she was perspiring, her curls stuck to her forehead. There was something ethereal about the photo. Her tenacity showed in the way she lifted her chin slightly towards the sunset, her lowered lashes dipped. It was a beautiful, striking photo.

Surprised, Seokyeong looked at Jebi.

She shrugged, a little bashful. 'I thought it'd be nice for everyone to have a solo shot. I took this on my phone when we stopped by the side of the road.'

'Look how photogenic our Jungmi is! Lovely! Come on, let's sing – Jungmi's favourite song!' Jeongsoon stood up, holding her chopsticks like a microphone, and began to sing with gusto.

Listening to the lyrics, about the sun rising again after a storm, the women broke into wide smiles, wrapping their arms around each other's shoulders. Everyone joined in the chorus, accompanied by the rhythm of the waves outside . . .

Seokyeong and Jebi walked the women back to where the minivan taxis were waiting. The group was still in high spirits as they headed down the hill. The photos would be mailed out to their separate addresses, Seokyeong promised.

The bike pack rolled down their windows and waved, as if reluctant to leave. Among the faces, Seokyeong saw Jungmi smiling widely.

The taxis moved off but, a moment later, screeched to a halt. Surprised, Seokyeong and Jebi turned around.

Jeongsoon had got down from the van and was heading purposefully towards Seokyeong.

'Did you leave something behind?' he asked.

'Take this. It's from me. Think of it as danger money!' she said, thrusting a folded envelope into his hands. He watched her walk briskly back to the taxi before slowly opening the envelope.

It was stuffed with 50,000 won notes.

Jebi's jaw dropped. Seokyeong turned to the taxi and bowed. A deep, ninety-degree bow.

Back in the photo studio, the two of them stared at the mess in the café and sighed. A happy sigh.

Jebi stood with her hands on her hips. 'Sajangnim, let's keep this going.' Her tone was firm, determined.

'*This?*'

'Yes. Let's make it our niche.'

'Make what our niche?'

'Vacation photography!' Without asking for permission, Jebi grabbed Seokyeong's laptop, opened Photoshop and started to edit their menu of services.

6

A Wedding Shoot

Jebi stirred awake at a loud clatter from the front garden. Lifting the edge of the curtain, she saw that it was just growing light outside.

Dressed in baggy work trousers of a lurid pattern and a checked shirt, Mokpo Granny was dragging a large bucket across the ground. It looked like she wanted to water the vegetable patch before the day got too warm.

Sighing, Jebi pulled the quilt over her head. Yesterday, she'd stayed late to clear up the mess at the photo studio before uploading the riding and party photos onto social media – with the owners' permission, of course. The moment she'd come home, she had fallen into bed and gone straight to sleep.

Jebi reached for her phone. There were six unread texts from close to midnight. All of them from Bora.

—Eonnie, I got dumped lol

—Eonnie, you told me he was no good, I should've listened to you haha

—How am I going to show my face at work?

—I guess that's why people say don't date your colleagues :(

—Fuck, I'm screwed hahaha

— Eonnie, you asleep?

Jebi sighed at the slew of messages. She didn't need to ask to hazard a guess at what had happened to cause the break-up. She started typing a reply.

—I told you!

Her thumb hovered over the Send button. What was the point of saying this when the thing had already happened? She deleted the message and typed a new one.

—Oh no, you must be upset

—Who cares about him, just go to work as usual haha

—The next guy will be better

Jebi added a cute sticker.

Her phone pinged.

—Wow Eonnie hahaha

—I thought you'd be angry lol

Bora's next message was almost instantaneous.

—Anyway, we got back together lol

—He came to find me just now and apologised lol

—So I acted pissy for a bit then took him back lol btw hope you're having a good time in Jeju!

The absurdity. Jebi tossed her phone aside and pulled up her quilt again. She felt like a fool for having worried about her friend. *What does she take me for?*

Jebi sat up abruptly and grabbed her phone, her thumbs tapping furiously on the screen.

—Is love a joke? How can you take him back just like that?

But once again she hesitated to press Send, imagining Bora's crestfallen face. Sighing, she swiped away the chat app and, instead, opened her contact list.

She had barely scrolled the length of her screen before reaching the end. Most of the names were ex-colleagues or people she knew from work. In that moment, Jebi keenly felt the preciousness of Bora's existence. She might not quite know if it was friendship, or solidarity, or just familiarity, but whatever it was, such relationships were rare for Jebi.

Is Bora a colleague? Or a friend? Jebi wondered. Perhaps both, or maybe neither. *If I stop putting in the effort, this weak link between us might break forever.*

Jebi's thoughts drifted to the bikers from yesterday – the middle-aged women cruising down the coast road. They had been high-school friends and, thirty years on, they remained a tight-knit group.

In thirty years, will I have friends like that in my life?

Jebi thought back to her high-school days. A few faces surfaced in her mind. What were her classmates up to now? Jebi had no idea. She had never reached out to them; nor had they tried to keep in touch with her. Then what about all the people she had met at university? Catching herself in time, she turned on her front and buried her face in her pillow. She didn't want to remember anything from those days. The darkest period of her life, where everything had derailed.

Is it too late to make friends now? Friends that I can rely on?

Jebi hugged her pillow tight and turned over restlessly. It didn't feel possible in this lifetime. She was past the age of trusting people readily.

Just then, she heard another loud scraping sound from outside. Crawling on her hands and knees to the window, she lifted the curtain slightly.

Mokpo Granny had finished watering the vegetable patch and was now raking the garden. Just for a moment, Jebi thought she recognised her own grandmother's silhouette, overlapping with that of her landlady.

'Why are all grannies so hardworking?' Jebi grumbled under her breath. 'Don't they ever take a day off?'

She returned to bed with her phone. Opening the photo gallery, Seokyeong's handsome face greeted her on the screen. She'd secretly taken a photo of him, right after snapping the one of Jungmi against the sunset. She'd managed to capture the moment he got off Jungmi's bike and was exhaling a sigh of relief.

'It was you. You got them to let down their hair and sing. Your photo did.'

That was what Seokyeong had told her, late last night, when he had given her a ride back to Mokpo Granny's house. She had quickly turned away in case he saw her blushing at this feedback.

'No way, it's not worth a second look compared to the photos you take . . .' she had replied shyly, letting her words trail off.

'It's good to be critical of your own work, but don't compare yourself to others too much Jebi.' Seokyeong had looked at her. 'As Stephen Gertz says, a good photo shouldn't only attract admiring looks. It should stir people's imagination and their curiosity to find out more. The best photographers spur action. And today, you achieved that with your work.'

It was the kind of affirmation Jebi had yearned for her entire life. Her heart had been thumping so hard in her chest that it had actually hurt.

'Drive safely!' She had blurted out, before fleeing to her room.

If only I could meet a man like him!

Yanghee's face had swum in her mind, and jealousy and sadness bit at her.

He would never be interested in someone like me. And besides, it's too late . . .

Closing her eyes, Jebi had fallen asleep.

After lunch, Jebi slowly got ready for work; Seokyeong had told her to take the morning off, since she had worked so late yesterday.

As she climbed the hill, she noticed that the door of the photo studio was already wide open. On the other side, the window was also ajar, welcoming the sea breeze into the gallery. The octopus wind chime tinkled loudly.

Seokyeong was sitting by the window, deep in concentration as he wrote; Jebi had come to notice over the past weeks that he kept a diary. Bell was noisily licking her paws by his feet but when she noticed Jebi in the doorway, she immediately ran towards her.

Jebi bent down and gave the puppy a peck on the forehead and a head scratch. Then, reaching up, she took down the wind chime from the doorway, and the surroundings quietened.

'Thanks. It was starting to annoy me too.' Seokyeong smiled and swept his fringe back.

The photos of the bikers were still up on the wall. As Jebi put on an apron with the logo of the photo studio on its pocket, she reappraised the pictures. Yesterday, everyone had looked full of life and passion, but today, she thought they looked slightly different. Perhaps because she knew that their trip had ended, and it was back to the daily grind for them. She imagined them all, going to work, speaking in standard Korean rather than the dialect of their youth. Somehow, it made her feel a little sad, and strangely . . . lonely.

'Be right back.' Seokyeong stood up and headed towards the bathroom. Bell following him adoringly out of the room.

Jebi began wiping down the tables. Condensation had pooled below Seokyeong's glass of iced coffee. As she wiped it away, Jebi couldn't help glancing at the page he had been writing. It detailed the expenses and revenue from the shoot and the after-party. Jebi smiled at his unexpectedly tiny handwriting.

In the bottom the corner, he'd put in a note: *Danger money, 1 million won: 20% for Jebi.*

Oh, my goodness! Jebi's heart started pounding, as though she already had the money in her hand. She wondered how and when he'd give it to her.

Seokyeong's voice started drifting down from upstairs. It seemed like he was on the phone. Just then, a gust of wind picked up the pages of the diary and flipped them, so that the book lay open at an earlier page.

'Oh no.' Flustered, Jebi took a step backwards – but as she moved on to wipe the other tables, she kept an eye on the stairs. Seokyeong was still on the phone.

Unable to contain her curiosity, Jebi inched towards the table again.

Was there anything else in his diary about her?

07.06.2022
Let my wife take a break so that she can go away for a weekend with her friends. I'll spend the time with our kid and take photos together.

Jebi's eyes rounded. *What? He's married?* She flipped a few pages over.

19.05.2022
Done with the renovations. Set aside a room for our kid. He can decide how he wants to decorate it. I'll be able to do it, I'm sure.

Oh my god. He has a child too?! Jebi turned several more pages.

25.07.2021
The first home to call my own. Here, I'll start my family, put my roots down, be a good father, a good husband. Within three years.

In a daze, Jebi stuffed the wet dishcloth into the pocket of her apron and stared at the diary. Just as she was about to start reading it from the first page, Bell barked loudly from upstairs. With a start, she quickly moved away, going into the kitchen area.

Seokyeong ran down the stairs, two at a time, waving the phone in his hand as Jebi rinsed the dishcloth.

'Jebi-ya, we've got a booking!' Seokyeong shouted. 'I just got off the phone with them! They want to do an outdoor pre-wedding shoot! They saw the motorcycling photos you uploaded and loved the vibe!'

Jebi spun around, her eyes wide in surprise, not noticing that water droplets were dripping from the dishcloth onto her trainers and the floor. Seokyeong hurried to turn off the tap for her, and slipped a little in the wet. As he collided with Jebi, his lips brushed her forehead.

Jebi held her breath, not daring to move an inch. The moment was broken, however, when Bell came running over, jumping up to join in the fun.

Jebi quickly turned back to the sink, wrung out the dishcloth and hung it up before scooping Bell into her arms, her heart calming at the touch of the puppy's soft fur.

'Sajangnim, have you done a wedding shoot before?' Moving Bell to one arm, Jebi opened the laptop, which was on the kitchen counter, with her free hand. Clicking into the inbox, there was indeed an email enquiry about a pre-wedding shoot.

'Yes, I've shot a ceremony at the wedding hall.' Seokyeong couldn't keep the excitement out of his voice.

Erm . . . aren't those two different things? Indoors versus . . . Jebi stopped herself from voicing this. Instead, she asked, 'Did they mention the concept they want?'

'The couple is leaving that up to us.'

Jebi narrowed her eyes. She didn't have a good feeling about this at all. 'Leaving it to us? The bride said that?'

'Yeah, she was like, "Oh, you guys will know best." All she said was that she wanted the shoot to be creative and hip – those were the words she used.' Seokyeong grinned, but Jebi didn't share his excitement.

'What about the location? Did they have somewhere in mind?'

Seokyeong shrugged. 'They're leaving that to us, too. Again, quoting her – "I don't like places that are too ordinary. Somewhere special, hip." She told me she hates anything that's too tacky or cheesy.'

'Oh . . .' For the first time in a long while, Jebi was dreading a shoot.

Seokyeong, however, seemed blissfully unaware of what was awaiting them.

Bell was squirming in her arms, so Jebi quickly put her down and she scooted away. 'Is it a full day shoot?' she asked.

'Yeah.'

Bell returned with a ball she had brought over from her basket in the corner. Seokyeong picked it up and threw it for her. Barking, Bell skittered after it.

'In that case . . . how about Bell?'

'I'll have to leave her with Mummy,' Seokyeong said, as he held out a hand for the ball.

'As in your mother?'

'No. Bell's! My mum hates dogs.'

Seokyeong threw the ball again; this time, in the direction of the garden. Bell ran out into the bright sunshine, and Seokyeong followed behind.

Left alone at the kitchen counter, Jebi immediately began researching pre-wedding shoots.

A week later, Seokyeong and Jebi hired an SUV and headed for Jeju city. The plan was to meet the couple at the bridal shop and begin the shoot there.

Seokyeong carried the camera bag, while Jebi unloaded the other equipment. In the elevator, they were silent. The bikers' shoot had come out of the blue and they had managed to wing it, but this time, there had been a lot to prepare. To plan the shoot and get in any equipment they'd lacked, they'd been working non-stop for the entire week.

At the bridal make-up shop, a woman in uniform greeted them politely.

'We're here for Lee Juhyeon's photoshoot.'

The woman stood up. 'Please follow me.'

'Oh, one moment, please.' Seokyeong and Jebi hurriedly opened their bags and took out the camera as well as the reflector.

The plan was to begin by taking photographs of the bride having her make-up and hair done. Because she hadn't wanted photographs of her bare face, they had only needed to arrive around the time the make-up artist was finishing up. The idea was to capture her excitement as she got ready for the day.

'This eyeliner's not even at all! God, look at that foundation caking under my eyes!'

The first thing they heard was the bride's raised voice. Entering a large room, they saw, in front of a mirror, a woman in a halter-neck wedding mini dress examining her face up close.

'That's her,' said the employee, neutrally, before returning quickly to the reception desk.

Seokyeong looked up from the viewfinder. Jebi, the reflector in her hand, turned around. The other customers in the shop, all of them brides-to-be, were staring at the woman.

'This is what I paid one million won for?' The woman glared hard at the staff.

A man, who looked like the groom-to-be, hovered awkwardly by her side. 'Let's start the shoot later,' he whispered to Seokyeong, with a tight-lipped smile.

'Ma'am, you look beautiful. The make-up is fine,' said the make-up artist, standing stiffly with her hands clasped in front.

'Fine? What's fine about this?' The bride whipped her head around. An angry flush had appeared on her cheeks. 'This is a disaster. *Fine?* Ha! Why can't you admit you've done a terrible job. Can't you see the foundation caking? There's no way am I paying for this!' The bride crossed her arms and sat back heavily in the chair.

A woman in a black jacket approached the bride. Her tag read 'Manager Jeong Jinshim'. She flashed a professional smile and spoke soothingly. 'Ma'am, you have a wedding photoshoot today, right?'

'So?' The bride jutted her chin out and glared at the manager, who had turned towards Seokyeong and Jebi.

'With a little Photoshopping, everything will be fine, right?'

'Excuse me?' The woman bounced up from her seat and jabbed an angry finger at the manager. '*Everything will be fine* if the make-up is done right in the first place! Why should they have to edit the photos? What a joke!'

Jebi was feeling more and more uncomfortable as the other employees and customers in the room cast anxious glances in their direction.

'Ma'am, you're disrupting our business,' whispered the manager, a cupped a hand around her mouth.

'Disrupting your business? How dare you! You're disrupting my *life*!' The angry bride snatched up her phone from the vanity table and started filming. 'Say it again. It's my pre-wedding shoot today. You've done my make-up like this and you tell me I look beautiful?' The bride flipped the camera and panned to a close-up of her under-eye area before turning the camera back to the manager. 'Say it to the camera. I'm what? "Disrupting your business"? What's with this bridal shop? Your name is? Manager Jeong Jinshim? "Jinshim" as in sincerity? I see absolutely none of that in you!'

'Ma'am, you can't do this.' Unable to watch any longer, the staff now surrounded the woman and made to escort her from the shop.

'Get your hands off me! How dare you touch me? Darling!'

In the ensuing chaos – the bride struggling to get away from the staff and the groom frantically trying to help her – Seokyeong and Jebi also ended up being pushed out of the shop.

'What the hell!' Sitting in the SUV in the basement car park, the bride swiped away her tears. 'Everything's ruined! My eyeliner is smudged! Oh god, the lashes are falling off!' The bride slammed down her hand mirror.

'Darling, it's okay. You're look perfect, as always,' the groom reassured her. 'And we got a fifty per cent refund—'

'*Perfect?* Are you for real?' The bride glared at him through her smudged make-up. 'I hate this – why are you telling such a blatant lie?' Stamping her feet, she started crying again.

'Alright, alright. You look terrible . . . but I still love you, all the same.' Her fiancé patted her consolingly on the shoulder.

Standing beside the SUV, Seokyeong and Jebi sent meaningful glances to each other.

We need to get our act together. At this rate, the shoot will be cancelled.

Quietly, Seokyeong stepped back a few paces and lifted the camera to take a picture of the silhouettes in the SUV.

Jebi, however, was finding it hard to breathe. The air-conditioning system in the basement car park obviously wasn't working properly; the space was hot and filled with exhaust fumes. She covered her nose and mouth with a handkerchief. As Seokyeong snapped away, Jebi's thoughts drifted to what had happened that morning; her mood hadn't improved since then.

Jebi had woken up early – two hours before her alarm was due to go off. Her mind had felt sluggish, her body heavy as lead. She'd hugged her quilt tighter around her and let her thoughts wander.

Can I say I'm too ill to go today?

She had been thrilled that the photos she had uploaded had scored the photo studio its first booking. It felt like she was finally earning her worth, and it made her proud. But why did it have to be a pre-wedding shoot, of all things? Why did their first client have to be a woman who was blessed to have met a man she loved so much she wanted to marry him, and the man felt the same way? That she had to spend an entire day following the bride around and taking care of her felt . . . humiliating.

When will I get to be the main character in my own life?

Jebi tossed and turned. It was the same during the months after she left university, when she worked at a nursery. She didn't want to spend her precious time caring for other people's kids; she wanted to take care of her own child. And she hadn't even been paid well. The Seoul photo studio had been no different, either – entertaining other people's babies while they were photographed had depressed her. In the end, she quit. And today, she had to waste an entire day tagging along on someone else's pre-wedding shoot.

Should I run away?

She had kicked away her quilt and got up. Run? Where could she run to? There was no place for her to go.

Her thoughts returned to the present. The bride she'd dreaded to meet was crying, because her once-in-a-lifetime wedding shoot was ruined.

Somehow, that made Jebi breathe a little easier.

'Excuse me, ma'am.' Jebi approached the SUV and knocked on the window. Seokyeong, witnessing the scene through the viewfinder, looked up in alarm. The window rolled down.

'What is it?'

The groom was sweating profusely while the bride looked stiffly ahead, sniffing.

Jebi bowed her head politely. 'If it's not too presumptuous of me, can I help with your make-up?'

'Oh?' Looking delighted, the man turned to his bride.

Reluctantly, the woman cast a glance at Jebi. 'Are you a certified make-up artist?'

'Nope.' Jebi swallowed nervously. 'But I do occasionally help to touch up make-up for our clients.'

Turning out of the basement car park, Seokyeong drove to a quiet park. Water cascaded from a manmade waterfall and bright sunshine lit up the surroundings.

Seokyeong and the groom headed to the café to buy drinks for everyone as Jebi turned up the air-conditioning in the car and started to clean away the bride's make-up. Luckily, she'd done her research on wedding shoots and had brought along all her make-up supplies.

'You should use better products,' the bride grumbled, when she saw the cheap brands and the flimsy plastic cases in Jebi's stash.

Jebi bit her lip. 'I'm sorry.'

'It's fine. You're not at fault. Your boss probably wanted to cut costs.' The bride cast a glance at Seokyeong through the window. 'At least you have a new powder puff. The shop was using a latex sponge – an old one too! It's obvious they just washed and reused it. I even spotted an employee drop a sponge on the floor, nonchalantly pick it up and continue dabbing it on one of the bride's cheeks! She had her eyes closed so she didn't notice, but I was fuming. I stopped myself from saying something then but, oh god, when I saw what they did to my face, that was the last straw.'

'I see.'

Soaking cotton pads and buds with make-up remover, Jebi gently wiped away the stubborn streaks around the bride's eyes. Then she applied moisturiser before taking a new powder puff and brushing on a light coat of foundation.

The bride appeared to be in her mid-thirties; there were some wrinkles and freckles under her eyes. The employee at the bridal shop had tried to cover them up with thick foundation that had only accentuated the creases. Now, Jebi did her best to apply the foundation in a light and even layer.

Putting on the false eyelashes was a challenging task that needed a steady hand and, nervous, Jebi accidentally jabbed the bride's eyelid.

She jerked back slightly but didn't say a word.

Jebi, braced for the woman's anger, blurted: 'I'm so sorry! That must've hurt.'

'It's okay,' the bride replied, her eyes still closed. 'These things happen. Thank you for apologising.'

Jebi heaved a silent sigh of relief.

'Hey, you did a great job!' the bride exclaimed, as she examined herself in her hand mirror ten minutes later. 'What exactly is your role here?'

'What?'

'As in are you a photography assistant, or a make-up artist?'

Jebi hesitated. She had never quite thought about it.

'That man over there, he's your boss?' The woman jutted her chin in the direction of Seokyeong.

Jebi nodded.

The woman looked at Jebi with shrewd eyes. 'Does he get you to do everything for him? The slave-driver kind of boss?'

'Um . . .'

'Be clear on your goals. You have to stand up to any bullying right at the start.' She raised her eyebrows. 'Don't let him trick you into working more than you should, with that charming smile of his.'

'Um, he doesn't really . . .' Jebi said, as she picked up the make-up brushes that were spread out on her lap.

The woman shrugged. 'Work hard, build your portfolio, and set up your own business. Don't let a man stand in your way. I see you as a little sister, that's why I'm telling you this.'

With that, the bride got out of the car and the groom hurried over to her.

*

On the way to their first shooting location, the couple were quiet, checking emails and replying to messages on their phones.

Seokyeong glanced at his watch. It was just after nine in the morning.

Every now and then, the bride would take a call. Not wanting to spoil her make-up, she put it on speaker mode each time, holding the phone away from her ear.

Jebi marvelled at the bride's perfect English. She could only catch a few words here and there – *approved, urgent*. From the way the woman was introducing herself, it sounded as though she had a high-profile job. She caught the name of her company – it was a well-known conglomerate. And it seemed that the groom worked at the same company, as an associate.

'. . . The Museum of African Art?'

The groom put his hands on his hips, looking flabbergasted.

Seokyeong glanced at the bride. 'You told me that you aren't keen on the usual tourist spots. This place is modelled on the Great Mosque of Djenné in the Republic of Mali. It's a mud-brick building, breathtakingly simple, impressive and yet soft at the same time. And today the sky is a beautiful blue, which will bring out the beauty of the mud wall.'

'Excellent!' the bride exclaimed as she changed into her white heels. 'I love how it stands out from the surroundings. Very different!'

In her enthusiasm, she failed to see her fiancé pulling a face.

Relieved that the bride was happy with his suggestion, Seokyeong swung into action. It was still early in the morning, so there was barely anyone else around, and shooting was a breeze. After capturing some shots with the museum in the background, Seokyeong directed the couple towards a garden where two leopard sculptures stood. He encouraged the bride to pose as though she were a leopard, chasing after the groom. The bride giggled as she acted her part.

After finishing there, they moved to the next location, in front of Starbucks Jeju Jungmun. The bride ran up the rainbow-coloured stairs and looked up at the building, which had been designed to resemble a brightly coloured coffee monster.

'But this is a tourist spot. It's teeming with people. How can we take photos . . .?' asked the groom as he hurried after her.

Right next to the steps was a busy six-lane road. At the sight of the bride in her wedding dress and holding a bouquet, the cars honked in greeting.

She straightened her shoulders. 'I love this! Totally retro!'

'I just want to do a normal shoot. There are too many people here,' the groom muttered to her.

'If it bothers you, I'm sure it'll be possible to Photoshop out the pedestrians. Right?' The bride held up her bouquet excitedly.

'No problem at all!' Seokyeong gave her a thumbs up.

'That's not my point. People are staring . . .'

'So what? It's not like you'll be seeing them again.'

The bride leant back in an exaggerated pose while Seokyeong clicked away. He sent the flustered groom a smile.

Jebi held up the reflector and followed them around, her face slightly flushed from the heat of the day.

After the shoot, the four of them retreated from the summer sun into the Starbucks and ordered iced coffee. Seokyeong and Jebi sat at a separate table and took candid shots of the couple enjoying their drinks.

Seokyeong was checking the photos on the LCD monitor when Jebi suddenly grabbed his arm.

'Sajangnim! What's with these photos?' This looked nothing like an ordinary pre-wedding shoot. None of the poses were traditional, affectionate; everything was edgy and arty. She glanced at the other table, where the couple was once again focused on their phones.

'It's okay. That's what they want,' Seokyeong said. 'Jebi-ya, do you know the origin of candid snapshots? It began with courtroom photos. In the 1920s, a German photographer, Erich Salomon, hid a Leica camera in his bowler hat, entered the courtroom and secretly took photos of the court proceedings.'

Jebi frowned and pursed her lips. 'Are you saying that you're trying to shoot as though it's a hidden camera? There's nothing sweet or lovely about that . . . they're going to ask for a refund. Have you forgotten what happened at the bridal shop this morning?'

'But she wanted creative shots. In her words, "hip".' Seokyeong sucked his coffee noisily through the straw.

'Sure, it should be hip, but it has to feel romantic, too.'

'Don't worry. They'll feel it. They love each other so much, that's why they're getting married, right?'

Jebi shook her head. She obviously wasn't getting through to him. 'Sajangnim, have you not dated before?'

Spluttering, Seokyeong put down his coffee with a thud. He clamped his mouth shut, colour rising in his cheeks.

Looks like he was writing about his dreams, not his reality in that diary. I don't think he's ever had a girlfriend, let alone a wife and child.

The ice cubes tinkled against the glass as Jebi picked up her coffee. She was dreading the bride's reaction when she saw the photos.

The sun blazed down as Seokyeong parked the SUV at Mulkkureok village. The bride had changed into a beautiful mermaid-cut dress. The groom was now in a short-sleeved shirt, paired with an orange bow tie for a pop of colour.

'This place is so . . . rustic.' The bride frowned, lifting a hand to shade her eyes from the glaring sun.

'You didn't want the usual touristy spots,' Seokyeong reminded her again, with a grin.

'It's good with me. I like this place. It's so rare to find a peaceful village like this.' The groom had brightened at the quiet surroundings.

Seokyeong got the couple to pose in front of the stone houses and their colourful rooftops. He snapped more photos against the background of the tangerine trees with clusters of fruit hanging from the branches, the unpaved mud road, the sea in the distance and the plots of carrot and peanut crops.

'I love these shots. The simple feel,' the groom said.

The bride held up her skirt to cool herself down in the heat. 'This goes beyond simple. It's shabby. Why are we taking photos here? It's not like we don't have the money.'

'We're not rich either,' the groom retorted.

'What I'm saying is that it doesn't feel right – as if we're deliberately going for the "poor but happy" look.' She frowned.

'Erm. The village isn't that poor . . .' Seokyeong spoke mildly, but the couple didn't hear him.

'So you prefer using a big franchise chain like Starbucks as a decorative prop?'

Jebi swallowed nervously as she watched them bicker.

Seokyeong put a hand on her shoulder. 'Just wait. A photographer needs to have patience. Wise words from Erich Salomon.'

Jebi gripped the reflector and whispered back: 'Sajangnim, that's the second time you mentioned this Erich person. Is he famous? A millionaire photographer?'

'Hmm.' Seokyeong cocked his head. 'I'm not sure if he's a millionaire. I only know that in the second world war, he was held in a concentration camp and later passed away.'

Jebi dropped the reflector.

Next, they drove to the beautiful coastal sand dunes. Standing on the white sand, the groom flapped his shirt uncomfortably. 'Finally! I've been waiting for a seaside location. It's so hot.'

'We didn't want the bride's hair ruined in the strong wind, so we had to make it the last stop.'

The couple posed on the uneven slopes of the dunes, laughing as they slid and staggered around on them.

Later, Seokyeong drove them to the octopus jangseung by the entrance of the village.

'Wow. This is *hip* indeed!' the bride exclaimed at the sight of the statue.

This time, perhaps feeling more relaxed in the country-side, the groom didn't say anything in protest. They slipped their hands into the octopus's mouth and made their wishes as Seokyeong caught the moment on camera.

And then, as if out of nowhere, rain started to fall from the clear sky. Jebi scrambled to use the reflector to protect the bride's head, although it didn't provide enough cover and her dress began to get wet. And in protecting the camera, Seokyeong didn't have time to care for the groom; soon, his white shirt was soaked through.

Seeing his nipples poking out, under the fabric, the bride giggled. 'Hey, take a photo of him, please!' and Seokyeong quickly pressed the shutter as the groom stood there, grinning and embarrassed.

As it proved impossible to shoot in the rain, they took a break in the SUV.

It was still raining a quarter of an hour later, and the bride looked sharply at Seokyeong. 'You have back-up plans, right?'

Taken aback by her sudden sternness, Seokyeong fumbled his words. 'Erm, w-we prepared . . .' A flush crept into his face as he scratched his head awkwardly.

Jebi jumped in. 'Yes. A shoot in traditional costumes.'

'Hanbok? Isn't the weather still a little too hot for that? And it's so commonplace, not original at all.'

'Not hanbok. I mean the traditional costume on the island – what the haenyeo wear.'

The bride's eyes lit up, and she grinned as Jebi took out the white jeogori and black trousers from the car boot. The bride clapped in delight at the bouquet of dried seaweed that Jebi produced next.

'It's certainly one of a kind,' Jebi said, pleased. While waiting for the couple to change in the car, Seokyeong and Jebi took a quick walk along the beach.

'I don't know what I'd do without you.' Seokyeong took out a handkerchief and helped to dry Jebi's hair. 'When did you pack those costumes? I bought them when I first opened the studio and promptly forgot about their existence.'

'I thought of them at the last minute. I was too busy getting everything together, so I didn't have time to mention it.'

Seokyeong let out a sigh. 'I was just thinking about it last night . . . This business would be failing if it weren't for you. I'd have to close up to pay off the loan, just like the previous owner.'

Jebi looked at him. 'But it's because you'd thought to buy the costumes that I was able to bring them today. What's that saying? The heavens help those who help themselves.'

Jebi shoved him good-naturedly and Seokyeong elbowed her back.

'Look at us. Showering each other with praise.'

They laughed before making their way back to the shoot.

Following Seokyeong's instructions, the groom presented his bride the seaweed bouquet on one knee, while she smiled widely with a tewak – a round buoy with a net attached to it, unique to the haenyeos – draped over her shoulder, like a veil.

Not far in the distance, a group of haenyeos were coming along the beach after a dive. Spotting Yanghee, Jebi's expression froze on her face.

'Samchon!'

Jebi glanced away at the sound of a child's voice. A young boy was running along the bumpy ground towards them; an elderly woman carrying a sun umbrella followed him. The next moment, Jebi felt a camera being shoved into her hands.

'One moment! Sorry!'

Seokyeong dipped his head in apology towards the couple and, in the next second, the young boy jumped into his embrace.

'W-who is this?' Jebi asked.

'Son.'

'What? *Your* son?'

'I'd love that. But no, he's Yanghee-ssi's son.' Seokyeong bounced the boy on his arm, making him chuckle in delight.

'Samchon, why haven't you been coming? My mum isn't feeling well,' the boy said in Jeju dialect.

'She's not well?' Seokyeong's voice was subdued. He'd been so busy preparing for the shoot, it had been a few days since he'd gone to the beach.

'Dongwon!' Yanghee came running.

With a smile the boy ran towards his mother, leaving Seokyeong to retrieve his camera and turn back to the couple on the dunes.

'Didn't you say Yoona was the only child in this village?' There was an edge in Jebi's voice.

'I said she's the only baby,' Seokyeong replied, as he took back the camera.

Jebi walked away a little distance, struggling to keep her feelings in check.

Just then, a familiar voice rang out behind her. 'What's going on?' Mokpo Granny was coming towards her, her expression severe.

'Granny! You've just finished a dive?' Jebi greeted her brightly.

'I'm asking what the hell you are doing? Did you not hear me?' Her face had flushed an angry red, and around her wrinkled eyes were the deep marks left by swimming goggles.

'Granny, we're doing a wedding photoshoot . . .'

But Mokpo Granny was beyond listening to her. 'Is our work a joke to you? We put our lives on the line every time we go into the water!' Throwing down her net, she made a move towards the couple.

Jebi quickly blocked her way. 'Granny!'

Too far away to hear what was being said, the rest of the divers looked on with indifference. But surely they could see something was going on? Why didn't they intervene?

Casting a glance over her shoulder, Jebi saw that Seokyeong had finished the shoot, and that the couple were now seated in the SUV.

He started the engine, rolled down the window and shouted: 'Jebi-ya! What are you waiting for?'

'Granny, I'm so sorry!'

Leaving her behind, Jebi ran back and got onto the front passenger seat. apologising profusely to the couple in the backseat.

As Seokyeong drove off, in the side mirror, Jebi could see Mokpo Granny giving chase for a short while before stopping and shaking her fist at the departing vehicle.

The gallery at Hakuda Photo Studio had been transformed to welcome the couple. Gold balloons spelling out CONGRATULATIONS and bouquets of white roses stood on every table. Through the window, the cobalt-blue sea sparkled. The couple seemed enchanted.

'Please feel free to relax and enjoy the space in the next two hours. We'll use the time to print the photos and prepare for your photo viewing party. And of course, the food!'

'I don't know if I can wait until then. I'm starving.' The groom rubbed his flat stomach.

Jebi quickly heated up some octopus buns in the oven. This was version 2.0 from the bakery – newly christened Yoona's Bakes – and they were an instant hit.

'It's the cutest thing I've ever seen!' the bride gushed, taking photos with her phone. Attached to a round bun were four short arms. The eyes, nose and mouth were drawn with octopus ink, making the pastry look even cuter.

'How is the inside so chewy when it's crispy on the outside? Wow, I love the aroma of the garlic spicy sauce. How delicious!'

The couple polished off all eight buns with gusto, along with the coconut juice that Yoona's dad had insisted accompany them.

'I feel alive again!' The bride had washed her face, removing the make-up and lashes. As she walked downstairs, she stretched idly. The groom then went up to take a quick shower.

Sitting by the window, the bride rubbed her tired eyes. 'Sorry, is there a place we can lie down for a bit?'

Jebi conveyed her request to Seokyeong, who was busily editing photographs in his small workroom.

Seokyeong came out to the gallery. 'There's a room upstairs we use as a studio. We don't have a bed, but we can put a clean rug on the floor for you.'

'Perfect.'

Tasked with making the necessary arrangements, Jebi took the couple to the studio. As she worked, they poked their heads into the other rooms. The first was kept very simple, with a chair in the middle and a wall where different backdrops could be hung. The set-up in the next room was more elaborate, with white flowers and a fake tangerine tree clustered with fruits. The last room had a rustic feel with two antique chairs, and a window looking out to the sea.

'Can I open that?'

From the doorway to the room, Jebi looked over to where the bride was pointing. There was an antique chest of drawers below the window, part of the decorative set-up.

'I suppose so.'

'Babe, it's a prop. There won't be anything inside,' the groom said, casting an embarrassed glance at Jebi.

'You never know! Perhaps there'll be old photos or mysterious treasure. When I was young, I used to be so fascinated by antiques.' Her eyes lit up as she pulled open a drawer. 'Oh my god! What's this?' She took out a box.

'Hey! We shouldn't be snooping, touching things that aren't ours!' The groom cast another awkward glance at Jebi.

'But it looks like it's for us—?' The bride held out the box she had found to the groom. Written on the wrapping paper was a message: *Congratulations on your marriage!* Without waiting, she tore it open. Inside was a blank photo album with the logo of the photo studio printed on its cover.

Jebi smiled. 'I guess Sajangnim prepared it as a surprise present.'

'How funny! Who prints out photos and sticks them into albums these days?' the bride scoffed, but a soft blush coloured her cheeks.

Jebi went into Seokyeong's room and took out a rug and a thin blanket from the cabinet. Back in the other room, she laid out the rug carefully, pulling out any wrinkles.

The couple came back into the room then, stepping on the rug with their bare feet.

'Ahh, that feels good.'

Jebi handed the blanket to the groom. 'It's summer but we're by the sea, so it can still get a little chilly.'

'Thank you,' he said, with a smile.

When Jebi came back downstairs, Seokyeong had just finished choosing the photos.

'I think we can go with these,' he said, handing her the external hard drive as he reached for his apron. Behind him, the printer whirred into action.

'Sajangnim, are you sure you can pull off the menu tonight?'

'Of course!' Seokyeong held out a fist. 'When I was working at the hoe restaurant, there was something I learnt from the chef – *If you're a beginner, don't do anything.*'

'What? How do you cook without doing anything?' Jebi asked as she tied her apron.

'What he meant was that if you have good ingredients, just serve them as they are. And here, what we don't lack are the freshest and best ingredients. This pig was selected from the village head's pen two days ago!' Seokyeong slapped a slab of pork on the chopping board, black bristles still visible on the skin.

Jebi let out a yelp and stepped backwards. Taking a butcher's knife, Seokyeong scraped away the bristles and washed the meat clean. Wrapping it with palm tree leaves, he carefully placed it in a steamer before tossing in a generous handful of peppercorns. While the meat cooked, he washed and peeled earthy potatoes before steaming them. As they cooled, he whipped up some mayonnaise.

Then he thawed frozen octopus in the microwave, sliced it and made a simple stir-fry. He served it all onto plates, sprinkling ground sesame seeds mixed with salt on top to complete the simple dish.

He finished serving just as the couple came downstairs, looking refreshed. A lovely piano piece was filtering from the speakers. Lights from the ceiling cast a warm glow on the table and the steamed black pork glistened tantalisingly. Looking like the chef of a Michelin restaurant, Seokyeong used a pair of wooden tongs to peel back the palm tree leaves and sliced the pork into thick pieces.

Holding her chopsticks in her left hand, the bride snapped photos on her phone.

'Enjoy the food. Leave the photos to us,' Seokyeong said, pointing towards Jebi, who shyly held up the small RX0 in her hand.

The bride smiled and swiftly moved the chopsticks to her right hand. Conscious of maintaining her figure for the shoot, she had only eaten a few biscuits that morning. Though the octopus buns had staved off her hunger a little, she was positively starving now.

'The tangerine wine makes an excellent pairing with the food,' the bride said, as she ate happily.

'Yeah, just when the food begins to feel a little rich, a sip of the wine cleanses the palate and makes me ready to eat more.' The groom smiled.

'Please enjoy the slideshow!'

Seokyeong had taken off his apron and was standing next to the screen. From the narrowly opened window, a cool wind blew in from the sea. Outside, it was a beautiful purple dusk. The couple sat side by side, looking relaxed and happy.

But when the first photo came up, they looked surprised. It was a photo taken at the bridal shop.

'Didn't I say not to take photos of that?' The groom was upset.

'No, wait. I actually like this . . .' The bride cupped her chin thoughtfully. 'When I look at the photos, it actually makes me feel better about the whole fiasco – like it was no big deal after all.'

Jebi let out a quiet sigh of relief.

Seokyeong shot her a meaningful look, reminding her to focus on taking the photos. However, Jebi was finding it difficult. Nobody had noticed her as she went around snapping photos with the big group of bikers, but now that there were only two subjects, she was afraid that it'd be too intrusive if she kept hovering around them.

'It's okay. They're focused on the slideshow,' Seokyeong whispered into Jebi's ear.

At the next photo, the couple burst out laughing. The bride was surrounded by the bridal shop staff, while the groom valiantly tried to fend them off. Meanwhile, the manager, dressed in a smart black suit, was attempting to block the bride's phone camera with her palm.

'Oh dear, my expression! I looked feral.' The bride turned towards her fiancé. 'Darling, am I always like that?'

He chuckled. 'Erm . . . not always.'

'You should've told me!' She mock-slapped his arm.

'I have . . .'

'You have? When?'

'Sometimes. Like that time when we were having a fight over the wedding gifts . . .'

'Oh! *That* time.' A scowl flashed across her face before she closed her eyes and then reopened them. 'Fine. Let's just watch the slideshow.'

Next was a photo of the bride crying in the SUV while the groom tried to comfort her. Through the tinted windows, only their silhouettes could be made out.

The bride yelped. 'Wait, you took this too?'

'I would have thought it would be quite obvious that we won't want a photo like that in our album!' The groom frowned at Seokyeong. 'Why did you bother taking it?'

'Because you wanted something hip, authentic, different. I thought it'd make for an interesting memory to include it here.'

The bride gave a little nod of approval while the groom, still frowning, shook his head.

With a change of image, the bride was exiting the SUV looking delighted, her make-up fixed.

The groom touched his fiancée's shoulder tenderly, and the two of them exchanged a happy smile.

The photos taken at the African Museum of Art were very striking. The bride's white dress stood out against the blue sky and the mud-brick building, while the groom looked suave in his black tuxedo. The images were faultless, the work of a true professional. The couple clapped, visibly impressed.

Watching the slideshow, Jebi realised that the photos she'd seen at Starbucks were only a small part of what Seokyeong had shot.

Seokyeong leant against the wall, enjoying their enthusiastic response, and Jebi realised he was wearing a completely new expression – one she'd never seen him make during their discussions of administrative and operational matters.

When the comedic photo with the leopard statues came up, the couple giggled; same with the photos taken at the colourful stairs in front of Starbucks. Seokyeong had captured the moment when the bride struck an over-the-top supermodel pose and a passer-by had given a thumbs up. Next was a close-up of the groom looking self-conscious, with sweat rolling down his cheeks, pooling into a stain on his collar.

The bride nudged him. 'Darling. Were you sweating like that for the entire shoot?'

'I told you I was having a hard time with so many pairs of eyes on us!'

'I didn't think you really meant that.'

'Why would you think that? Do you not take me seriously at all?'

The bride looked surprised at his sudden outburst. 'That's not what I mean. But those people were just strangers. Did you have to get so embarrassed?'

'It's not like I can help it!' The fiancé's face had turned an angry red.

'I don't get it at all.' The bride looked at him, then shrugged. 'Try not to care so much.'

'Try not to *care*?' The groom closed his eyes and gave a heavy sigh.

The beautiful piano melody played on in the background, a soundtrack to the slideshow, which had moved on to the images taken at Mulkkureok village. The bride had changed out of her wedding dress, into something more comfortable and her brows were knitted tightly together, her lips pursed as she wore a look of extreme annoyance.

'Oh god. Is that me again? Am I always like that?' She slapped her thighs in surprise.

Her fiancé sighed again.

The photo changed. The groom was grinning widely as he surveyed the fields and the multi-coloured rooftops.

'You look great in that picture!' the bride exclaimed, but then her expression turned stoney. 'I haven't seen you smiling like that in . . . years.'

'Nonsense, I'm always smiling.'

'Not like that,' she murmured.

Next came the photos taken on the dunes. The couple was walking hand in hand, avoiding depressions in the sand. Behind them, the sea stretched out seemingly to infinity.

As they looked at the photo in silence, the couple reached for each other's hand.

Jebi quietly took a photo.

At the sight of her fiancé's nipples showing through his soaked shirt, the bride doubled over in breathless giggles. He peered at the photo between the gaps of his fingers, stifling his laughter at how he'd tried to cover, rather unsuccessfully, his chest with his hands.

The image changed again, to one of the groom in the white jeogori and black trousers and the bride in the haenyeo costume. She had slung the orange tewak over her shoulder like a designer handbag, strutting in front of the camera as the groom chased after her with the seaweed bouquet. In the image that followed, he was down on one knee, presenting the bouquet to her while she had her nose in the air.

The final photo was of Mokpo Granny running towards them with her fist raised, and Jebi trying to block her. The couple clapped their hands, the bride laughing so much that she had to wipe tears from her eyes.

Jebi glanced at Seokyeong. He was still leaning against the wall, grinning.

'Thank you. I loved the photos – they're just what I was hoping for. So unique! Like you said, they'll become great memories,' said the bride.

It was the first time that they heard her speak with such warmth.

'Please join us,' said the groom.

Seeing their hesitation, the bride held up her wine glass. 'Yeah, do join us. Thank you so much for your hard work today. Cheers!'

Leaving the slideshow cycling in the background, the four of them sat down at the table. After clinking glasses of tangerine wine, the groom was about to say something when his phone rang.

'Damn, it's a customer. Doesn't bode well that they're calling at this hour.' He walked out, looking worried.

'I hope it's nothing serious.' The bride sighed as she

watched him step outside. There was a short silence. Suddenly, she downed her wine in one go. 'To be honest, I didn't want to get married.'

Seokyeong and Jebi exchanged a look of alarm. On the projector screen was a shot of the couple answering work calls in the middle of the shoot.

Her smile was replaced by a piercing gaze. 'Look. Don't I look confident in that photo?' she said. 'I spent four years working hard at university to get a place at the company I'm in now. Then I worked myself to death, rising up the ranks. In the past ten years, I've suffered all kinds of ailments – colds, flus, infections and so on – but I've never taken a single day of sick leave . . .'

She turned and stared out of the doorway. The groom was on the phone and gesturing with his hand as he paced to and fro.

'Four years in university, ten years at work. And over many group projects and assignments, he never once treated me badly. He is the only person who has never tried to stab me in the back. That's why I decided to marry him. But . . .' Jebi filled the bride's empty glass. 'Now I'm getting cold feet.' Her shoulders shook. 'I've seen so many of my colleagues stop working after they got married. So many men expect their wives to take care of their child alone. Isn't that like being stabbed in the back by someone you trusted? I'm afraid that when we get married, I'll finally be betrayed by the man who's never done that to me, and that fills me with so much dread. Just take today's shoot. We had so many disagreements, about the shoot locations, about the photos themselves. The whole time I was thinking that maybe we aren't a good fit . . . that when we get back to the hotel tonight, perhaps I should call off the wedding.'

Seokyeong and Jebi stared at each other in shock. The slideshow at that moment was showing a close-up of the groom's expression as he watched his fiancée take a work call.

Jebi looked at the photo. *Was* that look in his eyes more admiration than love?

'But . . . after seeing these photos, I've changed my mind. I'm going to keep the Let's Get Married project going.'

Jebi put a hand to her heart to calm herself. On the screen was a photo of the bride in the bridal shop, and the groom using his entire body to shield her.

'This year, I got promoted to manager. When I was making a wish at the statue just now, I prayed to become a board member within twenty years. But seeing these photos makes me think a little differently. All I have to do to become a board member is work hard. But can hard work earn a person's heart?'

Jebi shook her head, draining her glass at the same time.

Seokyeong glanced sideways at her.

'Jebi-ssi is right. Hard work can only go so far. It boils down to luck.'

At that moment, the groom came back. 'What boils down to luck?' he asked, as he returned to the table.

'Nothing much. Excuse me, I need the use the bath-room,' said the bride.

As she got up, Jebi followed suit, murmuring that she'd clear the empty dishes.

The groom munched on squid crackers as he fixed his eyes back on the slideshow. On the screen was a close-up of the bride pointing an accusatory finger at the bridal shop employee.

'This morning, I almost wanted to give up.'

Seokyeong whipped his head around, looking at the man with alarm.

'I was thinking . . . is it really worth it? Can I really live with that woman for the rest of my life?' the man confessed quietly, pouring himself more wine. 'But one photo stirred something in me. Oh, here it is. It's the way we were holding hands so that we wouldn't fall over on the sand dunes.' He rubbed his nose. 'Juhyeon . . . she's amazing. When she cares about something, she focuses and goes all in. I can never do that . . . I find it hard to put in 100 per cent into anything I do. Not that I don't work hard. I do. But that's just it. Everyone congratulates me for having gone to a good university and found a job at a well-known company . . . but it's not really what I want. It's not my dream.'

The groom stared hard at the screen as though trying to bore a hole through it. He continued calmly: 'But I realised something today. As I looked at that photo of us, I felt that I was truly giving my best. With her by my side.'

Seokyeong picked up his wine glass and swirled its contents around. He stared out of the window at the dark, cold sea, not saying anything.

Wiping her hands, the bride returned to the table. Jebi had replenished the snacks, too. They clinked glasses once more.

The slideshow continued, the music filling the gallery.

The couple called a taxi to take them back to their hotel. Seokyeong and Jebi cleared up in silence and by the time he was driving her home, it was past ten.

In front of Mokpo Granny's house, Jebi turned to Seokyeong. 'Those two . . . do you think they will be happy together?'

'Who knows if they'll be a good fit in the end.' He shrugged. 'But it looks like they trust each other a lot. Even if they do part ways, I think they'll break up amicably.'

Jebi crossed the dark garden back to her room. The lights were already out in Mokpo Granny's house.

Jebi lay down on her bed, thoroughly spent.

Break up amicably.

Seokyeong's words stabbed at her heart.

7

An Octopus on Land

On the morning of payday, Jebi's salary landed in her bank account. And just as she was finishing work for the day, Seokyeong put something into her hand.

It was a small envelope with the photo studio's logo on it. Back in her room, Jebi eased open the flap and saw something that looked like a voucher inside. She pulled it out.

Promissory Note
Amount: 2 million won
To be paid on your first work anniversary.

She hugged the note close and rolled around in bed, squealing. Then she jumped up, took out the green tape and stuck the note to the back of her door. She couldn't believe that she'd survived an entire month without touching her credit card. The complete lack of convenience stores within walking distance had certainly helped.

After settling her phone and insurance bills, she also paid for her second month's lodging at Mokpo Granny's house. Though she was always on the verge of wanting to run away from the room crawling with centipedes, she had decided to stay put as a favour to Seokyeong.

'But aren't you angry that she did that during a wedding shoot?' Jebi asked Seokyeong He shook his head. 'She's the only one who doesn't treat me as an outsider.' It was evening time and Seokyeong was sitting by the window in the gallery, cleaning the lenses of his cameras.

'When I first came here, Mokpo Samchon shared her meals with me. As you know, there aren't any restaurants nearby. I was basically surviving on cup ramyeon while renovating the place. After a month, I couldn't take it anymore. I went around the neighbourhood, knocking on doors, telling people that I really missed homecooked food and asking if they would please be kind enough to sell me a portion. But because I wasn't a local, they didn't want anything to do with me. Only Mokpo Samchon was different. She invited me in. One day, we were having dinner together and perhaps she sensed that I was having a difficult time, or she'd seen my efforts in trying to get closer to the villagers, but out of nowhere she told me this . . .' He paused.

'What? What did she say?'

Seokyeong imitated Granny's expression and voice. 'Have you heard of koendang?'

'Koendang?'

'Yes, in Jeju, that's what they call a family relationship, a bond of blood. It's what makes people look out for each other. But Mokpo Granny told me, "If you want to be koendang, the way to do it is to marry a local." So I asked if she became one that way. She nodded. And then she told me, "There's a lady called Yanghee. She's divorced and living at her parents' home with her young son. She's the only young woman in our village. Tomorrow I'm going on a dive. Come when we're almost done, and I'll introduce you to her." '

So that was how the one-sided love affair had begun. Jebi felt a stir of resentment towards Mokpo Granny. But it wasn't enough to drive Jebi out of her house. She was becoming attached to the old woman, and to her cooking even more so.

While Seokyeong sometimes invited her to join him for dinner at the photo studio, she was conscious of the fact that he was her boss. She felt obliged to do the dishes, and she couldn't have any say regarding the menu. At Mokpo Granny's, she never had to wash the dishes. And the food was always good. There'd be fresh kimchi made from the lettuce or chives grown in her vegetable patch, and she'd steam the fresh catch of the day, such as top shells or barnacles. Jebi would wolf down the food in the blink of an eye. Before coming to Mulkkureok village, she'd been in the habit of getting an after-dinner treat like ice-cream, but after tucking into Granny's home-cooked food, snacking never crossed her mind.

'How do you have enough energy when you're eating so little? Girls need to eat well.'

Jebi secretly liked it whenever Mokpo Granny nagged her. Her own grandmother had never been the caring type and growing up in that environment had made her crave the affection and attention of an older adult.

After deducting her outgoings, Jebi put what little was left of her salary straight into a savings account, where it would slowly gather interest. At first, she had thought of investing in the stock market, but after reading up on it, she had decided to put the idea aside for now. All the books on the subject advised only investing in an industry that one was familiar with, and Jebi didn't have any areas of expertise like that.

From the allowance she set aside for herself, she bought the most luxurious dog food she could find.

'Just as business is picking up at last, it's already the end of August,' Jebi lamented, as she poured salmon-flavoured kibble into Bell's bowl.

Her tongue flopping out, Bell made a beeline for the food.

'It's okay, Jebi. In Jeju, summer lasts till September. There are quite a lot of people who avoid the summer peak and come towards the end of the season.' Seokyeong was refreshing the photos hanging in the gallery. 'Here, take a look. What do you think?'

Jebi put down a fresh bowl of water for Bell before going over to him. On the wall hung a photo of the octopus jangseung, and beside it one of the pack of bikers speeding along the coast road.

The photo that caught her attention the most was the close-up of an opened mouth – a red tongue and glittering wisdom teeth. The photo was edgy, with a strange allure.

Next to it was the photo of Jungmi that Jebi had taken on her phone.

Jebi gaped. 'Are you sure you want to hang this here? It's nowhere near as good as your photos . . .'

'It's fine. And look, your name is there, too.' Seokyeong grinned and pointed.

Next to the frame was a small sticker with the date the photo was taken and the photographer's name.

Jebi's hand flew to her mouth. 'Oh my god! It feels like my debut as a photographer!'

Seokyeong smiled. 'Not quite. What I've given you is an opportunity. When customers come in and see this photo, they're going to be impressed. It's an image that evokes a reaction in people. But a real debut is when someone likes your photo enough to pay money for it.'

Jebi wrinkled up her nose, and said teasingly. 'It feels a little odd hearing an artist like you talk about money.'

'Of course! Money is important. Didn't I tell you I bought this building in an auction?' Seokyeong was using a microfibre cloth to wipe the frames. 'I'm not that great at dealing with customers, but luckily, I have you to help me now. Jebi-ya, some people think that money and art are separate. But in this world, after life and health, the most important thing is money. True art has value, it's worth putting a price tag on.

Jebi thought of her ex-colleagues at the photo studio in Seoul. She hadn't liked the way they worked and had even looked down on them a bit. But those people had been able to sell their work.

Suddenly, Jebi felt a newfound respect for them.

'I'll look forward to displaying more of your work in the future, if it's good enough,' Seokyeong said, smiling.

Jebi chewed her lip shyly. 'I'll . . . do my best.'

'That's the attitude! But it's not going to be easy. This was beginner's luck.' Seokyeong pointed at the photo of Jungmi. 'Remember. If you set your heart on taking good photos you're only going to end up with bad ones. You have to keep trying, nonetheless. And, one day, the moment will come where you forget about wanting to take good photos. That's when you become a real photographer.'

Jebi stood in front of the frames, tapping the ground absent-mindedly with her foot.

'It doesn't matter who the photographer is. What matters is whether the photos are good. Art, whether by an amateur or a master, will always be acknowledged.'

'Is that another quote from that Stephen guy?'

'Nope. It's Lee Seokyeong.'

Jebi suddenly noticed that his expression had darkened. *Come to think of it, he's been distracted all morning.* 'Sajangnim, did something happen?'

'Mm? No, nothing.' Seokyeong continued to dust the frames. The next moment, his phone buzzed in his pocket. He quickly pulled it out and answered.

He ended the call soon after, and did a fist pump. 'Jebi-ya! They told us to come!'

'Who? Where?'

Jebi was still confused when Seokyeong held out his spare helmet to her. They got on his motorcycle and drove off slowly: a thick fog covered the village.

He parked the bike in front of a long, white building. A wooden sign at the entrance read DAEMULLI ASSOCIATION.

Jebi stopped in her tracks at the sight of the crowd assembled in the spacious hall. Everyone was chatting among themselves in small groups. When they caught sight of Seokyeong and Jebi, they exchanged meaningful glances.

'What's going on?' Jebi whispered, as they retreated to a corner.

'Preparations for the festival. In February of the lunar calendar, the village will hold the annual giant octopus festival. We welcome the octopus which comes onto the land and then choose the envoy who will send it back into the sea.'

Seokyeong nodded at everyone with a smile. A few of the elderly haenyeos whom Jebi had met by the coast came up to him and shook his hand affectionately, but others in the room blatantly averted their gaze.

'A lot of people don't seem very happy to see us,' Jebi whispered.

'Well, you can't expect all neighbours to like one another, right? It's okay. Getting invited means we're being acknowledged as part of the village. I've been waiting so long for this day.' Seokyeong stood a little straighter and took a deep breath.

'It's your first time too? Wow. It took you a year, then?'

'Yup, and that's considered pretty fast.'

'I see . . . I don't see Yoona's dad here.' Jebi looked around for the family.

'Exactly. Because they only moved here six months ago.'

'But I've been here for less than six months.'

'They see you as part of my family. Here, it's not about the individual. Of course, some of them are unhappy that we're here. I heard they put it to a vote, and it was almost fifty-fifty. Just one vote decided it in our favour. Do you know who cast it?'

Jebi shook her head.

'Mokpo Samchon.'

Jebi spotted the old lady on the other side of the room, sitting with her eyes closed. From the way her lips were moved slightly, it looked like she was praying.

Just then, Yanghee and her son Dongwon came in, bobbing their heads in apology for their lateness. Spotting Seokyeong, Dongwon wriggled free of his mother's hand and squeezed through the crowd to get to him, leaving Yanghee looking put out.

'We're starting!' Having checked that everyone was now seated, the village head shouted for attention.

Two young men left the room and returned carrying a large rubber basin between them. Inside was a box-like structure wrapped in black cloth. Everyone automatically shifted to make space for the basin in the middle of the living room.

With his large hands, the village head unwrapped the black cloth to reveal a clear tank of water. Inside was a strange and wonderful sea creature. Everyone clapped and bowed deeply, murmuring under their breath.

Jebi stared in fascination, realising a little late that she ought to bow along with the others.

Dongwon giggled. With his natural curls and slightly upturned nose, he was an adorable child.

'What is it?' Jebi whispered to Seokyeong.

'You're silly! Can't you see that it's a mulkkureok?' Dongwon interrupted.

Jebi glanced at him before turning back to Seokyeong. 'Isn't it the closed season for giant octopuses now?'

'It was caught before the season closed, and kept in an aquarium until now.' Dongwon said, as he climbed onto Seokyeong's back.

'Who did?'

'The village head, of course. Who else? Samchon, this nuna knows nothing.'

On the other side of the room, Yanghee narrowed her eyes at her son and put an index finger to her lips. Immediately, Dongwon squeezed his eyes shut.

'The saja – the envoy – has to be chosen by a pregnant octopus. They catch the octopus before the closed season and take care of it. The village head has suggested several times to push back the start date of the closed season, but his proposal is always rejected during the voting,' Seokyeong whispered.

'Hurry up, let's get started!' someone urged.

At that, the village head put both hands into the tank and picked up the octopus. Not only was it huge and heavy, but its suckers gripped tight to the tank, so the two men who had carried it in hurried over to help.

'Check whether it's a female!' one of the elderly haenyeos called.

'You think I haven't checked that already, in the months

I was looking after her!!' The village head retorted, but the villagers continued to insist.

'Check it!' One of the experienced divers, a sanggun haenyeo, shouted.

Looking frustrated, the village head raised up the octopus and showed it to everyone. 'Look! Suckers on all eight arms. If it was male, one of its arms would be flatter, with no suckers on its tip.'

Everyone pressed in for a closer look and nodded.

The village head put the octopus back into the tank and covered it with the black cloth. Suddenly, he started turning the tank round and round.

'What's he doing?' Jebi was craning her neck to see over the crowd. The people around them turned to give her a quelling look, as if telling her to be quiet.

'He's trying to make things fair. Watch and you'll understand,' Seokyeong replied in a whisper.

Like a magician, the village head suddenly pulled off the black cloth. Everyone sat up a little straighter, putting their hands together in front of their chests.

The octopus, looking a little annoyed, started to climb out of the tank and manoeuvre itself through people's legs.

'Yikes! What's happening?' Jebi hid behind Seokyeong. Meanwhile, the villagers remained absolutely still with their palms together. At the touch of the octopus, they'd lower their gaze and murmur, 'Come closer,' or 'I'm at your mercy,' or 'Bless me'.

'The haenyeo the octopus chooses will have a bountiful year and harvest the best abalones,' Seokyeong said.

'And if it chooses a man, he will marry a lovely haenyeo and be blessed with many sons,' Dongwon added.

Whenever the creature crawled onto someone's knees, the person would look visibly delighted; each time it moved on their face would crumple in disappointment. As it was forbidden to influence the octopus's choice in any way, no one dared move an inch.

Jebi watched quietly. Slowly, the octopus came closer, crawling onto the lap and then the shoulders of the haenyeo next to her. She was a mid-level junggun haenyeo. Would she be the chosen one this year?

A few people were letting out disappointed sighs, but then the giant octopus climbed down again. The next moment, it slid an arm onto Jebi's foot.

Jebi yelped and tried to shake it off.

'Stop moving!'

'Misfortune will befall you!'

At the villagers' whispered admonitions, Jebi froze.

The pale brown giant octopus was using its tentacles to climb her; first, it crawled onto her thighs, then up her back. When she felt its suckers on the skin of her neck, it became too much to bear and Jebi screamed. She tried fending it off with her hands but the people around her moved forward to pin them to her sides.

'Sajangnim! Help me!' Jebi cried.

But Seokyeong sat back, looking delighted. Taking out the small RX0 from his pocket, he starting to snap photos.

'Nuna! Almost there! Hang on a little longer!' Dongwon jumped up and down excitedly.

The giant octopus crawled up past Jebi's cheeks and

ended up on top of her head. And as if finally satisfied, it settled there.

'Can you see?!'

'What's going on?'

There was a buzz of commotion.

'It picked the mainland girl?'

'How could that be?'

'Would you look at that!'

Suddenly, the octopus squirted its ink. Frozen with fright, Jebi allowed the lukewarm liquid to run in rivulets down her cheeks. 'P-please,' she begged, 'please get it off me . . .' Her voice was barely audible. She felt like she was about to pass out.

The village head waved his hand, and immediately, the two men came forward and carefully tried to peel the octopus's arms away from her neck. But the animal refused to budge.

Eventually the men were able to lift the octopus off her. As soon as they did, Jebi slumped to the floor.

Seokyeong hurried forward and, kneeling next to her, dabbed away the ink in her hair with a handkerchief.

'We should try again, no?' someone complained loudly.

'Hush, don't say that! Bad luck will befall us!' the village head shouted angrily.

'Well, we've no choice. She's the chosen one.'

'Hear, hear,' the elderly haenyeos chorused.

'That's why I said only village residents should have been invited,' a sanggun haenyeo complained.

'This is the will of the mulkkureok god. What can we do? If we interfere by repeating the ceremony, the octopus might not choose anyone.'

'Has that ever happened before??'

'There have been such years. And the village suffered a poor harvest, and haenyeos fell sick.'

'Fine, fine. Stop saying such inauspicious things.'

When the disgruntlement died down, everyone turned to Jebi. A silence fell. Jebi looked around with wild, fearful eyes.

'You're now the chosen one,' the village head declared solemnly.

'Yes. You shall be the one who carries the mulkkureok offering into the sea,' a sanggun haenyeo continued.

'Did you just say *into the sea*? But I can't swim!' Jebi waved her hands in alarm.

Everyone glanced at each other, the disdain evident in their eyes.

'So who's going to do it?' The village head broke the silence and looked left and right.

'Do what?' one of the elderly haenyeos asked.

'Someone has to teach this mainlander how to dive, how to swim.'

At this, everyone looked at their laps, waving their hands in rejection, muttering they were busy.

Looking sharply into the crowd, the village head suddenly smacked his palms together, as if an idea had come to him. 'Yanghee, you do it.'

She stood up, saying abruptly. 'Why me?'

'You're the obvious choice. The mainlander doesn't even know our language. How do you expect the sangguns to teach her? You're young, you two will understand each other.'

The village head's words were final. As Yanghee buried her head in her hands in frustration, Dongwon ran to her to comfort her with a hug.

Seokyeong hesitated. Of course, he could teach Jebi to swim himself. But this was an opportunity for Jebi to build a closer relationship with the villagers, and with Yanghee, which wouldn't be a bad thing.

Or rather, it'd be great.

8

Beneath the Waves

Bookings came pouring in as the photo of the giant octopus on Jebi's head which they posted online went viral, especially after a famous magazine editor 'liked' it. Perhaps this was the first of the blessings of the mulkkureok god.

Seokyeong and Jebi were doing shoots every other day. Most were holiday photoshoots, with families or groups of friends who wanted pictures in scenic spots around the island. Gaining experience quickly, the pair soon found these outdoor shoots were a breeze.

Everything was going well – except that, strangely, the baptism by octopus seemed to have robbed Jebi of her sense of smell and taste. The sense of touch on her face was gone too. Each time she washed her face or put on make-up, she was disconcerted by the sensation, or rather, the lack of it.

Worried, Seokyeong drove her to the hospital in the city.

'It's likely due to the toxins in the octopus's ink. But the symptoms should ease soon.'

The doctor prescribed several medications and told Jebi to return if she didn't see an improvement in her condition.

Back at the photo studio, the first thing Seokyeong had to do was call the village head and report that Jebi had safely returned to the village.

Bear in mind, you're not to leave the island. The day of her selection by the octopus, the village head had warned Jebi that if the chosen one were to leave the island before the festival next spring, misfortune would befall the entire village.

Added to all this, on days without a scheduled shoot, Jebi was expected to take swimming lessons in the sea, with Yanghee.

'Frosty' was the only way to describe the haenyeo's attitude towards her. Jebi didn't blame her: the woman had nothing to gain from this assignment. Despite calling it lessons, the village didn't pay her for her services, chalking it up to the obligation of every villager to volunteer their services to the chosen one.

While Yanghee didn't bother hiding her disdain for the job, Jebi tried her best to keep things friendly.

'Is it okay if I call you Eonnie? And what's your last name? I'm Jebi, Yeon Jebi.' In the changing room, Jebi stuck a foot into the wetsuit the haenyeos had lent her, twisting her body from side to side as she tried to pull it up. After a long struggle, she finally managed to fasten the float meant for kids around her neck.

In the other corner, several haenyeos were changing, chatting among themselves in the local dialect.

' "Go" is my last name.'

'Go . . . Yangyi. Oh, like *goyangyi* – a cat?'

'It's Yang-*hee*! Go. Yang. *Hee*!'

'It's okay, Eonnie. I grew up being teased about my name, too. People called me *sujebi* – hand-torn noodles, and *jokjebi* – weasel.'

'For heaven's sake! Just because you're okay with being teased doesn't mean I have to be. Enough of this nonsense and get your butt into the water!' Yanghee snapped, and then grumbled under her breath, 'I'd be better off harvesting abalones instead of . . .'

The haenyeos headed out of the changing room, and Yanghee and Jebi followed. Sitting by the shore, the divers rubbed mug wort on their goggles as the waves crashed on the sand.

Yanghee headed towards them. Behind, Jebi walked slowly, clutching some yellow flippers. 'I'm curious. How much do haenyeos earn?'

'Shh!' Yanghee shoved Jebi to silence her, casting furtive glances around to make sure none of the older haenyeos had heard.

Wobbling, Jebi lost her balance, and her feet plunged into the water. Startled, she quickly scrambled up the rocks, far from the reach of the waves. 'I mean, is it enough to raise a kid? Who takes care of Dongwon when you're diving?'

'You ask too many questions! Get into the water!' Yanghee gave her a shove.

'I'll get into the water after you tell me.' Still playing for time, Jebi clung to Yanghee's arm, only pulling away after a short tussle.

Shaking her head, Yanghee let out a resigned sigh. 'Fine. My mum looks after him. Are we done with the questions?'

'And how much do you earn a year?'

'Twenty million won.'

Jebi took a clumsy step back in surprise. 'But that can't be enough to raise a kid on?'

'That's why I have a side job,' Yanghee said, as she pulled on her swimming cap.

'What is it?'

Yanghee glared at her, exasperated. 'Am I obliged to tell you everything? I've answered your questions. You've got to keep your side of the bargain now!'

Jebi nodded. But she squirmed with discomfort, casting anxious glances at the sea. 'I . . . I'm afraid of water. I almost drowned at a swimming pool when I was a kid . . .'

Yanghee just looked at her.

'Eonnie, can I ask you something? What if the chosen one can't swim? What if she refuses to get into the water?'

Yanghee shot her another fierce glare, her lip curling in a sarcastic smile. 'The chosen one is blessed with abundance. But failing to do what she must will bring great harm upon her.'

'Like getting into a car crash?'

'Is that what scares you most?' Yanghee turned towards the sea. The haenyeos' tewaks bobbed like tangerines on the surface of the water . 'Surely there is something that you fear more than anything else?' she continued, as she sat down in the shallow waters and began rinsing her goggles. 'We believe that if you don't do this for the mulk-kureok god, what you dread will come true.'

Jebi's face blanched.

'Aha, you should see your face . . . looks like there *is* something. Then I'm sure you can do this.' Yanghee scooped up some water with her goggles and wet her head and shoulders.

'How about you, Yanghee Eonnie. What do you fear most?

'Hmph. Why would I tell you?' Yanghee slung the tewak over her shoulder.

'I bet it has something to do with Dongwon.'

Yanghee, who had stood up now, turned on her. 'Enough talking! Get in!' With that, Yanghee grabbed Jebi's arm and yanked.

Screaming, Jebi struggled and shook her off. Desperate to delay the moment she had to enter the water, she blurted out: 'Eonnie! By any chance, have you ever tried surfing?' Jebi was shaking as she clutched at her neck float.

'You're beyond help, aren't you?' Shaking her head in exasperation, Yanghee went into the sea by herself.

Jebi looked on as Yanghee's tewak bobbed away.

From the rooftop of the photo studio, someone had witnessed the entire scene. Lowering his binoculars, Seokyeong let out a small sigh.

All Jebi managed was to go in up to her ankles before she called it a day.

Back at the photo studio, she was leaning against the counter, checking Instagram out of habit, when she saw a fresh booking. She ran up to the rooftop where Seokyeong was preparing for an outdoor party. A wooden table and chairs were neatly arranged, and hanging across the walls were strings of multi-coloured fairy lights.

'Sajangnim! Can you freedive? We have a request for an underwater shoot!'

Bell came bounding over and begin licking her toes.

'Yep. I learnt not long after opening the studio,' Seokyeong said, as he switched on the lights to test them.

Jebi stared at the LED lights blinking in the sun. Scooping Bell up in her arms, she stretched out a hand and touched the bulbs.

'Oh . . . but do you think you can pull off an underwater shoot? Isn't it kind of hard to dive with a camera—'

Seokyeong pushed back his fringe. 'Don't worry. Stephen Gertz once took underwater photos of an oil spill. I picked up quite a few tips studying his work. I know what to do.'

'Amazing!' Jebi gave a thumbs up.

Seokyeong retreated downstairs to his room. He found his GoPro and its waterproof housing, and from a box below his bed he pulled out his diving equipment.

Jebi popped her head around the door. 'When you're shooting . . . what should I do? You know I can't swim . . . I don't think I'll be of any help.'

'Can you do all the preparations for the viewing party afterwards?' Seokyeong asked, as he checked the equipment.

Jebi bit her lip. 'But I can't cook.'

'Everyone starts from scratch. I'll teach you. Even if you could just get the ingredients ready, that'd be a big help. An underwater shoot is tough work.'

Jebi nodded solemnly. 'Where's the dive?'

'Here. Our neighbourhood.' Seokyeong took out his dive knife, opened the blade and examined it.

'Here? Like, from the hill?'

Seokyeong gaped at her. 'What are you saying? If you dived from here, you'd land on the rocks!' He looked pensive for a moment. 'Mokpo Samchon told me once that people have died here when they lost their footing. I think that's partly why this place was auctioned for cheap . . .' He shook his head, clearing his thoughts. 'Anyway, freediving isn't about diving from height. You know scuba diving, right? Where you dive with an oxygen tank? Freediving is essentially the same thing, except you dive in shallower waters, and without the tank. We can go where the haenyeos dive. Although that might be an issue . . .' Seokyeong folded the knife and packed it into his bag.

'Why?'

'Never mind. I'm sure it'll be fine, I guess,' he said, zipping the bag closed.

A few days later, a group of six, all looking to be in their mid-twenties, arrived at the photo studio in their fancy sports cars.

Putting on an apron, Jebi followed Seokyeong outside to greet the customers. When she caught sight of a familiar face, her knees nearly buckled.

'Y-Yeon Jebi? What are you . . .?' one of the men spluttered when he saw her.

'A friend of yours?' Seokyeong asked, as he reached out a hand to steady Jebi.

'No. I mean . . . he was . . .' Shaking her head, she allowed the sentence to tail off.

Seokyeong was going to take them freediving off the coast at the sand dunes. He been given permission from the Haenyeos' Association, who had agreed to let the group dive in the area at a fee of 30,000 won per person. However, they were strictly forbidden from gathering any seafood or damaging the ecosystem during the dive.

At the counter, Jebi was busy taking notes as Seokyeong briefed her on what to do in his absence. First, she was to thaw the frozen octopus and the horned conches. Next, she was to clean the conches with a brush as she steamed the octopus. Once it was cooked, she was to cut it up, ensuring that it was still possible to identify its different parts. When that was done, she would clean and prepare the freshly caught cuttlefish and the king prawns.

After checking that they had ample rice and ramyeon in the cupboard, Jebi clipped her ballpoint pen back onto her apron. She was nervous. What if she couldn't finish everything in time? How did Seokyeong manage to do it all on his own?

Meanwhile, the group was laughing and chatting as they looked around the gallery. Of the two women, one had hair down to her waist while the other sported a stylish bob. One of the men wore a hoop earring, and next to him was a man with a set of numbers tattooed prominently on his arm. The third man was big-bellied; the last man was a head taller than the rest.

At first it looked like there were two couples on the trip, but Jebi soon worked out that only the tattooed man and the girl with the bob were an item.

'Look at this! Can a person have that many teeth?' Short-bob exclaimed as she stared at Jungmi's wisdom teeth. The rest of them crowded around the framed photograph.

'Wow. That's someone's mouth?'

'Seems so.'

'That's impossible. I bet it's a composite photo. Right, Sajangnim?'

Seokyeong, who was making repeated trips to the SUV to load the camera equipment and an oxygen tank – as the photographer, he would be scuba diving – grinned at their reaction. 'Nope. All four of her wisdom teeth came out straight, so she has thirty-two teeth – a full set.'

There was a moment of silence as everyone used their tongue to feel around their mouths.

'This place is rad, I'm glad we came.,' said Tall Guy, as he turned his gaze to the rest of the photos.

'Yay, told you!' Short-bob clapped. 'Remember how sceptical you all were?' She glanced at them. She was wearing a simple necklace and bracelet, but they were clearly of high-quality, possibly even designer.

'It's not that we didn't trust you . . .' Tall Guy protested. 'Hey. Is this you?' He turned towards the counter, pointing at the photo of the creature on Jebi's head.

'Um, yeah.' Jebi nodded as she put the octopus into the steamer.

'Cool!'

'Weren't you scared?'

The curious group crowded around the kitchen area.

'This one could be edited too!' Short-bob laughed, standing in front of the frame.

'Nope. It's a real octopus. Caught in the waters right in front of the village,' Seokyeong said, coming back in from the car.

'Is it? Wow. So what did it feel like?' Long-haired Girl's eyes lit up as she wriggled her fingers above her head to mimic the octopus.

'Wet. Slimy,' Jebi confessed. 'I was so scared that my mind went blank.'

'Should I do this pose later?' Short-bob called out suddenly, changing the subject. Standing in the middle of the gallery in her white one-piece wetsuit, she spread out her arms in a ballet pose and did a standing split.

'Oh, looks good.'

Everyone's attention returned to Short-bob as they snapped photos on their phone and showed her.

She grinned. 'I'm so glad we came here!'

'Yeah. Nothing's worse than hitting the books in summer,' said Long-haired Girl as she ran her fingers through her tresses and tied them up into a ponytail. 'I swore that even if I had to retake my university entrance exam, I'd never let myself go through the civil service exam twice. But damn, it's already my third try! And I'm taking a break from school without knowing if I'll pass this time . . . I wish I could leave it all behind and live here. I could open a dive shop. And it's alright for you,' she said, turning to Short-bob. You're seeing the light at the end of the tunnel.'

Short-bob gave an airy laugh. 'Oh well, I'm stepping through the door straight into workplace hell.'

'Girl, I'd take that hell. Nothing could be worse than these exams.'

Tall Guy butted in. 'Ladies. Can we not talk about studying when we're on holiday? You're killing the mood.'

'Can't help it. It's on my mind twenty-four seven. You and Minah have both found jobs. You don't get it.'

'Well, if you're so miserable, give up on the exam and just get a job!' Tall Guy retorted. 'And don't think I don't know that you guys are secretly looking down on me for working at a small company. But I say it's better to take what you can get in the job market, people are still willing to hire you. Blink and you'll be hitting your thirties!'

An uncomfortable silence descended.

'Come on, no one's looking down on you.' Short-bob laughed awkwardly, and nudged his arm.

'Reality check, guys. If you care to look, there are loads of openings in smaller businesses.' Tall Guy's hand grazed Short-bob's waist before he moved away.

The interaction hadn't escaped the tattooed man's eyes.

'Small companies can be a total nightmare! I'd take the civil service exam over that, any day.'

Everyone but the tall guy broke out in raucous laughter and Tattoo Guy smirked at Tall Guy's reddened face.

'Can we just chill? We're on holiday! We're here to eat, drink and swim.' Big Guy protested, and patted his round stomach.

'Yeah! Let's enjoy it while it lasts and make memories to get us through the misery when we're back to the grind,' said the friend with the earring. Jebi noticed he had a habit of playing with it when he spoke.

Unnoticed by the rest, Tattoo Guy slid up to the kitchen counter.

Seokyeong cast a curious glance over at Jebi but didn't intervene.

'I heard you'd come to Jeju. Are you here alone?' Tattoo Guy asked, in a quiet voice.

At first, Jebi ignored him. But the man continued to hover, moving closer until she finally raised her head. 'Why? Is there a reason I shouldn't be alone?' she hissed, as she took the frozen horned conches from the fridge and placed them in a stainless-steel bowl.

'I didn't mean it that way. Why are you always so sensitive?' Tattoo Guy put a finger to his lips.

Jebi glanced at him. His dark eyebrows and hooked nose were as she remembered. His clear, fair skin, too. Jebi was glad that she had lost her sense of smell so she didn't have to breathe in his signature cologne, which never failed to make her heart squeeze.

Jebi's gaze landed on his arm. *10312*. The tattooed numbers. He must've had them done after they broke up. 31 October. Then what about the extra number? Jebi couldn't help but be curious.

'Must be nice to work at a place like this. I'm envious,' said Short-bob, as she slid up to the man and ran her fingers across his tattoo.

Jebi took the kitchen brush and started scrubbing the horned conches harder than necessary.

The man turned to his girlfriend. 'What's there to be envious of? You passed the civil service exam!'

She gave a tinkling laugh. 'I'll just be working for the customs office. Not very glamorous.' The woman slid her long, slender fingers over the wood of the kitchen counter as she spoke, her nail art crystals glittering in the light.

Jebi ignored the redness of her hands from the cold water she was running. The burning feeling in her chest was harder to ignore. It hurt that her ex-boyfriend had cut her off so rudely. The woman had been speaking to her, and she could answer perfectly well on her own. However great the woman's civil service job might be, Hakuda Photo Studio wasn't too shabby, either. Yet her ex-boyfriend made it seem so inferior.

She shook her head – it'd always been like this, him trampling over her feelings.

Jebi put the cleaned conches back in the fridge, resolving to never let herself be treated that way again.

'Don't be too stressed, just finish what you can.'

Jebi gave a start. While she'd been lost in thought, her boss had come over to stand next to her.

With a nod to her, Seokyeong rounded up the customers and left; only Bell and Jebi remaining behind.

*

At the stunning coastal dunes, the group was warming up for the dive, wearing underwater masks and lead weights. Of the men, only Big Guy had opted for a two-piece wetsuit; the rest of them were topless, their muscles glistening in the sun.

In a black wetsuit with a red belt across his shoulder, Seokyeong held his underwater camera in his hand. On his back was an oxygen tank. A depth gauge was pinned to his chest and a dive knife stowed at his calf.

'I understand that you're all professional freedivers,' Seokyeong began, and everyone puffed up with pride.

'Not quite professionals, but we are all level three divers – we met at our university's diving club,' said Long-haired Girl.

'Yup. We can all hold our breath for two minutes and thirty seconds, and dive up to thirty metres deep,' Tall Guy added.

'Hey, not me. I'm a level two. I can do twenty metres, and about ninety seconds each time.' Tattoo Guy went pink under his goggles.

Seokyeong nodded. 'Got it. Enjoy the dive. I'll be moving about and taking photos of the group. We'll take a short break later and decide on the order of the individual dives and shoots.'

Everyone nodded. 'Perfect.'

Seokyeong continued in a serious tone: 'Once again, please remember that you're strictly forbidden from gathering any seafood. Flouting the rule will incur a fine of up to ten million won.'

'Hey, hey, we may not be professionals, but we're all certified divers. You don't have to explain something that basic to us,' Earring Guy cut in.

Seokyeong smiled. 'Of course. I have no doubts.'

The group entered the water.

With the ninety centimetre-long fins on their feet, Seokyeong thought they were like six oversized fish, or mer-people who'd walked out onto the land for some fairy-tale reason and were now returning home. Their free and practised moves touched something in his heart and, for a moment, he forgot his task.

He was thirty-four. Still young, he knew. But he couldn't shake the anxious feeling that time was passing him by.

But would I want to return to those times?

His past was like a mouldy square of film, blotched and spotted. He was envious of the group's youth, but he didn't think he had the confidence to relive those days. For the past ten years, he had kept going with a single goal in mind – to open a photo studio. He had worked single-mindedly, sacrificing any possibility of finding love, to scrimp and save for his dream.

Perhaps this group of young people he envied were also going through the same tough times?

Seokyeong took a moment to slow his breathing before making his descent. As they dived deeper, the water became an inky blue. On the steep sides of pillow basalt were corals in different shapes and colours. Seaweed danced gracefully as a school of silver anchovies swam above like a passing rain shower.

Seokyeong signalled an OK, and the group returned the same gesture to confirm that everything was good. He stretched out his hand, palm facing forward, suggesting that they stop at this depth. Everyone signalled OK again and went off to explore the reef.

Seokyeong turned on the underwater lighting and manoeuvred the handles attached to the housing of his camera. He held the shutter trigger and got to work.

'That was the best!'

'The coral was gorgeous!'

'And not a single piece of rubbish in the water.'

The group was taking a break on top of the sand dunes, working their way through the sandwiches and coconut juice that Seokyeong had packed from Yoona's Bakes.

For the individual dives, it was decided that the women would go last, giving them more time to catch their breath. And among the men, Tall Guy would go first, followed by Tattoo Guy, Earring Guy and finally Big Guy.

For Seokyeong to maintain his stamina, everyone agreed they would limit themselves to two poses underwater.

Tall Guy cut through the water with a duck dive. When he was deep enough, he took off his fins and mimicked walking on the sand. Seokyeong caught the pose from several angles. Later, when Tall Guy emerged to get some air, he threw his fins onto the surface of the water and jumped on top of them, striking a surfing pose.

Tattoo Guy took some time to descend, staying dangerously close to the corals despite Seokyeong's signals to move away. When he inevitably scratched his calf and started bleeding, Seokyeong signalled at him to go back up, but he shook his head vehemently, instead turning back to the same spot and, for a while, glaring hard at the coral that'd injured him.

Big Guy was surprisingly flexible. He made several graceful three-hundred-and-sixty degree turns under-water. His bulging belly gave him the look of a puffer fish and he seemed to be more at ease in the sea than on land.

Earring Guy was also an accomplished diver. Instead of striking poses, he was more interested in admiring the beautiful underwater scenery. Spotting a clownfish wiggling its tail among the sea anemones, he approached carefully and even when he stretched out a hand, the clownfish didn't startle and swim away. Seokyeong caught the interaction on camera.

Then it was the women's turn.

Long-haired Girl, in a mint-green swimsuit, was the first one to dive. Her billowing locks spread out behind her like seaweed as she entered the water. Seokyeong clicked his shutter. Then, as a school of neon damselfish passed in front of her, the woman changed direction and followed. Seokyeong captured the kaleidoscope of colours on his camera.

Hadn't she said she wanted to open a dive shop?

Was she caught in the rat race of life, constantly pushing her dreams aside . . .? At least in this moment, Seokyeong thought, she was truly living. Out in the open ocean, she swam as one with the damselfish. It was his task to capture the moment, to help her never forget this feeling. Seokyeong centred her silhouette in his viewfinder.

It was time for the last shoot of the day. As he surfaced, Seokyeong was surprised to see that Short-bob had changed out of her white wetsuit into a tangerine chiffon dress. On her head was a garland of white roses.

'Make me a magical water fairy.'

Because her skirt kept getting caught up around her legs, Seokyeong had to swim close and help her adjust it. Putting her thumb down, she descended deeper. Seokyeong followed but signalled at her to slow down.

Short-bob floated just above the corals waving their stumpy yellow tentacles. Underwater, the giant sea anemones looked like blooming plum blossoms. Short-bob took off her fins and swam barefoot. Seokyeong snapped photos, darting back and forth to make sure that the dress didn't hide her face.

Taking a few breaths from his oxygen tank, she descended towards the sargassum beds and started twining them around herself, confusing Seokyeong as to what she was trying to do. Just then, a pale, ghost-like shape appeared behind her. Seokyeong quickly signalled to her that something was amiss.

Alarmed, she looked behind her. A giant jellyfish, the size of a human child, was swimming among the sargassum. She gave a start but instead of swimming away to avoid it, she signalled a square with her hands for Seokyeong to keep going. Slowly, she swam towards the creature, stretching out her fingers as if to touch it.

At that moment, however, wafted by the currents, the jellyfish started drifting towards her. Seokyeong knew that if he didn't do something, the girl would get caught in the creature's tentacles and be badly stung.

Thinking quickly, he took out his dive knife and threw it at the jellyfish.

It jerked back, then swam away with the currents.

Back on the beach, Seokyeong was completely exhausted. Just as he was about to suggest that the group head back to the photo studio, he paused. Something was missing. *Someone.* 'Hey. He's not here. The guy with the tattoo.'

Seokyeong looked around. The men were resting on the dunes after changing back into their clothes.

'He said he was bored and went into the water.'

'How long has he been under? His limit is ninety seconds, right?'

His friends looked at one another blankly. Because the guys had changed and the girls were still tired from their dives, Seokyeong went back into the water alone.

But Tattoo Guy was nowhere to be seen – not on the surface, nor where he had posed for photos earlier. Dread welled in Seokyeong at the thought that the man might have met with a mishap.

Suddenly, a figure appeared in front of him. A black wetsuit – it was a haenyeo. Through the clear dive mask, Seokyeong could make out her features. Yanghee.

She signalled for him to follow her to the surface. Among the dunes, a group of haenyeos had gathered. In their midst lay the tattooed man, his eyes shut.

'He's breathing,' said the president of the haenyeos.

'We saw him trying to catch an octopus. He was sticking his hand in between the rocks when his foot got caught in the sargassum. The president saw him struggling and saved him,' Yanghee said, as she pulled off her swimming cap. Her tone was ice-cold.

'An octopus?' Shocked, Seokyeong stared at her.

'We sent it back to the sea, of course,' the president said, staring daggers at Seokyeong. 'I warned you about this. For heaven's sake, can you imagine what would happen if he had caught that octopus?'

Seokyeong bowed his head. 'I-I'm sorry. I should've paid more attention.'

'Look, a person almost died! Is a damned octopus really that important?' Short-bob spoke up from behind the ring of haenyeos. The rest of the group had followed her and were also glaring at the local women.

'*A damned octopus?* Then why try to catch it? It's our guardian deity, our lifeline!' The haenyeos were beside themselves. 'How *dare* you lay a finger on one when it's the closed season!'

'But it was right there, among the rocks . . .' The tattooed man spoke up, coughing weakly, as if sympathy would help him worm his way out of the situation.

'She's watching over her eggs, of course she was staying put! Do you expect her to leave her children behind to save herself?' the president thundered.

'Those ajummas killed the mood,' Short-bob complained, as she pushed open the entrance of the photo studio.

Everyone's expression was dark.

'Can you blame them, though? Why would anyone in their right mind go after the octopus?' Long-haired Girl shot the tattooed man a disgusted look as she squeezed water out of her wet hair. 'You just had to make it obvious, didn't you?' Tall Guy sank onto the sofa and looked scornfully at the troublemaker.

'What do you mean?' Tattoo Guy shot back. Over his shoulder was a diving fin bag.

'That you're not a proper diver. That you were a transfer student from a community college and joined the club much later than the rest of us.'

'What the fuck?' The tattooed man glared at him, an ugly look on his face.

'Never touch the marine life. That's the number one rule! A fucking idiot like you wants to be a civil servant? When you can't even follow the most basic instructions? What a joke.'

'Fuck you.' Tattoo Guy threw down his fin bag and lunged at the man.

Tall Guy stood up abruptly and shoved him hard.

The rest hurried to hold them back.

'Oh my god, stop embarrassing yourselves!' Short-bob shouted. Belatedly, the group realised that Seokyeong and Jebi were staring.

'What's done is done. Come on, drop it.' The man with the earring patted the shoulder of the tattooed guy.

'Yeah. We still have the viewing party to look forward to. I can't wait to see what's served,' Big Guy said, in a falsely cheerful tone, as he pulled Tall Guy away.

Seokyeong went to the kitchen to check on Jebi. 'Everything okay?'

'I've finished all the prep. The barbecue is set up on the rooftop. All that's left to do upstairs is to light the charcoal,' Jebi said, as she ran through her to-do list.

She'd ticked off her tasks with a pen as she had finished them.

'Amazing. I didn't expect you to get through everything. Great job!' Seokyeong's gaze swept over the neatly prepared ingredients. 'Was it all okay?'

'It was fine, except that I still can't smell anything, so it felt like I was handling play food.' Jebi shrugged. 'By the way, what's going on?'

Seokyeong briefly explained what had happened.

Jebi's jaw dropped. Her ex-boyfriend had almost died trying to catch an octopus.

Shaking his head, Seokyeong combed his fingers through his damp hair. He walked back to the customers, who were hanging around awkwardly in the gallery. 'The barbecue is ready on the rooftop. We have prepared lots of seafood and pork belly for you. There's beer in the ice box, and we have noodles too. While you guys enjoy the party, we'll be going through the photos from today's shoot. Once we're done, we can have the photo viewing party upstairs.'

'Sure, take your time.' Short-bob smiled warmly. Since he'd helped her chase away the jellyfish, she'd begun to take more notice of him.

Seokyeong was lighting the grill as Jebi carried plates and brass bowls of food to the rooftop. Bell tagged along, wagging her tail.

In the day, the lights had looked lacklustre to Jebi; after sundown, they were beautiful. Soon, the meat and seafood were sizzling tantalisingly on the grill, their mouth-watering aromas drifting on the evening breeze.

'Thanks for preparing all this. Please join us,' said Earring Guy.

'Yeah, have some food,' said Big Guy, as he took a thirsty gulp of beer.

'Thanks for offering! But I have to take photos of the party too . . .' With a grin, Jebi flashed the RXo in her hand.

'Aw, that's too bad.'

The guests connected a phone to the speaker and as electronic dance music blasted out, their bodies bobbed along like the waves. Laughter and chatter filled the rooftop as they enjoyed the freshly grilled conches and octopus, and washed them down with beer.

Tattoo Guy leant against the wall and drank alone. Nobody bothered to talk to him.

'Get away from me!'

Jebi quickly lowered the camera and turned to see her ex-boyfriend aiming a kick at something.

'Letting a dirty mutt run free when there's food around? That's just stupid – and unhygienic!'

Anger flared in Jebi's stomach as Bell gave a frightened yelp. Her tail between her legs, she scuttled over to Jebi. 'Our puppy has short fur. She's cleaner than you!' Jebi yelled so loudly that the entire village probably heard her.

An unnatural silence followed. The music, which continued blaring through the speaker, did little to cut through the tension.

Just then, Seokyeong arrived on the rooftop with a bucket of ice. 'Jebi, what's going on?' He turned to the gaping customers and apologised.

'Hey. Come with me?' The tattooed man caught Jebi's eye. Without waiting, he headed for the stairs.

'They know each other?' Long-haired Girl asked Short-bob, who shrugged and said nothing.

Jebi handed over the camera to Seokyeong and went downstairs.

Jebi and her ex walked down the hill and stopped at the edge of the small beach at the bottom of the cliffs. The rough waves seemed ready to swallow them at any moment as they thundered onto the rocks.

'What's your problem? Don't tell me you're still holding a grudge?' he said.

There was so much Jebi wanted to say but she was suddenly struggling to form a sentence.

It seemed, however, that he interpreted her silence in his own way.

'You should know . . . it wasn't easy for me to go from a community college to a four-year accountancy degree at a university. The transfer exam was hell, and trying to gel with those people was even harder.' He jutted his chin towards the top of the cliff. 'Right now, all that's left for me to do is to pass the civil service exam, and then I'll finally be able to tear off the "transfer student" label.' He sighed, heavily. 'I almost made it last year; I missed the passing grade by one question.' He turned to Jebi and held out the arm with the tattoo. 'Look! I even tattooed the answer here.'

Jebi's heart dropped. So those numbers had had nothing to do with her.

'Do you know why I went back into to the sea today? I wanted to catch something and cook it at the party. I wanted to impress them all by catching an octopus with my bare hands. If only my leg hadn't got tangled in those weeds . . . That octopus was weird too – it barely even struggled. I spotted that gap between the rocks; there were lots of white eggs in there, attached to the wall, swaying like flowers in the wind. I couldn't breathe so I kept kicking, to free myself. I must've hit those eggs, because I saw those tiny balls come tumbling out like bubbles and get washed away in the current. Just as I was blacking out, someone freed me from the weeds, thank god. Do you know what I realised in that moment?'

Jebi shrugged, mute.

'Fuck the civil service exam. Who cares whether I'm a transfer student? It's no big deal. I almost died, but I survived. That's what matters. I'm telling you, you should forget about the past, too. We're alive right now, and that's good enough.'

'We're alive, and . . . that's good enough?' The rage surging through Jebi's body felt pure. 'How *dare* you? Do you have no shame?' she screamed at him.

Her ex looked shocked. 'Shame? Why should I be ashamed? What about you? You really think you're the better person.'

'What do you mean?'

'What happened four years ago, it was hard for me. When you broke the news, do you know how shocked I was? In fact, *you* owe *me* an apology!'

Jebi couldn't believe her ears. 'Me? Apologise to you?'

'Why are you acting all innocent? I can't believe this!' He strode forward, stopping inches from Jebi's face. 'Fine. I got you pregnant. But that's your fault as much as mine, right? You should have been practising proper contraception. You didn't even tell me it wasn't a safe day. All because of you, I have to carry around this horrible guilt—'

'What are you talking about?'

The two of them turned at the voice. Short-bob was standing only a few paces away.

'Minah, no, it's not what you think . . .' The man pushed Jebi aside hastily.

'Not what I think? You're disgusting!' The girl turned and started crossing the angular rocks.

Jebi's ex gave chase, shouting at her to be careful.

Jebi heard her angry reply: 'We're over! That's what I came here for, anyway. To make a few last good memories before going our separate ways. It's a break-up trip!'

Jebi fled.

When she reached Mokpo Granny's, feeling like she'd left her soul elsewhere, the old lady was just watering her garden.

'Back so early? Didn't you say you'd be late because there's a shoot?'

At the sound of her familiar voice, the tears burst out of Jebi.

She ran into her room and started packing her bags. But the note stuck to her door gave her pause: 'To be paid on the first work anniversary.' She tore off the paper and ran out of the house, leaving Mokpo Granny staring after her, perplexed.

When Jebi stopped to catch her breath she realised she was at the entrance of the village. Staring severely at her was the octopus jangseung with its sea-urchin hair. Jebi remembered the first time she had seen the statue. She had been dripping wet, her phone dead, at a loss for what to do. She remembered noticing the banner, which now flapped noisily in the dark. And how she'd slipped her fingers into the statue's mouth and made a wish.

Wiping her tears away with the back of her hand, she fished out her phone from her pocket and made a call. It was picked up immediately.

'Jebi-ssi! It's been a long time. How've you been?' said a woman's voice. 'Don't hang up, please Jebi-ssi. Don't hang up! The child is well. In a good home. Your letter, I passed it on to them . . .'

It was more than Jebi could bear. She dropped the phone and felt her legs give way, until she was slumped forward, forehead against the ground. She was gasping, great sobs racking her body. She had planned to say thank you, to the woman on the phone, to the octopus jang-seung, to say it ten, no, hundreds of times, but the tears wouldn't stop.

Rubbing her swollen eyes, Jebi trudged back to Mokpo Granny's house only to see that several people had gathered in the narrow garden. Next to Seokyeong, Granny was pacing anxiously. When she saw Jebi, she rushed forward and embraced her.

The village head threw down the cigarette he'd been smoking, crushed it with his foot, and walked over briskly. 'How many times do I have to tell you! If you leave, misfortune will befall our village!'

'She's back. Say no more,' Mokpo Granny hushed him.

'You're right. It's fine. She's back,' the haenyeo president heaved a sigh of relief. There was a murmur of agreement. Yanghee was among the crowd.

'I'm sorry.' Jebi sank into a deep bow.

When everyone had gone home, Mokpo Granny made some roasted barley tea and poured Jebi and Seokyeong a cup each.

'Why are you here? What happened to the customers?' Jebi asked him.

'I offered them a thirty per cent refund and asked them to leave. I told them I'd mail out the photos.'

'I'm really sorry. Please deduct it from my salary.' Jebi hung her head, her thumb running back and forth over the rough rim of the mug.

'Very well. But thank you. Thank you for coming back.' Seokyeong reached out and brushed dirt from Jebi's forehead. She must have picked it up when she'd fallen to the ground, crying.

Jebi couldn't help but laugh. The warmth of his big hand lingered, the smell of soap in her nostrils. Everything had returned to its rightful place.

9

The Man at the Cliff Edge

The next morning, Jebi woke at first light and helped Mokpo Granny water the vegetable patch. She volunteered to rake the garden, and then, when it was time, she set out for the coast.

Half an hour later, when all the haenyeos had started diving, Jebi was still standing stiffly on the beach. Her lips, blue from the cold, trembled.

'For the water to kill you, you'd have to be submerged up to here,' Yanghee said as she tapped Jebi's nose.

Jebi shook her head violently and scooted back several steps.

'So it's okay for the water to reach here, no?' This time, Yanghee jabbed Jebi's chest.

Still, Jebi refused to move an inch.

'Come on, I'll hold you.' Yanghee pulled Jebi forward.

Alarmed, Jebi wriggled away and ran further up the beach. They'd done this dance several times already, with Jebi returning to apologise and then fleeing the next time Yanghee tried to get her into the water.

Exasperated, Yanghee rounded on her. 'You're scared of the sea. And you don't trust anyone! Then why keep coming back? Just run away, as far as you can.' She pulled out the swimming cap tucked at her waist with a snap and jammed it on her head.

'I-I have nowhere else to go . . .' Jebi lowered her head. The clear water swept over her feet.

'There *must* be something you're more afraid of than drowning.' Softening a little, Yanghee looked at her. 'Focus on that. Tell yourself that should you fail to get into the water, the thing you dread will happen.'

As Yanghee stretched and warmed up, Jebi inched towards the sea. The water reached her shaking knees. Just as she was about to turn back, she screwed her eyes tight and took another step forward. Several steps later, the water came up to her thighs, her butt, and finally, her chest.

'Good. Fight fear with fear.' Yanghee slung the tewak over her shoulders. Like a duck, she dipped her head into the water, neatly dived under, then surfaced again. 'One step forward. One step back. Do it one hundred times before you go home.'

With that, Yanghee pulled her tewak after her and began swimming further out.

Jebi lifted her head and squinted her eyes. The sun was dazzling, and she felt her skin prickle with it. On the horizon, fishing boats bobbed on the waters.

'One step forward. One step back,' Jebi muttered under her breath. As she edged further into the water, she realised she was pushing past the fear that gripped her.

Fight fear with fear. Yanghee's voice rang in her ears.

The thing worse than drowning. Jebi willed herself to focus on that single thought. If she learnt to dive and did what was required of the chosen one, that thing she dreaded wouldn't happen. Hope lit a flame in her chest, melting away her fear. One more step, and one more . . . Jebi continued to push herself forward. She'd never gone out this far. She laughed out loud for the thrill of it, and suddenly the salt water was rushing into her open mouth.

She choked, stumbling. *I can't touch the ground!* Panicking, Jebi flailed her limbs wildly. The waves lapped at her, water filling her ears, deafening her.

I'm going to drown!

The sea was swallowing her up. Jebi tried to scream, but she couldn't make a sound. Her heart lurched. She gasped for breath, but it was as if her lungs were on fire. Through blurred vision, she could make out the glow of the orange in the distance.

The next moment all she could see was darkness.

Confused by the rapidly changing scenes as her head bobbed up and down in the water, Jebi closed her eyes. Memories flashed past like a film being rewound . . .

Jebi, nudging her sleeping baby awake and feeding her from a bottle. When the baby had drunk her fill, she had dressed her in her best clothes and taken a taxi to the orphanage. The director, whom she'd met several times, had greeted her with a smile, but her eyes had been sad. With the last form filled and signed, Jebi had stared at her baby sleeping soundly on the sofa. 'It's time to say goodbye,' the director had said. Jebi had bent down and hugged the child close to her, the baby gurgling and reaching sleepily for Jebi's neck. She knew then that she would never forget that moment, not until the day she died.

'Live well, be happy,' Jebi had whispered.

As the director had picked up the baby, the unfamiliar smell and touch had caused her to squirm and start crying. Jebi had watched, helpless, and then it had been too much to bear. Covering her ears, she had turned and run . . .

Jebi screamed, and her eyes flew opened. Flailing her arms, she gasped for air, inhaling yet more salt water instead.

The last thing she saw was a huge wave surging towards her.

'Breathe! Jebi-ya, come on!'

Jebi stirred awake to a searing pain in her chest. Someone was pumping her chest repeatedly – fast and steady. Then it clicked. *CPR.* Someone was performing CPR on her.

Feeling a wave of nausea, she threw up a mouthful of salt water and curled over onto her side. Looming above her was Seokyeong's face, deathly pale. Jebi felt him shaking her. Dongwon, too, stood wide-eyed beside his grandmother. He looked terrified, his curls flying wildly in the wind as he bit his nails in anxiety.

Jebi felt a sourness shoot up to her nose and, groaning, she threw up again.

'What happened?' A group of sanggun haenyeos crowded around them.

Seokyeong didn't turn around. Neither did he say anything as he continued to massage Jebi's limbs.

Yanghee set down her heavy net and pulled off her swimming cap. 'What's going on?'

'You're asking *me*?' Seokyeong whipped around, his body stiff with anger. Dongwon went on biting his fingernails. Without waiting for a response, Seokyeong turned back and helped Jebi to a sitting position, before picking her up in his arms and carrying her to his motorbike.

He tried to set her down on the seat, but she kept slumping backwards.

'At this rate, the chosen one is going to fall and get hurt.'

An employee from the local fishery cooperative who had come to collect the haenyeos catch rushed forward to help.

Promising the haenyeos that he'd be back, the cooperative employee lifted Jebi into his truck and headed for Mokpo Granny's house.

'How did you know . . .?' Taking off her swimming cap, Jebi sank onto her mattress.

'I saw what happened through the binoculars. From the rooftop.' Seokyeong said, pulling a blanket over her.

'Wow. Spying on your employee . . . Isn't that a criminal offense? You're going to be on the news.'

'I guess you're feeling better if you're cracking jokes like this,' Seokyeong replied drily.

Jebi pulled the blanket closer and sniffed it. The scent of the laundry detergent mixed with the smell of Mokpo

Granny's house steadied her. 'Why were you so angry? Because of me?'

Seokyeong sat down next to her. 'Yeah.'

'Why?'

'What?'

'What made you so angry? Do you . . . care about me?'

At that moment, Mokpo Granny pushed open the door. In her hands was a bowl of warm honey water.

'Yeah, of course I care about you,' Seokyeong replied. He ruffled her hair as he got up. 'Samchon, I'll leave her in your good hands.'

'Don't worry about a thing. You get back to work.'

Mokpo Granny spooned the honey water into Jebi's mouth. Jebi was feeling strong enough to feed herself, but she continued to lie there obediently. It was the first time in her life that someone had taken care of her like this.

She must have fallen asleep after that, because when Jebi next opened her eyes, the room was dark. Hearing voices outside, she sat up.

'Mokpo Samchon, are you at home?' a voice called out.

'Who's there at this hour?'

Jebi heard the creak of the front door. There was a moment of silence.

'Yanghee, what are you doing here?'

Jebi thought she detected a trace of apprehension in Granny's voice. Perhaps she was just feeling weary after a difficult day.

'I'm here to visit Jebi,' Yanghee replied, although her tone was so frosty it would have been less surprising if she had said she was there to collect an overdue debt.

Jebi kicked away the quilt, stood up slowly and opened the door. 'I'm sorry for all this trouble.'

'Not at all. I'm here to apologise.' Yanghee came into Jebi's room and sat down primly in the corner, tucking her legs beneath her.

'Thank you.'

Jebi didn't know what to say. *Was 'thank you' an appropriate response?* she wondered. Why was it that whenever she received an apology, her first reaction was gratitude? 'Er . . . but why?' Jebi cast a furtive glance at the haenyeo.

'As in why am I apologising to you? Well . . . you're the chosen one.' Her cold eyes swept across the room. 'Do you not read? I don't see a single book in here.'

A flush crept up Jebi's cheeks. 'Um, I just haven't had the chance to go book shopping.'

'Is there a book you want to read?'

'Er . . . many. I want to learn more about photography, cooking, and make-up . . .'

'You can just watch YouTube for that. Noone reads these days to pick up a skill. You should read to feel.'

'Feel? Feel what?'

Yanghee pursed her lips, as if the question wasn't worthy of an answer. She shot a glance at Jebi. 'I got an earful for letting you come to harm. From my mum, from our president, and from the village head.'

Jebi bit her lip. 'I'm sorry.'

'You're a very blessed girl. In the village, we all learnt to dive on our own.'

Jebi tilted her head. 'You didn't learn from your mother?'

'What?'

'Diving.'

'I guess some people do.' Yanghee let out a snort. 'But when you have a haenyeo as your mum, you're expected to know how to swim and dive practically from birth. All of us haenyeos are on our own; we have to find the courage to dive every day into the dark, cold water, as if entering the afterlife.' Yanghee got up quietly and walked towards the window. She lifted the corner of the curtain, peeked at the garden and sat down again. 'The best way to become a haenyeo is through marriage.'

Jebi blinked. What was Yanghee trying to tell her?

'The best way is to marry a Jeju man.' Her tone suggested she was letting Jebi in on a secret. 'Between a haenyeo's daughter and the wife of a Jeju man, the wife is more qualified to be a haenyeo, even if she is an outsider. And our village's haenyeos' association has only one opening to fill.'

'There's a limit?'

'Of course. Can you imagine hundreds or thousands of people diving into the same small stretch of ocean? Marine life needs time to reproduce. In order not to upset the balance of the ecosystem, we limit the number of haenyeos.'

'I see.'

Yanghee cast another meaningful glance at the window. 'The old lady from Mokpo became a haenyeo after marrying a man from here. At first, the villagers treated her like an outsider, but not for long. My grandmother on my mum's side befriended her. My grandma was a sanggun haenyeo, one of the most experienced and skilled. She was the one who taught that old woman the ropes.'

'Oh.'

'My grandma died in the sea. She went out with that Mokpo old lady one day, and never came back.' Yanghee glanced towards the window again. 'To this day, I don't know whose fault it was. I don't even know how she died! That old lady refused to ever speak about it – her mouth clamped tighter than a clamshell. My mum grew up lonely, having lost her mother at the age of ten. She became afraid of the sea, making it impossible for her to be a haenyeo.'

Yanghee met Jebi's eyes. There was no animosity in her face, only frustration at those who feared the waters. 'I never thought that much about my grandma's death. That was until I got divorced and moved back to this island.' She tucked a lock of stray hair behind her ears. 'It's not easy to raise a kid and make enough money to live on as a single mother on the mainland. I knew that if I moved back here, at least Mum would be able to help me look after Dongwon. And being a haenyeo is like being a free-lancer.' She bent forward and stretched. 'It is hard work. But it's a matter of survival for me. I just have to grit my teeth and do it. Nobody taught me the ropes. So why should I have to teach you?'

'Then how . . .' Jebi swallowed hard. 'How did you learn?'

For a while, Yanghee didn't respond. 'Grit, and resilience. And by thinking about the octopus.'

'Octopus?'

'Yes, everyone who grows up here knows about octopuses. We know that male octopuses die after they mate. And that the females are left to lay the eggs and care for them alone. They find a crevice between the rocks, and until the eggs hatch, they have to keep moving their arms to create bubbles so that the eggs have a constant supply of fresh air. The eggs take at least five months to hatch. In that time, the females don't eat. When the eggs hatch, the females die. The elders in the village always say, "Eggs that have lost their mother go rotten." I knew that if I didn't want my Dongwon to suffer that fate, I must become a haenyeo. I must learn to hold my breath underwater, just as mothers on the island have done for generations.'

'I . . . I guess that's why I can't even swim. Because I'm a terrible mother,' Jebi whispered.

Yanghee cocked her head, as if wondering whether she'd heard correctly.

'I . . . I had a child.' Jebi's voice was a whisper.

Yanghee jerked her head back. 'No. Don't confide in me.'

'Please. Listen to me. I have to tell someone. Please . . .'

'No! Why should I be the one?'

'But didn't you say that you're sorry? Aren't you here to apologise?' Tears fell from Jebi's eyes.

Yanghee, who had been about to get up, paused. She sat down heavily and leant against the wall. Without saying anything, she looked at Jebi.

'I wasn't the one who initiated things. He asked me out.' The words tumbled out of Jebi like vomit. 'He had just returned to school after completing military service. To me, he seemed like a real adult. We started dating, and I found out that I was pregnant just a few months later. At first, I was delighted. I imagined us raising our child together. I thought he loved me, that he would work hard and we would get through it together. But . . . I couldn't have been more wrong. He told me to my face that he'd never thought of marrying me. That the idea had never crossed his mind. "I'm going to transfer into a four-year university," he said. The way he stared at my stomach, it was as if he was looking at something disgusting.'

Jebi wiped her tears on the quilt.

'I gave birth alone. I was so scared I didn't dare go to the hospital . . . It was so painful, I thought I was going to die. In the end, I called an ambulance. I was living with my grandmother at the time, but . . . she simply watched me, her eyes cold. She'd given birth to four children, but she refused to lift a finger to help me. When I brought my baby home, and she laughed or cried, my grandmother simply pretended not to see, not to hear.'

Jebi's voice grew desperate.

'I had no idea feeding the baby would be so demanding, so painful. After taking care of her for a week, I finally understood how my own mother could have abandoned me. I had always thought I'd hate her until the day I died, but considering she took care of me for three whole years, I began to feel grateful instead.' She looked up, appealing to Yanghee. 'Eonnie, all I ever wanted was to be a normal university student, to enjoy life. I wanted to turn back time, to return to the moment when my child was still an unfertilised egg. And him? He moved to a new city, and started dating someone else right away, posting their couple photos on Instagram as if nothing had happened.'

Jebi balled her fists at the side of her head and howled. 'But I didn't give up my child because of that man! I left her because I couldn't love her! I . . . I couldn't stop crying, the anxiety was overwhelming . . . My own childhood had been lonely, loveless, and I was terrified it would be the same for my daughter. I couldn't stand that thought!'

There was a silence. Then: 'If you're hoping that I'll comfort you . . .'

'No, I'm not!' Jebi buried her face in the quilt.

'Where's the child now? Who's raising her?'

Jebi's breathing was ragged. 'She was adopted. To a good home.'

'Oh? Then what are you so afraid of?'

'I'm afraid that something will happen to her.' Jebi bundled up the quilt and hugged it close. 'What if her adoptive parents are bad people?'

'But you gave her away. And they took her in.' Yanghee shrugged. 'Don't you think you're being illogical?'

'I know. But . . . I'll never know why they adopted her.' Tears fell from her bloodshot eyes.

'So?'

'If I can complete my mission – learn to swim and be an envoy to the octopus – it feels like my child will be blessed with a good life, and her adoptive parents will continue to shower her with love.'

Yanghee snorted. 'That's ridiculous. Whether you can dive or not will not change the personalities of these people you've never met.'

Jebi nodded, still sobbing.

When Yanghee next spoke, her voice was gentler. 'But learning how to swim is a good thing you can do for your child.'

Jebi looked up. 'How so?'

'She may fall into the water one day. Who knows? And you may happen to be there, in the right place, at the right time.' Yanghee shrugged again. 'You never know what's going to happen in life. Maybe you'll save a woman from drowning, and she'll turn out to be your child's adoptive mother . . .'

Jebi swallowed hard. 'Eonnie, do you believe in the mulkkureok god?'

Yanghee frowned. 'Your own faith shouldn't be influenced by what others believe.'

She glanced at her watch, and ran a hand through her hair, before going on. 'If a mulkkureok god does exists, and you fail to get into the water and suffer its wrath as a result, you will live your life in regret. You'll cry, as sorrowfully as you're doing now, and tell yourself "I should've completed my mission *no matter what*!". But if you succeed, you'll never regret it, even if suffering befalls you all the same. So, learn how to swim. In life, the hardest things are always the most important.' Yanghee got up and smoothed out the wrinkles on her clothes. 'Come to the beach the day after tomorrow. I'll do my best to teach you.'

Jebi scrambled out of bed and saw her to the door. And even after Yanghee had disappeared down the road, Jebi kept her head bowed low.

*

Seokyeong spent the whole afternoon wiping, cleaning, dusting. But no matter how hard he tried to tire himself out, the anger in him wouldn't dissipate. The memories the events of the morning had dredged up felt so *raw*, as though they'd happened only yesterday. His mother, his father, and the immeasurable pain and sadness . . .

In the evening, Seokyeong decided to take Bell for a walk and stop by Mokpo Granny's house to check on Jebi. He picked up the little dog, attached her lead, and reached for his windbreaker in the closet. In September, Jeju was still as hot as midsummer in the day, but at night, the wind was crisp; he could feel autumn approaching.

He locked the door behind him and was about to cross the garden when Bell let out a bark. She was straining at her lead, trying to head in the direction of the precipice behind the stone wall. Seokyeong tugged gently, but she resisted. The next moment, she pulled free and, as the lead slipped through his fingers, she disappeared under the safety fence.

Alarmed, Seokyeong followed behind and caught Bell before she ventured too close to the cliff edge. Straightening up, he paused. Someone was standing by the window of the gallery, not far from the precipice. An old man.

Were the rough waves too loud or was he deep in thought? For even when Bell barked sharply, the man didn't move an inch. Seokyeong wondered if he should call out to him. He didn't want to surprise the man in case he fell, but leaving him standing out there wasn't an option either.

'Hey! You can't pee here!' Seokyeong swallowed hard. It was all he could think of to say, but now it sounded ridiculous to his ears.

The man turned, looking aghast. 'What? What kind of person do you take me for?' His voice was gruff, reminding Seokyeong of broken shards of pottery grinding together. 'I was just admiring the view. This place has rather a magnetic pull.'

Despite the man's calm and friendly tone and body language, Seokyeong approached carefully. 'We have a much nicer view from the rooftop.'

'Really?' Unthinkingly, the man stepped backwards, closer still to the edge, and looked up at the building.

A chill ran down Seokyeong's spine. *One more step and he'll fall.*

Closing the gap between them quickly, he grabbed the man's arm. 'If you haven't had dinner, come and join me. A booking got cancelled and we have more than enough food in.'

'Dinner? At a photo studio? Well, now that you mention it, I am feeling peckish.' The man rubbed his stomach. 'And what an intelligent-looking puppy.'

As they made their way carefully into the garden, Seokyeong thought back to the man's words, about the magnetic pull of the precipice. *This man has something of that mysterious charisma too*, he mused.

As Seokyeong held the gate for him, he thought he caught a glint in the man's eyes – was it menace or intelligence he saw in them? Seokyeong couldn't quite tell. He'd noticed that the man was strong when he'd grabbed his arm before, and now he found himself stealing nervous sideways glances at the stranger.

*

'My goodness, what are these?' The man's eyes widened at the freediving photos scattered on the table. With a wide smile, he bent forward, his hands clasped behind his back, taking his time to look at every single one. 'The best years of life, indeed. I never got the chance to try something like this,' he continued.

In the brightly lit room, Seokyeong looked the man over properly. He was dressed in a red Hawaiian shirt. He looked to be in his early seventies, but his protruding cheekbones and wide jaw spoke of strength and an iron will. His sinewy arms had a healthy tan to them, too.

'That's the same for most people.' Seokyeong had meant it as a comforting, neutral remark, but the man didn't reply. Instead, he pursed his lips and stared at Seokyeong.

'I'm sorry if I misspoke.'

'Not at all. I'm just thinking of how a young man like yourself could understand me . . .'

'What?'

'Oh no, it's nothing.'

Seokyeong placed some seafood in the ice box, stuck it under his arm and began leading the man to the rooftop. At the top of the stairs, the man made a muffled sound as his gaze took in the rooms on the first floor. Was it because the man's eyes were so big that every little action of his seemed magnified?

Out on the rooftop, Seokyeong lit the grill and when the coals were hot enough, he arranged horned conches and king prawns neatly on the mesh. Then he tore open some freshly microwaved rice and poured hot water into a cup ramyeon. In a saucer of soy sauce, he added a small lump of horseradish to make a dipping sauce as the brine in the conches bubbled vigorously. Noticing that the grilled prawns were ready, he placed a couple on the man's plate.

The night air was cold, but the warmth of the barbeque kept the chill at bay, and the man seemed to be comfortable, keeping his back straight even as the sleeves of his Hawaiian shirt flapped noisily in the wind.

'I love the scent of that charcoal. What have I done to deserve this hospitality?'

'We use palm charcoal. And don't worry, I was fretting over finishing all this food by myself, so I'm glad to have you here.'

The man picked up his chopsticks and chuckled. 'Thank you. What an unexpected treat.' He put on the cotton gloves Seokyeong handed him and reached for a horned conch. He tried to poke the meat out with the chopsticks, but the conch slipped out of his hand and dropped to the floor. Then he took a second conch and smashed it hard against the one on the floor before casually picking the meat from the shell and slipping it into his mouth.

Seokyeong stared as the man finished a serving of rice in four mouthfuls and slurped the ramyeon in three.

Bell, disgruntled that she hadn't got her walk, was zooming around the rooftop.

'You have a lovely view of the sea from here.' Having eaten his fill, the man had stood up and was now walking around, with his hands once more clasped behind his back. The beam of light from the lighthouse on the breakwater pierced through the darkness, illuminating the night fishing boats on the horizon.

'Hang on. It looks like I can still enjoy the view while sitting down. Young man, did you make these?'

Round holes had been cut into the walls of the rooftop at regular intervals, like circular photo frames.

When the man sat down again, Bell trotted over to his ankles and whined. He reached out a hand to stroke her ears.

'Yes, I did.'

Seokyeong wondered if he should try smashing the conches too, but after a moment's hesitation, he decided against it.

'It's very well done,' the man commented, as he reached out to touch one of the holes.

'Are you interested in architecture?'

'I only know the basics. Just the common-sense stuff. Enough to help in investigations.'

'Investigations?'

'I'm a detective. I've done it all my life.' The man made a loud sucking sound as he tried to remove a piece of food stuck in between his teeth.

Bell scampered back to Seokyeong.

'I see.'

Stroking Bell, Seokyeong poked at the charcoal with a pair of tongs. Then he took a piece of jerky from his pocket and held it out to Bell.

With his back towards Seokyeong, the man shrugged. 'I should say I *was*. I recently retired, although I should've left much earlier . . .'

*

After clearing the table, they went down to the gallery. While Seokyeong was washing the dishes, the man took his time looking at the photos on the walls, lingering again at the table with the freediving photos.

'There are so many different ways to live, as many ways as there are people in this world,' the man mused. 'But in my line of work, I so often saw the worst of people and, gradually, I came to equate that with life. Seeing these photos makes me reconsider. I used to think that no matter how faultless a person appears to be, there's always dirt if you dig deep enough . . .' The man paused, spreading out his palms in front of him and then putting them close together, with a small sliver of a gap in between. 'This is me, stuck in my own narrow view of the world.'

Brows knitted together, he picked up the photo of the young man smiling at the clownfish.

'Life should be like this. Full of moments that shine brightly.'

This is a man who has gone through life seeing only the worst side of humanity. Seokyeong felt a rush of sympathy towards the old man.

'Can I offer to take a picture of you?'

'Me? An old man?' The man was shocked.

'I'll make sure it's a good one.' Seokyeong began untying his apron.

'Hmm. But I'm not wearing my uniform, nor do I have my medals.' The man fingered his Hawaiian shirt absent-mindedly. But from the way his eyes lingered on the photos, it looked like he was interested. 'To be honest . . . I've always wanted to have a portrait photo taken. Something I can leave behind in this world.'

He must be thinking about his funeral portrait.

'Naturally. Please just give me a moment. I'll get everything ready upstairs.'

'Can I watch you while you work? Just the natural curiosity of a detective.'

In one of the rooms on the first floor, Seokyeong set up a black backdrop that would nicely set off the man's red shirt. As he adjusted the camera and the lights, the man watched him closely. He had fished out a small notepad from his pocket and was busy scribbling notes.

'What are you writing?'

The man looked up, slightly embarrassed. 'This? Ah, it's an occupational hazard, I'm afraid. Just a few observations here and there. I can't break the habit.'

'I see. Like how to set up a tripod, how to hang a backdrop, that kind of thing?'

'Nope.' The man slipped his pen back into his shirt pocket. 'Like the fact that you're a right hander with a small scar on your left hand, and how you appear to be a little near-sighted.'

There was a loud, impatient scratch. Bell was at the door.

'One second, please. She must be tired.' When Seokyeong opened the door, Bell slipped in and settled down in a small basket that was kept for her in the room. The man got into position at the same time.

'It's funny, but I can't settle on the right expression for the photo,' the man murmured, as he swept back his grey hair.

'You're fine the way you are now. Try to forget the camera.' Seokyeong approached his tripod, looked through the camera's viewfinder and positioned his finger on the shutter.

'Wait . . . shouldn't I at least smile?' The man stretched his lips, awkwardly.

'Sure. But don't force it. Think of something funny.'

'Funny? I can't think of anything.' The man stared up at the ceiling. 'Maybe the joker who broke wind right in front of me, as I was writing my report of his crime at the station? But that's not what I want to be thinking of when taking my last photo.'

Last photo? Seokyeong felt goosebumps rise on his arms.

For the rest of the shoot, the man didn't say anything.

Later, the old man sat down by the window in the gallery and looked out at the sea.

Seokyeong poured some omegisul for him. 'It's a traditional liquor from the island, made by fermenting omegi millet rice cakes. It'll help you feel more relaxed.'

Seokyeong handed the old man a glass, before going over to the projector screen and pulling it down. When the first photo came up, the man's eyes widened.

From more than a hundred photos, Seokyeong had chosen ten. He looked at the subject in each of them. A faint, benevolent smile, and deep wrinkles. Straight eyebrows, a wide forehead, age spots on his skin and piercing eyes. There was something familiar about the man's features, as if he'd seen them somewhere before.

Looking from the photos to the man himself, Seokyeong noticed that the anticipation on his face had clouded over. 'You don't like them?' he asked.

'Hmm . . . it's not that. I know this is my face, but there's something . . . different, something *fake* about it.'

Seokyeong felt his heart sink.

'No, there's no need to feel bad. It's nothing to do with your skill. It's my face.'

'But you look fine to me,' Seokyeong said, looking at the screen as he sat down next to the man.

'Get a glass for yourself. Drink with me.'

Seokyeong obliged.

'This is the first time I've seen my face so close-up. It's as if I'm zooming in on a map of my life. Just this morning, I saw myself in the mirror at the hotel. But I don't recognise the face in these photos. Look at my eyes there.' He pointed at the screen. 'They're scary. Like a wild beast's.'

'So why do you think the photos turned out this way?' Seokyeong countered.

'No idea.' The man suddenly laughed. 'Oh god, I sound like a suspect.'

'A suspect?'

'Yeah, those lowlifes who always insist it isn't them in the CCTV image.' The man tut-tutted. 'You must be thinking the same as I always did whenever they said something like that. *Ridiculous, when the evidence is literally in your face!*'

'But a photo is just one piece of evidence.' Seokyeong chuckled. It was as if he was playing detective. 'Would that be enough to prosecute a suspect?'

'Well, it's what we call conclusive evidence. No matter how you try to deny it, even if you hire an expensive lawyer, you won't be able to wriggle your way out of it.'

'And then what would happen?'

'They'd have to be persuaded to confess. That's what you should be doing right now, young man: making me acknowledge the truth.'

'Me?'

'Yes. You should say, "Whatever you think of the eyes or nose, this is indisputably your face." You have to go hard, to convince me.'

Seokyeong sighed. It would be hard for him to be so forceful with a client. Instead, he took out his phone and checked the time. It was almost midnight and his heart gave a lurch. *It's already so late.* 'Do you have a place to stay tonight?'

'Nope. I've just been wandering around. I'll have to find a room somewhere.' The man topped up his glass. 'I went all out for this trip. Today is my fourth day here. On the first day, I ate at a posh hotel and spent the night there. Same for day two. I walked into the biggest seaside restaurant and ordered the most expensive set meal. I had grilled cutlassfish – the meat was four centimetres thick – with abalone and sea urchin, all just for me. That night, I checked into the most luxurious room at the hotel. What do you call that? A *suit*? No, *suite*. Inside was a beautiful cypress wood bathtub. I sprinkled in some salts or whatever you call them and had a good soak. Alone. All by myself . . .' He knocked back the shot and reached for the bottle again.

Seokyeong beat him to it. 'Take it slowly. This one's pretty strong – thirteen per cent,' he said as he poured just a little for the stranger. *At this rate, he won't be able to make it back down the hill.*

This thought gave Seokyeong an idea: 'If you'd like, you can spend the night here,' he offered.

'It's okay. I've imposed on you long enough,' the man said, staring at his half-filled glass.

'It's no problem. Spend the night here and, next time, you can come back with your family.' Seokyeong winced. *Damn. Why did I say that? Maybe he doesn't have one.*

'Family.' The man laughed faintly. 'It's been a long time since I last took a family portrait.'

Seokyeong was greatly relieved. He led the man upstairs again, showed him the bathroom, and was about to suggest he slept in the room with the antique chairs when the man stepped into the neighbouring room. He stood there, captivated by the fake tangerine tree.

'This is not possible.'

'Hmm? What do you mean?'

'The tangerine tree. There are flowers and fruits growing at the same time.' The man reached a knobbly hand out to touch to an artificial flower.

'Oh, that. It's just a prop. I use it as a backdrop.'

The man nodded. 'It's a fact of life that flowers bloom and wither, and in their place, fruits grow. To hope for flowers and fruits at the same time is foolish, greedy.'

Seokyeong mumbled a vague response. The man wasn't criticising him, but Seokyeong felt his face redden all the same.

'But it can happen.' The man turned to Seokyeong. 'Sometimes. There are people for whom life bears fruit when the flowers are still blooming.'

'Sounds like a blessed life.'

'Is that so?'

Seokyeong gave an awkward laugh as he passed the man a clean rug and a blanket.

Seokyeong lay on his bed. He was wide awake. *What a long, tiring day.* He had opened the photo studio in hope of making a living, settling down and starting a family, but nothing was going right. He wasn't making any progress with Yanghee. Jebi had almost died. He had chased away his customers. Maybe they'd leave him a bad review. His head throbbed.

'Excuse me.'

At a sudden knock, Seokyeong jumped. 'Coming!' He got up immediately and went to the door. 'Is there something you need?'

The man, who had changed into Seokyeong's pyjamas, stood outside. He cast his deep-set eyes down.

'I need to give you this.' The man held out a small envelope, the kind that photo studios had used decades ago. Seokyeong took it, and eased the flap open. Peeking from inside the stained and mouldy paper was a piece of plastic. He knew what it was immediately.

'Oh, it's a negative.'

The man nodded. 'Do you think . . . it might still be possible to develop it?'

*

Downstairs in his workroom, Seokyeong closed the door and drew the curtains, throwing the small space into darkness. He turned on the red safelight and held up the negative against it. The edges were rough, fingerprints ran all over the surface and the film smelt of age. In the glow, he could vaguely make out what appeared to be bushes, and the outline of a person. There was someone in the photo. Someone in a dress. But he couldn't quite tell which way up the image should be.

Seokyeong took a cleaning pad and wet it generously. Carefully, he started wiping the negative. It was a gamble – if he pressed too hard, the old film might be damaged further, or even disintegrate. Already, there were scratches all over it, not to mention mould and dust. Luckily, nothing of that sort happened. The greenish mould and the overlapping fingerprints – every stain was wiped away.

Seokyeong took out the liquid concentrate developer, a stop bath and fixer, and with a practised hand, diluted the liquid in a plastic tray. After making sure that the negative was securely held in place, he prepared a piece of photo paper.

In the studio, there was absolute silence. Seokyeong glanced up at the ceiling. What was the man doing? Sleeping? Waiting? Or maybe he had slipped away unnoticed.

Seokyeong refocused on the task in front of him. Holding the paper in place with wooden tongs, he held his breath as the image slowly materialised.

The photo appeared to have been taken on a hill. The surrounding trees were oddly stumpy, but the main image was of a girl . . . lying in a pit. Seokyeong reared back in surprise.

Outside the room, the gallery was empty. He went upstairs. The thin blanket was folded neatly but the man was nowhere in sight. Trying to ignore his growing unease, Seokyeong climbed up to the rooftop. Empty. His gaze swept past the round holes in the wall and, suddenly, he spotted a familiar figure.

Like the first time he'd seen him, the man was standing at the edge of the cliff, to one side of the garden.

Seokyeong tore down the stairs and swept through the gate like a gust of wind. 'I've done it!'

The man turned around.

'The photo! It came out.' Seokyeong shouted, breathing heavily as he stopped in front of the old man.

The man staggered.

Alarmed, Seokyeong grabbed him and pulled him back. The old man fell forward on his knees as a few pebbles tumbled down the precipice.

'After all this time . . .' As the man laughed to himself, the beam from the lighthouse swept past, illuminating his grotesque smile.

'You really did it . . .'

The man sat at the table by the window and stared at the photo. He brushed his hair back from his face, frowning. 'You have talent. This negative is decades old, yet you've made it look as though the photo was taken yesterday.'

Seokyeong swallowed hard. 'Wh-who is this?'

The man silently placed the photo back on the table. 'Do you have any more of that liquor?'

'We finished the omegisul, but I have some gosorisul.' Seokyeong got up to fetch the bottle. 'This is a soju distilled from the liquor we had just now. It's strong. Forty per cent.'

'Good, I need it.' The man lifted his glass.

Seokyeong poured out the clear liquid, and his hand shook despite himself.

'You have some, too.' The man took the bottle and poured Seokyeong a shot.

In silence, they savoured the fragrant alcohol. When the man started fanning out his shirt as though the burning heat of the alcohol was getting to him, Seokyeong pressed the switch below the window, and a panel slid open. Immediately, cold air rushed in. Seokyeong hunched his shoulders slightly.

'Who is that? The person in the . . .'

'The child I killed . . . a long, long time ago.'

The man put down his empty glass and looked frankly at Seokyeong. 'This was a coin toss. If the negative couldn't be developed, I was going to put everything behind me.'

Seokyeong spluttered. It felt suddenly as though his chest and throat was on fire.

'In my long career, I've saved countless people,' the man continued, as he tilted the bottle once again over his glass. 'Put many criminals behind bars – no shortage of thieves, of course, an arsonist who burned his family to death, a scammer who ran off with all my village's money,

187

gangsters who butchered each other in their wars. All of them caught by me. And there were those who'd been falsely accused for years, finally getting the justice they deserved. The people I saved, their relief and gratitude aren't something you can put a price on. I was paid to do my job, of course, but a good deed is still a good deed. And I found myself foolishly thinking . . . perhaps everything I'd done would balance out the single instance of wrongdoing . . .? Is there a god who'll tell me, "It's okay, you've paid your dues, we can call it quits . . ."'

The man tilted his head back and emptied the glass.

'Take it slow. This one is strong . . .' Seokyeong reached out to take the bottle.

'I killed someone,' said the man, as he knocked away Seokyeong's hand. His eyes were bloodshot. 'Not with my own hands, but I was to blame, it's impossible to deny it.'

Seokyeong tensed, waiting for him to continue.

'That child . . . she was only nine. She died in my jurisdiction. Thirty years ago. A victim of Park Jun-gu. She was killed by that monster . . .'

Seokyeong gasped. 'Oh no.'

'He snatched her while she was on the way to school, strangled her to death, buried her in the hills. Crazy bastard.' The man reached out a gnarled hand and turned the photo face down.

'But you caught the murderer, didn't you? So what's the issue?'

The man shook his head. 'I couldn't have people finding out about the killing. At least not at that time, in my jurisdiction, under my watch . . . Not another one.'

Seokyeong tilted his head, confused.

'Three people had been killed in my jurisdiction that year. The angry families kept coming to the police station, refusing to leave. Our chief was under huge pressure. All of us were. The media was in a frenzy; the murders were on the news every day, house prices in our district were free-falling . . . If that girl had turned up dead, it would have been the last straw for us. So I . . . I saved her.'

'What do you mean?'

'I turned her . . . into a missing person. Her father came to the station, pleading with us to find his daughter, telling us that she was still so young. I promised that I would find her, and I told him that she must be alive somewhere out there. His expression still haunts me – the hope that flashed across his face at my words. He kept coming back to the station. For weeks, months.'

The two of them fell silent.

'Young man. Are you going to report me?'

'Me?' Seokyeong was alarmed. He had not thought about that. All he'd done was to develop a photo. Now, he remembered a crime novel he'd read back in university, in which a photo had been the critical clue in a murder investigation. In the book, seven people had looked at the photo and each one noticed something different in it. But that had been a story, fiction. He'd never thought that, one day, he'd experience something like it in real life.

Seokyeong reached for the photo and studied it for a long moment. 'The child . . . she looks too clean,' he said.

The man didn't answer.

'She can't have died there, in that pit.'

'Yeah, she wasn't killed there.' The man filled his glass again.

'There are two shovels,' Seokyeong said, pausing. 'By the way, who took this photo?'

'I did.'

'You dug the hole?'

'I did.'

'And there are two spades. Who was there with you?'

'A young man from the village. He was the one who discovered the girl's body and alerted me.'

'And he agreed not to say anything? Even when you asked him to help you bury the body in secret?' Seokyeong couldn't keep the shock out of his voice.

The man bowed his head, his shoulders shaking. It looked almost as if he was laughing. 'Yeah. That's what people were like back then. Whatever happened, they protected themselves first. It was forty years ago. People couldn't just speak up, not if they wanted to survive. It had only been thirty years since the war ended.'

'Where is he now, the young man that helped you? If the truth can be revealed now . . .'

'He died.' The man picked up the empty glass and stared at it. 'In those days, people died easily. A small ailment left untreated could kill you.'

Seokyeong's head throbbed. A dead girl. A dead witness. A detective. A War. Everything was a tangled mess in his head. 'You called this a coin toss . . . what are you planning to do?'

'What do you mean?'

'You said you were going to put everything behind you if the photo turned up blank. So what now, now that the photo has been developed?'

'I had decided to send it to the TV stations. And then to kill myself. That precipice would do the job.'

'The TV stations? Why not the police . . .?'

'Indeed why not?' The man replied carelessly, wiping a trickle of liquor from the corner of his mouth.

Seokyeong was suddenly aware that he was starting to get fed up with this game. 'Is that what you're going to do now then?' he asked, his voice hardening.

'No,' the man said, his voice cracking. He picked up the liquor bottle and shook it to see if it was empty. Then, without warning, he smashed the bottle onto the ground. The shards flew. 'I have children! Both are in the police force. They wanted to follow in my footsteps.' The man stared at Seokyeong with his bloodshot eyes. 'If I tell the world what I did, what will become of them? There'll be no place for them anywhere, not just in the police force; They'll never be able to hold their heads up again.'

The man tugged at his shirt agitatedly. He stood up and staggered to the gallery. His gaze swept past each of the frames – the bikers, the bride in a wedding dress, the open mouth full of teeth.

He turned to Seokyeong. 'Young man, I made her a missing person. Then do you know what I did?'

Wordlessly, Seokyeong shook his head.

'On the way home, I bought fried chicken. Back then, we called it tongdak. I got it half dipped in the sweet spicy sauce, and the other half original flavour. Then I went home. My son and daughter ran into my arms at the door. They were six and four. I passed them the treat. My wife was pleased – even though she grumbled about it being a waste of money, she was smiling. When I looked at my daughter holding a drumstick, I thought to myself, *She looks really happy.*'

The man cracked a smile. A smile that didn't quite reach his eyes.

And Seokyeong finally realised why he'd found the man's face familiar.

It was a déjà-vu moment of sorts: a face captured in one of Stephen Gertz's works. It was a photo taken in 1982 of a dictator who had just locked down a city, plotting a massacre. In the photo, the man was resting in a chair, stroking his daughter's hair affectionately. *Portrait of a Dictator*, as it was now known, was originally *Portrait of a Father*.

'Young man. You're going to expose my crime, aren't you?' The stranger, who was standing in front of Jungmi's teeth, turned sharply. The gallery light bounced off his forehead harshly.

'Me? No, I . . .' Shocked, Seokyeong gripped the arm of his chair.

'You're going to reveal what I did when the sun rises. Yes?' The man came closer. 'You're going to tell everyone that a retired cop confessed to covering up a dreadful case. You're going to do interviews here in this village in the middle of nowhere, become famous, and earn lots of money!'

Seokyeong, glued to his seat, could only stare up at the man. Though he was an ex-policeman, he was also elderly.

Seokyeong was still in his thirties. He could overpower him if he had to. Hadn't he wielded a sledge hammer when he was renovating the studio all by himself? But he couldn't move an ich. It was as if he was a kid again, looking up at his angry father.

'You musn't tell!' The man raised his arms. 'All my life, I was a model father. And I want to remain that way in the eyes of my children, protect them as every parent should!'

'You're right.' Seokyeong's voice was no louder than a whisper.

'Really?' The man lowered his arms.

'Of course.'

'So you understand. Young man, thank you.' The man sat down heavily in the opposite chair, rubbing his palms nervously. Then he got up, went to the fridge and, without asking, took a bottle of soju and opened the cap.

'My dad died young . . .' Seokyeong suddenly said.

'Oh? What happened?' The man poured himself some soju and filled Seokyeong's glass too. His hand shook, and he over-filled the glass, so that the clear liquor made a small pool on the table.

'It was because of me.'

'Because of you?' The man was standing up, the bottle still in his hand, a look of pity on his face.

Seokyeong knocked back the shot of soju. 'So, yes, . . . I've killed someone too. Not by my hand, but I also can't say with confidence that it wasn't me.'

'What do you mean?' The man lowered the soju bottle and sat down opposite Seokyeong.

'My family moved to Jeju when I was ten. I don't know if there was any particular reason we left Seoul, other than that my parents were sick of city life. Occasionally, I heard them talking about how they had their honeymoon here; the island was filled with happy memories for them. But the reality of life on Jeju was very different. They had been factory workers back in the city, so they had to find labouring jobs here, or work on the farms. Things were tough. Then my sister was conceived. My mum had a conception dream of a swallow swimming in the sea, so she decided to name my sister after the bird – *jebi*.'

Seokyeong poured more soju for himself.

'My parents were busy working all the time, so I became the primary carer of my sister. I would carry her on my back to the beach every day to pick godong shells. Mum was always pleased when we came back with a full bucket. We either ate them dipped in soy-sauce or boiled them in a soybean paste stew. I remember how my mum would always kiss us on the forehead after we'd eaten .'

'That's mothers for you.' Locked in his own memories, the old man chuckled lightly. 'When I was young, I'd sometimes steal pumpkins from a neighbour's garden. My mother would scold me, but she'd still make banchan with them – seasoned pumpkin with salted prawns. Absolutely delicious!'

Seokyeong nodded, before picking up the story where he left off. 'One day, when my sister was about three, we went down to the beach as usual. She was difficult to handle at that age, and when we couldn't find many godong shells, she began fussing and crying. I couldn't get her to stop. Tired of trying to soothe her, I left her by the beach while I went a bit further hunting for shells. When I had finally filled a whole bowl, I returned to where I left her . . . but there was no sign of her.'

'Oh god.' The old man nodded wearily.

'Four days later, her body washed up on the shore.' Seokyeong knocked back another shot.

'Your parents must've been devastated.'

'Yeah.' Seokyeong's voice was a monotone. 'My father drowned himself in alcohol and soon followed my sister. He walked into the sea and never came back.'

The man reached out and patted his arm. 'Your father was in the wrong. He didn't stop to think of you.'

'He loved my sister more.'

The man nodded slowly. 'Parents will always say they love their children equally, but it isn't true. There'll always be one they love more. It's the same for me.'

Seokyeong buried his face in his hands. Tears spilled from his eyes.

'But you must bear this in mind, young man. Even if you are the child they love less, they'll still love you more than anyone else could . . .'

'Not all parents are like that, especially not the fathers!' Seokyeong retorted.

'Sure. But I'm not talking about those exceptions – just decent people in general.' The man's tone left no room for disagreement.

Seokyeong didn't remember what happened after that. When he awoke the next morning with a splitting headache, the sun was already high in the sky.

Jebi was shaking him, her nose wrinkling. 'Sajangnim, why did you drink so much? Like a whale! Did you have company?'

'Oh, yeah. A customer.' Seokyeong frowned. He could feel nausea welling up.

'What's this?' Jebi picked up an envelope on the table. It had the Hakuda Photo Studio logo on it.

Inside was the negative, a couple of 10,000 won notes and a page that looked like it had been torn from Seokyeong's diary, with a note penned in sharp letters.

I saw your price list and I enclose the cash. Below is the address of the child's father. He still lives there, waiting for his daughter to return. I'll leave this negative with you. What you do with it is up to you. If you go to the press, I'll confess my crime to my children. Otherwise, I'll live out my life as a respected father. The coin is in your hands.

Seokyeong let out a deep sigh. He felt his world spinning.

10

The Haughty Geologist

As October came to an end, fluff-headed silver grass was blooming everywhere in the village, heralding a change of season.

It was a Wednesday, and the photo studio was closed as usual. Jebi, dressed in a wetsuit with an octopus design on the chest, held out an arm and let the grasses tickle her palm as she headed down to the coast. Sunlight bounced off the glistening water and onto her face

Jebi had been training hard, reminding herself of what might happen should she fail to learn to swim, disappointing the octopus god. Two or three times a week, she learnt diving from Yanghee, and on days the haenyeos didn't go out to sea, Seokyeong took over. In the evenings, Mokpo Granny would always have a table of food ready, and because she ate well every day, sleep came to her easily at night.

The first time Jebi managed to submerge herself fully using her flippers, Yanghee had let out a high-pitched whistle, a sumbisori, as she surfaced again. Jebi had never seen her teacher smile so brightly. She had panted hard, trying to catch her breath, and when she'd turned around in the water, she noticed a few haenyeos had also returned to the surface, making their own sumbisori to catch their breath. Seeing Jebi's, they had waved. And even though the autumn waters were cold, Jebi had felt a warmth course through her. Even without taking a photo, Jebi was sure she'd remember this moment for the rest of her life.

All the villagers seemed to have embraced them at last, and Jebi and Seokyeong were grateful. They'd fallen into the habit of staying after the Wednesday training sessions to help with the haenyeos' heavy nets and to clean and prepare the seafood they'd harvested.

Today was the first Wednesday in November. Amid a light drizzle, the haenyeos were sitting under a faded tent set up on the beach, preparing the freshly caught sea urchins. Jebi's job was to halve them with a knife before passing them to Yanghee, who would scoop out the innards into a bowl. Dongwon, who'd come with his grandma to wait for Yanghee, was having fun with Seokyeong, taking photos of the haenyeos at work.

Jebi scooted closer to Yanghee and whispered in her ear. 'So why don't you like our sajangnim?'

'What?' With half a sea urchin in one hand and a teaspoon in the other, Yanghee quickly looked around. The rest of the haenyeos were chatting among themselves and none of them seemed to be looking their way.

'You heard me. Why do you dislike him? Where else will you find a man like that?'

'He's only interested in me because he wants to put roots down in this village. Not because he likes me,' Yanghee said, as she went back to scooping out entrails with a practised hand.

'What makes you think so?'

Yanghee snorted. 'I can tell. He wants to be accepted here, to be koendang.'

If you want to be koendang, best to marry a local. She remembered Seokyeong telling her that. Or rather, he had been quoting Mokpo Granny. In any case, perhaps there was some truth in Yanghee's words.

'But you're letting him bond with Dongwon—?'

Yanghee glanced towards the pair. Dongwon had climbed onto Seokyeong's back, as if he was still a toddler.

'We don't have many younger men here, and Dongwon seems to like him very much. What can I do?' Yanghee let out a sigh and elbowed Jebi. 'Girl, you'd better hurry up. We're losing speed.'

'Oh.' Turning her attention back to her task, Jebi grabbed a sea urchin that was attempting to escape and sliced it open.

When they were finished, Seokyeong insisted on giving Yanghee and her family a lift home, overriding her protests by pointing out that it wouldn't do to make the elderly woman and the young child walk in the rain. Because Dongwon wanted to ride in the front passenger seat, Jebi sat behind with Yanghee and her mother in the SUV; Seokyeong had rented it for the long term in light of their increased bookings.

Yanghee's home, a five-minute drive away, was a traditional stone house with a grey slanted roof. There,

Dongwon's grandmother insisted that their guests should be invited in.

After renovations, the interior didn't look too different from a modern apartment. The living room, with traditional maru flooring, was small but neat. Wildflower-patterned curtains hung on the window overlooking the garden. And two walls of bookshelves were crammed with books.

As they sipped tangerine peel tea, Jebi felt a little embarrassed thinking back to Yanghee's surprise when she saw that Jebi's room had not contained a single book.

Who reads to study? You should read to feel. Yanghee's voice rang in her ears.

Jebi was curious. What had all these books made her feel? What made her keep reaching for a new one? Had she found the feeling she was looking for, or was she still searching?

'You have lots of books.' Seokyeong voiced Jebi's thoughts, ruffling Dongwon's hair affectionately as he looked around the room.

Yanghee had disappeared into her room after serving them the tea, and Dongwon was fiddling with Seokyeong's film camera.

Reminded of the last negative she had seen, tucked into an envelope at the photo studio, Jebi glanced at her boss. He hadn't brought *that* up in a while. She'd have to ask him about it tomorrow. *It's high time he makes a decision*, she thought.

'Yeah. My mum does English translations,' Dongwon said, puffing up in pride.

'Translations?' Seokyeong and Jebi spoke at the same time.

Jebi remembered that Yanghee had mentioned a side job. Was this it?

The next morning, the sky had cleared to a brilliant blue again. Strong winds had swept the clouds into a distinctive formation resembling a camera lens high above.

As usual, Jebi and Seokyeong began their Thursday morning cleaning. To get rid of the stale air in the gallery, they opened the windows and door. Today, they were unusually quiet as they went about their tasks, and Bell's ears twitched as she cocked her head in confusion.

After wiping the tables, Jebi put the dishcloth to soak in boiling water before removing her apron. Then she went to a drawer and took out a neatly ironed one and put it on.

Seokyeong wrung the dishcloth dry and hung it on the clothes line behind the palm trees.

'You've got to send that negative!' Jebi blurted out, as he came back in from the garden.

'I know, but . . .' Seokyeong went to wash his hands before removing his apron. Once again, Stephen Gertz was grinning on his T-shirt.

Jebi held out a new apron to him when he returned to the counter. 'I don't get it. Why are you dragging this out? Imagine if you were the father of that missing girl!'

'But . . . what about the detective's family?' Seokyeong unfolded the apron, shook it out with a snap and tied it around his waist.

'Well, they've been living a great life.' Jebi huffed.

'So what? Must we punish people for being happy, send misfortune their way to make them pay their dues? I don't think so.'

'The misfortune was brought about by their father, not by you!' Jebi shook her head in frustration.

Bell watched them bicker and licked her lips anxiously.

'You can't exactly say that either.' Seokyeong scooped Bell up into his arms. 'Do you think that old man has it easy? He's probably living each day in uncertainty and fear, not knowing if or when I might expose what he did. That kind of suspense is worse than going on trial, or even prison.'

'That's just your guess!' Jebi shook her head. 'Fine. We'll toss a coin.' She fished out a coin from her pocket: a hundred won coin so shiny it looked newly minted.

'What?'

'That's what he wrote in his letter, didn't he? That giving you the negative was like a coin toss. So let's do it for real. Heads, mail it. Tails, forget about it. Sound good?'

Seokyeong didn't answer.

Jebi faced the entrance to the studio and flipped the coin. Thinking that they were playing fetch, Bell tried to wriggle out of Seokyeong's arms but he held on tight to her in case she pounced on it and swallowed it accidentally.

The coin rolled noisily across the polished floor, out into the garden, hitting a rock – before dropping into the drain.

Jebi and Seokyeong ran out and peered down the hole. All they could hear was the sound of flowing water; there was no sign of the gleaming coin.

'Ah.' Their shoulders drooped at the same time.

At that moment, Seokyeong's phone buzzed. He hauled it out of his pocket and answered the call. 'Hajun Hyung, what's up?'

Because the volume was on high, Jebi could hear Yoona's dad's voice filtering out.

'I've sent a customer your way. She's been taking photos at the sand dunes for the past two days and stopping by the bakery for some lunch. Oh, she told me something important—'

'Sweetheart, that's not why you're calling,' a gentle voice admonished. Jebi could hear Yoona's mum, and a baby cooing, in the background.

'Er, right. That's not what's important. The camera . . .'

'What camera?' Seokyeong frowned.

'Well, I don't know if you can do it, but I told her to look for you all the same.'

'Wait, what is this about?'

Just then, they heard the crunch of tyres as a black compact car pulled up outside. With the phone still clasped to his ear, Seokyeong dipped his head towards the car. Jebi quickly smoothed the creases in her apron and straightened her shoulders.

'I think she's here.'

'A black Chevrolet Spark? That's the one. Okay, I hope you can help!' With that, Yoona's dad hung up.

A woman got out of the car. Unlike most of their customers, she wasn't dressed for a beach holiday, having opted instead for a wide-brimmed hat, sunglasses, checked shirt, outdoor trousers and hiking boots. She moved with a tired gait, as if she'd just climbed a mountain.

She leant into the front passenger seat and picked something up, waving it in their direction as she approached. 'Can you do something about this?'

Seokyeong looked at the object in her hands. It was a camera. Or rather, what used to be a camera. The body was smashed so badly that he could even see inside.

'The mirror is broken. This is beyond my abilities. You'll have to go to a professional. I'm afraid. Or . . . it might be easier to just replace it.'

The customer lowered her head and cursed under her breath.

Seokyeong and Jebi exchanged a glance.

'In that case, can I rent a camera? I don't have time to get it repaired.' She took off her sunglasses, and now Jebi could see that she was a young woman, in her late twenties.

'I'm sorry but we don't offer rentals. If you'd like some photos, we can take them for you,' Seokyeong said.

The customer placed a hand on her hips and let out a bark of scornful laughter. 'No. You won't be up to it,' she said.

'What do you mean?'

The woman jutted out her chin haughtily. 'The kind of photos I want. Not just anyone can take them.'

Jebi raised her voice slightly. 'My boss isn't just *anyone*! He's a great photographer!'

Before Seokyeong could stop her, Jebi took the woman's arm and propelled her into the studio. The woman tried to reclaim her arm but to no avail. Bell crouched low and wagged her tail enthusiastically.

'Look!' Glaring at the customer, Jebi jabbed a finger at the wall behind the counter where the prize certificate and the award-winning photo were hanging in frames. Caught in the sunlight, the glass gleamed.

Seokyeong turned away, embarrassed. Bell followed him to the gallery and lay at his feet, rolling over for a tummy scratch.

Rubbing her elbow, the woman looked at the certificate. Her eyes widened and her lips moved slightly as she read the details. 'I see. So he's a certified photographer?' The woman nodded. 'As someone in research, I respect that. And his name . . . Does it mean "quartz"?'

She walked briskly over to Seokyeong. Stopping in front of him, she held out her hand. 'I'm Choi Songhwa. I'm doing my PhD at Jeju National University. My main research focus is on Jeju's coastal sediments.'

Seokyeong, who was still giving Bell a tummy rub, stood up. He quickly wiped his hand on his apron and held it out tentatively.

The woman shook his hand firmly. 'As you may have guessed, I don't take photos of people, but of rocks.'

Seokyeong didn't respond.

'It doesn't matter how great a photographer you are, you won't know what I'm looking for. Your studio sits on a columnar joint – those prism-shaped stacks of basalt you see at the base of the cliff. You must have noticed them—? But as to which aspects of the rocks I'm interested in, and what angle to shoot them from, you would be clueless. That's what I meant. That you don't know how to take photos for academic fieldwork.'

'It's still photography. There are no photos our sajang-nim can't take!' Jebi insisted.

'Jebi, enough.' Seokyeong shook his head discreetly at her.

The woman fixed Jebi with an amused stare. It wasn't dismissive or angry; she was simply observing her.

Seokyeong grabbed Jebi's hand and pulled her out into the garden, so that they were standing under the palm trees. Through the window, they could see the woman looking at the photos in the gallery.

'Jebi-ya, what's got into you?'

Jebi pointed to his T-shirt. 'You can simply study his photos and learn, right?'

Seokyeong looked down at the grinning Stephen Gertz on his chest and shook his head. 'I can't.'

'What?'

'None of his photography was ever used for research papers, nor has he ever photographed a rock.'

Jebi's eyes widened in surprise. 'Really?' She pondered this for a moment, and then flashed a grin. 'Okay, then learn it now.'

'Huh?'

'You can't let a customer go like this!' Jebi rubbed her index finger and thumb together, indicating that there was money to be made. 'Get her to teach you. And tell her you'll offer her a discount. It's no loss to us: we don't have any shoots planned today.'

'What am I supposed to ask her to teach me? How to take photos?'

'Fine. If you can't work out what to say to her, I'll do

it myself.' Jebi grabbed his arm and looked into his eyes. 'Don't forget that the first floor still belongs to the bank.'

While this whispered conservation was going on, the woman had sat down and begun playing with Bell. The puppy pressed her paws on the woman's shoes and wagged her tail vigorously.

'What's her name?' Stroking Bell's head, the woman looked up as the two of them returned.

'Bell,' Jebi answered.

'As in jingle bells?'

'Nope. It's Jeju dialect for "byeol" – star,' Seokyeong explained.

It was the first time Jebi had heard this and she felt a stab of jealousy. The woman had only been here five minutes and already she was hearing important secrets.

Seokyeong had seemed to relax a little with the small talk. He walked over to the woman, shooing Bell away. 'I'm sorry, but we just don't loan equipment here. It's a matter of principle,' he said.

'I see.' The woman stood up to take her leave when Seokyeong, smiling shyly, stepped in front of her.

'But I can offer you a discount . . . if you teach me how to take the photos you need.'

'I don't understand. Why would you . . . when you're already a professional . . .?' The woman looked in turn at Seokyeong and then his certificate on the wall, clearly surprised by his request.

'Professional or not, I need to make a livelihood too.' He rubbed his neck in embarrassment.

'I can't give you much. I'm still a graduate student . . . and my area of research isn't well-funded.'

Jebi quickly brought out their price list.

The woman nodded. 'An outdoor shoot, with a fifty per cent discount. Okay?'

'Thirty per cent,' Jebi interjected.

The woman jutted out her chin and looked at Jebi. 'Forty.'

'Thirty-five.'

The customer sighed and glanced at her watch. 'Fine. But I'll need you to carry my equipment.'

Stowed in the boot of the woman's car was a large plastic container, the kind used for moving house. Inside was an assortment of tools including a hammer, various electronic devices, and a helmet. The geologist transferred everything into a backpack and stuffed it into Seokyeong's arms.

'I'm studying the formation of sand dunes and columnar jointing, specifically on this side of Jeju Island. I'd just finished taking photos of the dunes when I slipped and dropped my camera. All I need now are photos of the columnar joint below your studio. I also want to get a panoramic view of the landscape, so let's head to the breakwater first.'

Seokyeong put the backpack in the SUV before returning to the photo studio for his own gear. Though they weren't doing an underwater shoot, he packed his GoPro too, along with its waterproof housing.

As the white SUV cruised down the hill, Jebi lowered her window slightly, allowing the dry autumn air to seep into the car. Pretending to look at the scenery, she stole a quick glance at Seokyeong.

Since the freediving shoot, something had changed between them. Her feelings for him had begun to evaporate. Her encounter with her ex may have had something to do with it. But that wasn't the entire reason. Seokyeong was different somehow. Jebi suspected the old man who had visited later that night was responsible. Every time she looked at the portrait of the ex-detective hanging on the wall, she was more convinced.

His visit had shifted something in the photo studio.

At the breakwater, the geologist climbed out of the car and stretched. From where they stood, across the bay they could clearly make out the photo studio and the columnar jointing it sat on.

It was the first time Jebi had looked at the little building from this vantage point, and her heartbeat quickened. She felt as if she was about to witness something wondrous.

'I need you to take photos of everything.' The geologist raised her finger, swiping it from left to right, indicating the entire length of the cliff, which stretched for at least two hundred metres along the coast.

From here, the cliff looked somewhat like the cross-section of a cake. *A blueberry cheesecake with green tea powder sprinkled on top*, Jebi thought.

'Evidence of basaltic lava flows has been found over there.'

'Basalt . . . what?' Seokyeong and Jebi looked blankly at the geologist.

'Basaltic lava. Basically, there are signs that lava once flowed in that area, and formed the basalt you see right now,' she explained. 'Take a few panoramic shots here, please,' she instructed, waving her arms. 'Then we'll head back over there to take close-ups and collect samples. That's pretty much all there is to geology fieldwork – we walk, observe, then we gather rocks to take back for analysis.' The woman was sounding increasingly excited. 'After this, I'll have to return to my lab to investigate the composition of the rock, starting with cutting out a thin cross-section.'

'A cross-section?'

'Yes. I'll carve out a nought-point-nought-three-of-a-millimetre slice of the rock, so that I can mount it on a glass slide and view it under the microscope. That work will be the basis of the paper.'

'A research paper?' Jebi jumped in to ask. 'So will my boss's name also be mentioned? Like a photo credit?'

Seokyeong's face reddened. 'Jebi, hush!'

'Of course you'll be credited. Especially as you've given me such a generous discount,' the geologist promised.

Following her instructions, Seokyeong took one shot after another. Even through the viewfinder, it was a breathtaking landscape.

The geologist peered over his shoulder to look at the LCD screen. Her eyes widened. 'Wow. I didn't think photos for fieldwork could look like this. The composition, the lighting. Amazing.' Seokyeong's ears and neck flushed and he hurried to change the topic. 'But . . . what's the purpose of these photos? Where are the signs of lava you were talking about?'

'Right here.' She pressed the button to zoom in on the photo. 'Look at these beautiful patterns. Lava flows created the intersecting shapes. Look at this reddish layer at the bottom. The gently undulating surface suggests a smooth lava flow. Above it, the lava must've flowed more rapidly. Weathering by the winds over a long period of time, also helps form the patterns. Imagine! Once upon a time, red hot lava flowed all the way from there' – the geologist turned to indicate the wide stretch of coastline – 'to way over there!'

'It's so odd to think of it flowing through our village,' Jebi murmured. 'I knew that Jeju is a volcanic island, but still . . .'

'The land the village sits on probably came into existence around 530,000 years ago,' the geologist added. 'After the fiery lava from a volcanic eruption cooled to form the rocks.'

'Woah, I'm glad I wasn't around back then.' Jebi laughed.

'For sure. But the same thing could happen again, at any time. It's entirely possible.'

At her firm tone, the two of them looked at each other in alarm.

'Technically, Hallasan is an active volcano. It's been quiet for the past one thousand years, but from the earth's perspective that's the blink of an eye.' She chuckled.'

The three of them walked shoulder to shoulder along the breakwater back to the car.

In the backseat, the geologist leant comfortably against the headrest and looked out of the window. The seaside village rolled past. In the fields, an old man was using a sickle to cut back silver grass that was encroaching on his crop of carrots.

'Volcanic eruptions don't only bring disaster,' she said. 'They create life too, giving the fields their fertile soil. Without them, this village wouldn't exist, and neither would our paths have crossed today.'

They parked the car and walked the remaining way to the base of the cliff. Seokyeong and Jebi trudged heavily across the rocks with the equipment on their backs, while the geologist moved ahead with light steps. But as they got closer to the columnar joints, she slowed down, hunching over to observe every nook and cranny, to the point where Seokyeong and Jebi began to get frustrated. To their eyes, the rocks were all the same, but she didn't seem to think so.

After a while, the woman straightened her back and turned towards them. 'I need some photos of this section here.'

'You found something?' Jebi stifled a yawn.

Seokyeong, who had the camera to his eye, turned in the direction the geologist was pointing.

'Can't you see? Near sea level, there's a block-like sajilcheung.'

'A . . . what?'

Seokyeong moved closer – and his feet plunged into the water. Jebi was impressed when he didn't flinch, and that he'd had the foresight to bring the waterproof housing for the camera.

'Here, get one of this layer of sand deposits,' the geologist said. She walked carefully to where Seokyeong stood. 'And here are the mud deposits – the orange-brown nijilcheung. And this stratum with a purplish glint. Come closer and look carefully. You can see there's a thin layer of volcanic ash mixed inside. Wait.' She stiffened. 'Isn't this a fossil? Oh my god!'

'A fossil?' Jebi, who had been photographing the scene with the RXo, moved closer to take a look.

The geologist's eyes narrowed. 'Are you taking photos of me? Why?'

'She's my apprentice, I hope you don't mind.' Seokyeong dipped his head slightly.

'Oh, a student?' With that, the woman turned her attention back to the fossil. 'Mmm, there appear to be a few longish lines . . . What could it be? A sea snake?' the geologist muttered to herself as she ran her fingers over the rock.

Jebi scooted closer still. She tilted her head in thought and, suddenly, the answer flashed across her mind. 'I know!' she cried. 'I know what this is!'

The other two turned around, looking dubious.

'A mulkkureok! It's an octopus!'

'An octopus?'

The geologist peered at the fossil again.

Seokyeong moved his lens closer, adjusting the focus.

'Well, the lines are long, and look, they do seem to get thinner towards the tip . . . and can you see these round patterns? Don't you think they look like suckers. Jebi could be right! I bet it's a giant octopus!'

'I think you're right! Sajangnim, photos, please!' The woman clapped her hands in delight. While Seokyeong was busy photographing the fossil, she took out her phone and began typing furiously. As she scrolled through the relevant research she'd pulled up online, she let out a cry of joy. 'An octopus fossil is super rare!'

Jebi's heart was pounding. Maybe this geological – or was it zoological? – discovery would make her famous. She imagined scoring interviews on the news and meeting the big names of academia. She'd better insist that they film the interviews at Hakuda Photo Studio as a backdrop. That'd bring the customers in.

Seokyeong tilted his head. 'An octopus, really? How does such a fragile, malleable life-form leave a trace in the hot lava?'

'There's a famous ammonite fossil of a mollusc from the Jurassic period and octopuses are molluscs to. If the animal is rapidly buried in sediment, it's not impossible.'

Marking the area to return to later, the expedition continued on over the rocks.

'Sajilcheung . . . nijilcheung . . . sand . . . clay . . . Amazing. I thought the rock was just basalt.' Seokyeong paused to wipe his forehead with his handkerchief.

'Well, we aren't *just humans*, right? Same for rocks. Look here. The wall is uneven, with layers jutting out, yes? That happens when the upper layers shift horizontally, pulling in a different direction from the lower layers. And see these glittery bits? Under a microscope, you'd be able to tell that it's pyroxene – a mix of minerals including magnesium, iron, titanium. There's a high possibility that this is a special kind of basalt, called olivine.'

Jebi and Seokyeong just stared at the geologist.

'Come, let's climb!' Nimbly, the geologist started clambering up the basalt cliff. Stuffing their cameras into backpacks, Seokyeong and Jebi followed.

From afar, it had looked like a bare rock face, but, in between the layers, vegetation was growing.

'Isn't it amazing that there are pockets of soil in between the rocks? They're formed during a break in volcanic activity. This cliff isn't just a single layer of basalt created during one eruption.'

Jebi's thoughts drifted. She was envious of the geologist's knowledge, her ability to identify the rocks with a single glance. Was it also possible to look at a person and do the same?

Who am I exactly? Jebi found herself wondering. *A woman in my twenties. A failed mother. A photography assistant. Like the rock, she was more than just one thing.*

Jebi shook herself out of her thoughts.

'No way! Trachyte in between the tuff? Please photograph this section.' The geologist squatted down while Seokyeong zoomed in. 'Wait. Let me put this here.' She took out a fifteen-centimetre metal ruler and placed it next to the rock.

'Oh. You need to know the size?'

'Of course. This is scientific research. Everything needs to be quantified and measured,' she said. 'Wait, I should collect a sample too.'

With a hammer and chisel, she knocked a chip off the trachyte. Jebi photographed the process, finding it inspiring to see someone so fully focused on their work.

'It must be really cool when a group of academics gets together to discuss their research.' Jebi spoke softly. 'No matter how difficult the terminology is, everyone will understand each other.'

'Not exactly.' The geologist sighed as she chipped at the rock. 'When we present our work to colleagues, we might as well be talking to a computer – the data and figures need to be absolutely accurate and robust, so that they won't be questioned. As for terminology, you have to speak in the language that the computer understands. If not, you either get an error or it just stops working. Or maybe even explodes.'

As she slipped the rock samples into yellow cotton bags, a wide grin spread across her face.

Jebi hurriedly captured the moment, responding to a nudge from Seokyeong.

Her boss was scrolling through the photos he'd taken. The black-spotted rock looked so plain, dull even. Until now, he'd mostly taken photos of humans, who smiled, or at least wore some kind of expression. But basalt was just basalt. Even landscape photos of the sea or forests had more life than these; some kind of mood or atmosphere.

Stephen Gertz flashed into his mind. Seokyeong had thought he was giving his utmost for the shoot, yet he didn't really know what he was taking photos of. If the geologist hadn't been there to guide him, he would've been unable to find meaning in these shots.

His thoughts turned to the woman who had commissioned the shoot. Why had she chosen to study rocks? What happiness was there to gain – and for whom? – by understanding how sand dunes and columnar jointing were formed?

Or is it knowledge that everyone should have?

Seokyeong hesitated for a moment. 'Don't you get bored looking at rocks? What made you interested in such things?'

' "Such things"?' The woman looked up.

Seokyeong turned the LCD screen towards her. 'Look. There's no background in this photo, no expression . . .'

'What do you mean "no background"? And how is there no expression?' The geologist's eyes flashed. With a hammer in one hand and a chisel in the other, she looked a little intimidating.

Baffled, Seokyeong looked to Jebi, who rolled her eyes at him for having put his foot in it. She seemed to be siding with the geologist.

'What . . .?' His voice trailed off.

'The background is the time and era, of course. I told you that the magma spewed out of the volcano some 530,000 years ago, right?'

Next to her, Jebi was nodding.

'And what do you mean rocks have "no expression"? Can't you see that this one is standing stiffly, upright and unmoving?' She reached out a hand and touched the rock. 'With eyes like yours, however did you win that photography award?'

'Hey, don't be so mean.' Jebi nudged her.

'Okay, I'm sorry,' the geologist said. 'But to claim that rocks are expressionless – well, it's not a very nice thing to say to a geologist.'

Jebi nodded.

The rocky path up the cliff had become narrower, so the two women set off again in single file.

Left behind, Seokyeong stood scratching his head. He'd forgotten that photography at its heart was a quest to understand the subject. Everything that had been going on had made the most basic and important things slip his mind. *I should meet more customers and put more care into listening to their stories,* he resolved. Shaking his head to snap out of his thoughts, he followed behind, taking a few shots of the women ahead of him as he went.

Their fieldwork shoot ended just as the sun set over the darkening blue sea.

The geologist checked over her samples before slinging the bag over her shoulders.

'Here, I'll help you.' Seokyeong held out his hand, but the geologist put out her palm to decline the offer.

'I'll carry this myself. These are important.'

Her stomach growled loudly just then, making the three of them jump.

Jebi averted her face as she tried to stifle her laughter.

'Join us for dinner before you go,' Seokyeong said, mildly.

'I don't have that kind of money. After paying for the shoot, I'll need to tighten my belt this month,' the geologist said, as she adjusted her backpack strap.

'We're going to eat, and it's just an extra pair of chopsticks. Please, have some food before you leave,' Seokyeong said, as he strode ahead.

'Yeah, join us.' Jebi smiled, slipping her arm through the geologist's, and the woman hesitated for only a fraction longer before nodding.

The three of them walked back to the car together, each carrying a bag.

'Usually, we offer our customers a viewing party after the shoot.' Jebi was chattering away to fill a prolonged silence.

'A viewing party?'

'Yeah, that's what we call it– we create a slideshow of the photos for the guests to watch, and serve a delicious meal.'

'That sounds amazing! I'd love to do it next time.'

'We can do it today,' Seokyeong said, abruptly.

'Oh, but I don't have the—'

'It's okay. You taught me how to take fieldwork photos. Think of it as payment in kind. I'm also curious to see how the photos turn out.'

Back at the photo studio, the three of them quickly freshened up. The geologist took off her wide-brimmed hat and, after washing her face, she put on a hairband stitched with a crystal gemstones.

As Jebi cleaned a batch of sea urchins the haenyeos had given her, and the geologist chopped the vegetables for the bibimbap, Seokyeong sat down in front of his computer.

He had been about to start picking out the best photos, as usual, when he paused. He wasn't the right person to go through them: he didn't have the eye for it. This was something that the geologist had to do for herself, back at her lab.

Happily, he returned to the kitchen where he cleaned some top shells that he'd picked with Dongwon on his day off and then, oblivious to the tangerine-coloured sun dipping below the horizon outside, the three of them sat at the table and enjoyed the food. The sea urchin bibimbap was delicious, but the top shell soybean paste stew was a masterpiece.

Only when she had finally put down her spoon did the geologist look out of the window. Rubbing her full belly, she leant back comfortably into her chair. 'Wow. This place is great. It'd be nice to have a dissertation defence party here.'

'Dissertation defence party?'

'Yeah. The final interview of a PhD is notoriously difficult, so people often hold a party when they pass. But I don't really have anyone I'm close to at the university . . .'

'Why not?' Jebi asked, as she began clearing the plates.

The geologist stood up to help. 'I'm not local, unlike the other students. They're always cracking jokes in the local dialect. I think they see me as someone who's just passing through.'

'You plan to settle down on the island?' Seokyeong asked, as he folded the dishcloth and wiped the table.

'I'm not sure yet. Well, if I can get a job. But everyone else is probably thinking the same thing.'

*

'It's your turn.' Jebi turned to Seokyeong as she stacked the plates in the sink.

'Again?' Seokyeong picked up the dishcloth and sighed as Jebi pulled a face at him.

While Seokyeong handled the dishes, Jebi opened the windows to let in some fresh air. Then she pushed open the door too.

Bell ran out with a pleased 'Wuff!' She was sniffing enthusiastically at the ground when she suddenly turned and barked properly. Someone was walking up the hill.

Jebi smoothed down her apron, wondering who was visiting at this hour. The person's silhouette sharpened.

It was a middle-aged man in a stylish shirt. He looked European.

'Oh my god.' Jebi was completely thrown. 'Wait. Just a minute. Please,' she said in halting English. She ran into the kitchen. 'S-S-Sajangnim! He's outside!'

'Who?' Seokyeong turned around, holding his hands up, washing up gloves still on.

With a shaking finger, Jebi pointed at his T-shirt. 'Him! The person on your shirt!'

'What are you talking about?' Seokyeong turned back to finish rinsing the bowls.

Meanwhile, the stranger had walked into the shop. 'Excuse me?' he called out.

Jebi took out the camera in her pocket and started snapping shots of Seokyeong's bulging eyes, his slack-jawed expression, the running tap behind him. In his shock, he almost lost his balance, his arms flailing. It was

221

as if a hole had opened in mid-air and he was being sucked into another dimension.

Gotcha! I'll be able to tease him about this for the rest of his life. Jebi grinned.

'He says he's on holiday. The civil war he was covering has ended.'

The geologist was acting as an interpreter for Jebi's sake; Seokyeong's English was good.

But how does she know that I can't speak English? Do I look stupid? Jebi was a little put out, but she kept quiet. She would hate to miss out on what Stephen Gerz had to say.

'W-why are you here?' Seokyeong had stammered as he tried to pull the damp gloves from his hands. They hadn't wanted to come off, so he'd ended up pulling them down inside out.

The man shrugged. 'My feet brought me here.'

'C-can we offer you some dinner?'

'I ate. I'm looking for a place that will serve me a drink. I followed the waves and walked until the sun began setting. It's been a long time since I last saw the sea.'

'Then drink here. Let's all have a drink together,' Jebi said, making the gesture of knocking back shots while giving Seokyeong a meaningful glance.

Seokyeong's eyes widened.

Without waiting for a response, Jebi guided Stephen to the table next to the window.

'Lovely!' Stephen exclaimed, as he settled into the chair with a smile.

*

'How long are you going to keep making that expression? You look like a goldfish.' Jebi poked Seokyeong in the ribs.

'Is he famous or something?' the geologist murmured.

'Yes, he's a very famous photographer. A war photographer, and my boss's idol.'

The geologist nodded and then turned to Stephen. 'You're his idol, apparently.'

Embarrassed, Seokyeong tried to shush her. Jebi also hadn't expected her to translate that.

'Oh?' Stephen Gertz turned to Seokyeong. His gaze landed on his face before sliding down to the T-shirt he was wearing. He chuckled. 'I didn't think anyone would know me here. Not in this peaceful country.'

Seokyeong's eyes darted around. Jebi realised he was trembling. And it wasn't just she who had noticed.

Stephen got up to explore. 'It's a photo studio? I came here thinking it was a café.'

Seokyeong looked like he was about to faint, so Jebi sat him firmly down on a chair. At the table, three pairs of eyes followed Stephen as he walked slowly around the room. Every action of his seemed to be magnified in their eyes. They watched him lower his gaze at times, crossing his arms as he studied each of the photos on display. Passing the group of bikers, he paused in front of Jungmi's wisdom teeth and began whispering something urgently under his breath. But it was too low to hear what he was saying. He grinned at the photo of the young couple, and when he reached the photo of Jebi being chosen by the giant octopus, he jerked his head back in surprise.

'Is this real?'

'He's asking if it's real,' the geologist repeated in Korean.

'Yes, I hear him. Of course! It's real. Very real. Specially real!' Jebi bobbed up and down excitedly as she replied in English.

'Is that you in the picture?' When Stephen's eyes widened, horizontal lines creased his forehead.

Jebi nodded. 'Yes, me!' She stood up and draped a hand over her face, as if that would help him recognise her better from the photo.

The geologist went on translating what Stephen was saying.

'He said, "Wow, amazing. I'm heading for Ukraine tomorrow. I'd like to buy this as a good-luck talisman." He's asking how much it is.'

Seokyeong's jaw dropped.

'It's free.'

'One hundred dollars.'

Seokyeong and Jebi spoke at the same time.

Stephen laughed. 'A hundred?'

He rummaged in his backpack for the money. Seokyeong tried to decline it, but Stephen wouldn't let him. His expression was stern. 'They say it's bad luck to accept a good-luck charm for free. Can you print it out for me in a smaller size, so that I can carry it around in my wallet, too?'

While Seokyeong was printing the photo in his workroom, Gertz went back to the framed photos, looking at the underwater shots with particular interest. There was the young woman with the long hair diving next to the jellyfish, the man walking on the sand of the seafloor. In front of the portrait of the retired detective, he paused. Stroking his beard, he let out a soft sigh.

Seokyeong returned with the printed photo and held it out reverently with both hands to Stephen.

Gertz accepted it and slipped it into his wallet. Then he looked at Seokyeong, as though declaring something important, said: 'Will you be my son?'

Seokyeong froze.

Jebi and the geologist looked on, wide-eyed.

'Well, what do you say?' Stephen was smiling.

'Yes, of course!' Seokyeong replied at last. He lifted his head and looked steadily at Gertz.

'Awesome! That's my boy!' Stephen cried.

The geologist smiled at Jebi and repeated what he'd said in Korean. 'He said it's a wonderful day. That even though he isn't married, he now has a son.'

Stephen spread his arms and hugged Seokyeong, who looked as though he was having an out-of-body experience.

Four chairs were placed side by side as they got ready to view the photos taken during the fieldwork trip; Seokyeong and Stephen sat in the middle, with Jebi and the geologist on either side.

Jebi had brewed coffee with whole beans that had been roasted with tangerine peel, and placed the cups on the table.

'Didn't he say he was here for a drink?' Jebi said quietly to Seokyeong, mimicking downing a shot.

'He doesn't drink alcohol. He says he's used to being on high alert all the time.'

Seokyeong started the slideshow using the remote control. He kept quiet and pursed his lips tight in anxiety.

Stephen picked up his cup, took a sip of coffee and swirled it in his mouth as though tasting the notes, all the while staring intently at the photos on the screen.

The geologist was also rapt.

'These are great. Really amazing.' Gertz exhaled at the panoramic photos. The geologist was explaining to him, in fluent English, how columnar jointing is formed.

Jebi tried to follow the conversation but there were too many technical terms, so she turned her attention back on the screen. The columnar jointing had looked like a cross section of a cake in real life, but in the photo, the resemblance was less obvious. She wanted to tell Stephen this, but in the end she kept quiet.

Stephen was listening to the geologist, nodding along. When he saw the close-up photos of the sand and clay layers of the rocks, he grinned. 'It looks like a child took these photos!'

Seokyeong's face reddened, like a child in a classroom receiving poor feedback. Jebi was also a little shocked.

'Actually, they're great. He only learnt how to take photos like this today,' the geologist replied in English.

'Oh . . . You've been teaching him?'

'Yes. He'd never taken fieldwork photos before.'

Stephen nodded. 'Same.'

'He's a great student. I just have to tell him something once and he immediately gets it.'

'It's so wonderful to be travelling in a safe country, to take an evening stroll and to stumble upon such lovely photography,' Stephen said, putting an arm around Seokyeong's shoulders.

'Have you taken many photos on your trip so far?' the geologist asked.

Stephen shook his head. 'None at all. I don't want to work when I'm on holiday. I just want to enjoy myself to the fullest.'

'But you'd be taking *holiday* photos.'

'Photos are still photos. You're wouldn't analyse a soil sample when on holiday, right?'

The geologist rolled her eyes. 'Indeed.'

The four of them fell into a comfortable silence. On the screen was a photo of the octopus fossil and trachyte.

Stephen picked up his coffee and took a sip. 'If you don't mind me asking, I would love to know . . . why geology? Why rocks?'

The woman hesitated before she began speaking. 'There was a teacher I respected . . . I was a liberal arts student, and we didn't have to decide on our major during our first year. I was taking various courses, exploring my interests, when I met a really amazing professor. He was poised, patient; there was nothing he didn't know. He was a geologist. And that was that.'

'That was that?'

'Yeah.'

'Let's suppose that teacher had told you not to pursue geology. Would you have given it up?'

'Maybe. But he never told me that. He recently retired, actually, and his students got together and held a party for him. We drank a lot. I got a little emotional, Told him: "I got into geology because of you, Professor. How can you leave us before I graduate?" I completely spoilt the mood of the party.' She grimaced. 'But the professor placed a comforting hand on my shoulder. He told me, "I'm happy that you feel you chose this field because of me. But if you think carefully, you'll find that's not entirely true." I was confused. I had no idea what he was talking about. But he spoke kindly. "There must be something else that attracts you to it. You have to find what it is." '

'And what happened? Did you find the reason?' Stephen sipped the last of his coffee.

The geologist laced her fingers together. 'I think I'm figuring it out. I like things that are fiery, like lava that sweeps everything away in its path. I like the way we can trace its flow, reading the clues in the rock . . . maybe that's why I'm drawn to this topic . . .'

Stephen nodded. 'Interesting. However, you need to think deeper. What exactly it is that you hope to sweep away and make disappear? And could you find the power in yourself to do it? To carve your own path, rather than tracing the path of something else?' He looked at her. 'Tell me. Have you lost someone close to you? Or was there someone who . . . I don't know – hurt you, perhaps?'

'W-what are you talking about? There's nothing like that!' the geologist retorted loudly, her face red.

Stephen shook his head, gazing at her with concerned eyes. 'Don't be too quick to answer. You're smart, that's why you must think more deeply. Smart people trying to make up for what they've lost, they always have it the hardest. You can't use work to fill a gaping hole in you; neither should you wear yourself out without knowing what you're trying to achieve.' His words were cryptic.

'More coffee?' Jebi put down a new cup.

'Thank you.' Stephen flashed Jebi a bright smile and the four of them fell into their own thoughts once again as the slideshow continued.

This time, it was the geologist who broke the silence. Looking at Seokyeong, she asked: 'What made you get into photography?'

At the question, Seokyeong's body stiffened.

Gertz appeared to notice Seokyeong's reaction with interest.

'M-my mother . . .' It was as if the words took him a lot to say. 'When I was a child, our family wasn't well off. My mum had to borrow a camera to take photos of me and my sister. Then she'd get them printed out and carefully slot them into an album. I'd often hear her say she wished she could've taken more photos of us.' Seokyeong cupped his hands around his coffee cup, which was now cold. 'Then . . . my younger sister died. Suddenly. She was only three years old.'

Stephen and the geologist looked at him with compassion.

Jebi was stunned. This was news to her too.

'After the funeral, my mum said the same thing, crying: "I should've taken more photos." Then she asked me, "Do you remember her first steps? She looked so pleased with herself. If only I had captured that moment . . . And she

229

loved eating strawberries with her hands. Oh, how those little fingers of hers would stain red! I should've taken a photo of that too . . ." It was then that I told myself I'd be a photographer when I grew up. I want to take photos that people can look back on years later, to remember the important moments; and for those left behind, hopefully the photos will offer some solace.'

The wind had picked up as they spoke, and suddenly the windows were rattling in their frames. Perhaps a storm was coming. It would match the heavy mood in the gallery at that moment.

'It's not possible for every single moment to be captured in photos,' Stephen said reasonably. 'And even if it were, your mum would still be sad. Because her child died.' He paused. Stroking his beard, he added, his tone careful: 'But come to think of it, isn't it strange? Your mum hadn't forgotten. She remembered every single detail, the first steps, the strawberries. So why is she regretting the lack of photos so much?'

It was as if something hard and icy that had been lodged in Seokyeong's chest for years, crumbled in that moment. It hit him. His mum was . . . scared. She didn't want Seokyeong to forget. She wanted her daughter to be remembered, not just by her, but by everyone else. Or at the very least, by her son . . .

Stephen stretched and yawned.

Surfacing from his thoughts, Seokyeong turned to him. 'Are you tired? I can give you a lift back to your hotel.'

'Hmm. Would it be too much trouble if I stayed the night? I'm so sleepy.'

'Of course!'

The two of them went upstairs, and Seokyeong insisted that Stephen take the bedroom.

'That's very generous of you. Normally I would decline,' the older photographer replied, rubbing his eyes that were tearing up from yawning, 'But I'm leaving tomorrow, and I'm not sure if I'll ever see you again, my son, so I suppose it's fine for me to impose on you for a night.'

Seokyeong took out a new blanket for him before drawing the curtain to shut out the dim moonlight. He was about to leave the room when Stephen spoke.

'Don't go yet. I want to chat with you a little more, at least until I fall sleep.'

Seokyeong sat on the floor and Stephen lay a gnarled hand on his shoulder.

'I haven't told you my name, have I? I'm Seokyeong. Lee Seokyeong.' He knew English speakers found his name difficult. He thought he should tell Stephen the story behind his name, to help him to remember it. 'I was born on the winter solstice, the longest night of the year. It's one of the solar terms in the lunar calendar. That's what my name means. In hanja characters, it means "longest night" . . .'

At that moment, Stephen's hand slipped from his shoulder. It looked like he'd fallen asleep.

Seokyeong tiptoed out of the room and went downstairs. The geologist had left, taking the photos with her on a USB drive.

'I made a copy, don't worry.' Jebi yawned.

Seokyeong looked at his watch. It was getting late.

'I don't think I can take you home tonight. You wanna take Bell with you?'

'Okay.'

Seokyeong put on Bell's lead. The little puppy seemed excited at the prospect of a nighttime walk. The two of them left, and for a while, Seokyeong could hear Jebi trying to stop Bell from pulling, before their voices faded away.

The next morning, the father and son duo sat by the window looking out to sea, eating breakfast together. The rough waves had quietened, and the sun shone wanly through the clouds. Seokyeong had asked Yoona's Bakes to send a loaf of bread, which he sliced, grilled and topped with braised sea urchin roe.

Stephen nodded approvingly, making sounds of pleasure as he devoured it.

After breakfast, Seokyeong drove him to the airport. He would be flying to Europe before getting a contact's help to enter Ukraine.

Stephen was at the check-in counter already when he turned back and walked towards Seokyeong. 'If you don't mind, I want to give you a name? As a father.'

Seokyeong nodded nervously.

'I'd like to call you Quartz.'

Seokyeong blinked.

'Yesterday, while you were printing the photo, the geologist told me your name is Seokyeong, and that one of the meanings in English is "quartz". She said that quartz can come in the form of rock or crystals, depending on the level of impurities. But either way, it is one of the strongest and most valuable minerals on Earth, as well as being one of the most common. And that whether we know it or not, we're all walking on top of layers of quartz every day.' He patted Seokyeong's back with his broad palm.

As Seokyeong watched him turn away, sudden anxiety seized him, as if he were at an important crossroads in his life. 'Stop! Please! Take me with you!' he shouted, hot tears beginning to stream down his face.

Stephen turned, waved and shook his head. Then he walked back to Seokyeong. It was almost time to go.

'In a war zone . . . everyone has to fight . . . Where I've just been, the soldiers leave their families at home or send them to a safe place. And it's the same for me . . . I don't think I'll ever marry and start a family in this lifetime. I won't ever get the chance to father a child. But humans don't just reproduce through genes. A famous biologist, Dawkins, says that while genes are passed on in sperm and eggs, memes propagate by leaping from brain to brain.' He looked at Seokyeong for a long moment, smiling fondly. 'Quartz, do you see what I'm trying to say? I hope that you'll stay here, in this peaceful country, and live a long life. That's all I hope for you.' Stephen pulled Seokyeong into a hug, then gently patted his cheek with his large hand.

When he returned to the photo studio, Seokyeong flipped open his diary for the first time in a while. His long-time dream was to fulfil what his father had tried and failed to do on this island – to start a family, put down roots, and live a good life here. So, every day, he wrote in his diary, describing the life he hoped to one day have.

The last entry had been written on the day the detective came. He flipped to a new page and wrote the day's date. At the table by the window looking out to the sea, he sat down and started writing.

Some men become a dad on the day their first child is born. For others, it's when the child gets old enough to start to recognise him as a father figure. As for Dongwon . . . instead of trying to rush things, I hope that one day he'll come to think, 'This person is my dad.'

II

Polaroid Pictures

Winter solstice – the longest night of the year. Winds had howled since daybreak, and a hailstorm was raging.

In Giant Octopus village, the haenyeos decided not to go out to sea. Keeping their windows and doors securely locked, they busied themselves with tasks – sending dried seaweed to customers by post, cleaning the fridges they stored their catch in, settling insurance claims for the treatment costs for diver's disease, which many of them suffered from. That they'd been putting all this off for a while. They also used the time to mend the holes in their wetsuits and fix torn nets.

The day passed by in a blur. That night, they sat with their families, eating their way through baskets of tangerines as they listened to complaints and small sadnesses from work and school. To be a listening ear was one of the many things the haenyeos had to do.

But on most days in winter, even when snow or hail was falling, the haenyeos in Giant Octopus village went out to the sea. Jebi's training, too, continued.

'I'm freezing to death! I already know how to hold my breath underwater. Can't we start again in spring?' Jebi shouted, her lips blue. The waves felt like cold, sharp knives slicing at her jaw and cheeks.

'No haenyeo has ever frozen to death in our village,' Yanghee snorted. She was wearing a puffer jacket over her wetsuit and standing on the shore on top of a basalt rock, far from the reach of the waves.

'Must be a gene passed down among haenyeos!' In the water, Jebi gave another violent shiver.

'Maybe. Before wetsuits were invented, haenyeos wore cotton shorts and sleeveless tops. Because we are responsible for the livelihoods of our families, we have always needed to withstand the harsh environment and adapt. I read somewhere that Jeju haenyeos have a stronger resistance to the cold than Inuits.'

'Are you kidding? But Alaska is far colder than Jeju.'

'But we're talking about deep water here, not dry land,' Yanghee shot back. 'My grandma went back to work four days after giving birth to my mum. And that was in midwinter.'

Jebi thought back to that terrible summer, four years ago. The contractions had been excruciating. How to describe it? A terrible toothache that had racked her entire body? It wasn't just her stomach that had felt like it was being torn apart, but her limbs, too. Even that couldn't accurately express the pain . . . She had felt like a limp piece of cabbage rubbed in salt. Added to which, during the birth her vagina had torn, so that for a whole month, she couldn't walk properly.

The thought of going into the sea after a mere four days made Jebi shiver.

Taking a deep breath, she lowered her head into the water and swam breaststroke against the waves, sweeping her arms out and kicking hard like a frog.

Yanghee crossed her arms. 'This is rare. No more complaints?'

Because I want to be strong, Jebi wanted to say. *To be a strong woman like your grandmother*. Four years ago, when she had found out that she was pregnant, she had felt lost and afraid. She had, however, been confident of one thing. She had known she would be a better parent than her own mum and dad; and unlike her unfeeling grandmother, she was going to be warm and nurturing.

It was a lifelong dream of hers to start a family with a man she loved. That was why she had chosen to major in early childhood studies at community college. But then she had been dumped unceremoniously, left to deal with the pregnancy alone. And when her child had come along, she'd realised that all the theory she'd learnt was useless. A mum has to be strong, physically and mentally, as strong as a warrior. But like a soldier dragged into battle far too young, Jebi had failed miserably. And the experience had left her battered and bruised, barely surviving.

She imagined Yanghee's grandmother swimming in the dark, bitingly cold sea, her body still swollen, her postpartum belly jiggling . . . How did that same brave sanggun haenyeo end up dying in the sea?

Perhaps Mokpo Granny did know that secret.

'Why do you dislike our sajangnim?' Jebi had waded back to shore. She towelled herself and quickly put on her padded jacket.

'I told you before. He's using me to get what he wants,' said Yanghee, as she took off her jacket and passed it to Jebi to hold. Stretching out her arms, she started warming up.

'How can you know without going on a single date with him? It might be true love.'

'I'm just an object to him, a tool.' Yanghee said, rotating her neck.

Jebi cocked her head. *Tool.* She mulled over the word Yanghee had used. 'Eonnie, by the way, why don't you speak in dialect to me?'

'And why would you want to hear me speak in dialect?' Yanghee's legs were already in the water when she turned around. She dipped her goggles under and splashed her thighs and arms.

'It feels more . . . honest somehow, more intimate? As if you're speaking from the heart.'

Yanghee clucked her tongue in disbelief. 'People can speak dialect and still be liars, you know.'

'That's true . . .' Jebi nodded first, then shook her head. 'But our boss is not that kind of person.'

'How would you know?'

'He keeps a diary,' Jebi said. 'He writes in it every day, about all the things he'll do when he becomes a father. Do you know any other man who does that?'

Yanghee slung the tewak over her shoulders and cast her net out. 'Standard Korean is just as effective for conveying sincerity. I hate it when an outsider insists on speaking in dialect. They never speak it well. It gets on my nerves.' With that, she dived into the sea, her body cleaving the water.

Jebi stood up. The only thing on her mind right then was a good hot soak in the changing room.

The wetsuit stuck to Jebi's skin and she hopped up and down on one leg, cursing. She thought suddenly of the geologist and the way she'd cursed under her breath at her broken camera. Jebi giggled.

She filled a big basin with hot water and lowered herself into it. *How did she end up becoming a geologist? Was it really as Stephen Gertz had suggested? That she was trying to heal some kind of wound? Or was what she had said true – that she was simply inspired by her professor?*

Jebi scooped up some hot water and poured it over her shoulders. *Who knows*, she thought. Seokyeong was clearly trying to fill the emptiness left by his sister's death by becoming a photographer. Was it the same for the geologist? Stephen's voice rang in her ears.

"You can't use work to fill a gaping hole in you, neither should you wear yourself out . . ."

Maybe there's an emptiness in me too, Jebi thought.

As her body relaxed in the hot water, Jebi leant back against the basin, nodding off and falling into a vague dream.

In the fog-filled scene, she pushed open the door to the daycare centre where she had once worked, but instead of the familiar feelings of the frustration and fatigue that a workday brought on, a different emotion engulfed her.

Guilt.

Jebi woke up to the revving of a motorbike outside. The water in the basin had turned cold and there was a chilly draft.

Sneezing loudly several times, she quickly dried herself and put on her clothes. Perhaps she'd better take some paracetamol before bedtime – she could feel a cold coming. Putting on her padded jacket, she opened the door.

'Samchon! Can we do a few more loops, please?' Dongwon's voice was excited.

'Your grandma will be worried. I told her we're only going round once more before heading back,' replied Seokyeong in dialect.

'You're here early,' Jebi said, as she stepped outside.

Attached to his white motorbike was a sidecar in the same colour, from which Dongwon's small head was sticking out. Under his helmet, Dongwon's eyes were shining and because of the cold wind, his cheeks were like rosy-red apples.

'Yeah, we went for a test drive along the coast road,' Seokyeong replied.

To attach a sidecar to the motorbike had been an idea he'd come up with after the shoot with the bikers last summer. But he'd been so busy he'd only ordered it recently.

After spending the whole autumn practising, Jebi had successfully got her motorbike licence. The other day, she had ridden the bike with Seokyeong in the sidecar and the test shoot had been a success.

'That was much safer. The time with the bikers, I thought I was going to die.' Seokyeong had grinned as he unfurled his body from the cramped sidecar.

Now, Seokyeong spoke: 'Why don't you take the rest of the day off? We'll be starting at the crack of dawn tomorrow.'

He leant forward and restarted the engine. Dongwon spread out his arms and whooped in joy.

Watching the motorbike disappear into the distance, Jebi grinned. It'd been a long time since a child had brought a smile to her face.

The next morning, Jebi woke at daybreak to the sound of her alarm. A family who was visiting Jeju for three days over the new year holidays had booked a shoot with them.

In the past few months at Hakuda Photo Studio, Jebi had met customers of every description, but it was rare to see a young family. Her heart still ached whenever she saw loving parents with their kid. Nevertheless, she got up and showered. Seokyeong was waiting for her.

Because the family wanted to capture every moment of their trip, Seokyeong and Jebi had decided to start the shoot at the airport. Now, they stood in the arrivals lounge, carrying a small sign: WELCOME TO JEJU, LEE HYEYONG AND FAMILY ❤

A throng of people spilled through the doors, and among them was a family of three. Seokyeong recognised them immediately: a dad, a mum and a child in matching winter coats – the exact same ones in the photo they'd sent via email. Their seven-year-old daughter was wearing sunglasses in the shape of red-rimmed hearts.

'Hello! You must be Hyeyong? Nice to meet you!'

After snapping photos of them collecting their bags, Seokyeong held out a hand to the girl. He had always loved kids, and after spending so much time with Dongwon, he was getting more and more at ease with them.

Hyeyong ignored his hand, instead smiling shyly and hiding behind her dad. But he could tell that she was in a good mood. When she grinned, he saw that her front teeth were missing. This gave her an impish look.

Jebi guided them to the SUV while Seokyeong took their two large suitcases and loaded them in the boot. He got into the driver's seat and set the tangerine farm as the destination on the GPS. The plan was to go tangerine-picking and horse-riding today; tomorrow, on New Year's Day, they would climb Hallasan mountain.

The family were chatting away in the back seats.

'Wow, palm trees even in winter! It's so warm here.'

'Is that Hallasan in the distance, with the snow on its peak?'

'Look! There's a river over there.'

'Of course there's a river. They're not exactly rare,' the dad said to his wife, laughing.

'Well, actually . . .' Hyeyong piped up. She pushed the sunglasses higher on her nose. 'Jeju is a volcanic island, so most of the rainwater goes underground. The stream is usually dry, it only flows when it rains. It probably rained in the last few days.'

Seokyeong glanced in the rear-view mirror. 'Yeah, it rained yesterday.'

'Wow! Is there anything our girl doesn't know!' Hyeyong's dad exclaimed, delighted.

Seokyeong smiled at the sight of this happy family and, in that moment, he was grateful to be doing this for a living.

He stole a glance at Jebi. Though she was also smiling, her eyes were sad. Seokyeong had seen a similar expression on her face each time they did a family shoot. He wondered what he could say to offer some comfort, but couldn't think of anything appropriate.

Click. Znnng. There was a mechanical whir. Hyeyong's mum was taking Polaroid photos.

Jebi turned. Hallasan was still visible in the distance.

'Mum, don't use them all up.'

'Got it.'

Jebi wondered why they had brought that camera along, when they'd hired a photographer. The Polaroid in Hyeyong's mum's lap was starting to come into focus. Jebi glanced at it. It was a good shot and she began to worry – what if they were fussy customers?

The SUV cruised past the camellia shrubs that lined both sides of the road, their blooms like clusters of red velvet bells.

'So pretty!' Hyeyong's mum exclaimed, taking several Polaroids one after the other.

'Just like the baubles on a Christmas tree,' said Hyeyong's dad.

Hyeyong put her hands on her mother's back as she strained her neck to look out of the window.

Pulling into the farm, Seokyeong stopped the car.

243

Hyeyong and her dad got out immediately. 'Wow, the tangerines are such a bright orange! And there are crates and crates of them. Oh, one's rolling towards us. Come on, Yong-ah! Let's catch it,' the dad shouted and they ran, holding hands.

The owner of the farm, who was carefully tipping tangerines from a basket into a crates, paused and looked up. Straightening his back, he smiled to welcome the father-daughter pair.

'I'll park the car and come back,' Seokyeong said to Hyeyong's mum, who was still sitting in the back.

'Alright.' She smiled, then bit her lip slightly, as if contemplating her next words.

Seokyeong and Jebi exchanged a glance.

'I . . . Our daughter can't see.'

Seokyeong and Jebi both turned to look out of the window. Hyeyong was skipping around, listening to the owner talk about his farm.

'Have you ever heard of anophthalmia?'

Seokyeong and Jebi shook their heads.

'Hyeyong was born without eyes. The doctors say it might be caused by a genetic disorder or chromosomal abnormality. When she takes off her sunglasses . . . you'll see what I mean,' the mum added, her voice calm, as if she'd repeated the same thing hundreds of times. 'She tried wearing glass eyes, but she kept getting infections from them . . . I'm telling you this so that you won't be surprised later.'

'I see.' Seokyeong nodded. Jebi, too, her heart heavy.

'I'm sorry I didn't mention this earlier.' There was a pause. 'I hope you won't treat her any differently . . . I know you might have preferred to know this in advance, but . . . we didn't want any fuss to be made. What you've been doing is great.' She smiled, and then hurried off to join her husband and daughter.

'Does my expression look odd to you?' Seokyeong asked, as he glanced at Jebi.

'A little. Kind of stiff.'

'Yours too, actually.' Seokyeong sighed and looked at his watch.

'Come on, let's just get going.' Seokyeong opened the boot of the SUV. He took the camera from its bag, slung the bag over his shoulder, and passed Jebi the reflector.

Jebi took it but then just stood there, looking slightly dazed. Then: 'Right,' she said decisively. Going back to the front of the car, she opened the glove compartment and reached for a box of sour sweets in there. She'd bought them to combat sleepiness on the road, and she was desperate for some now.

They both popped a few into their mouths and, as they chewed, their faces scrunched up at the same time.

Glancing at each other, they burst out laughing.

After paying the farm owner the agreed fee, Hyeyong's family each received some pruning scissors and a basket.

'Take as many as you can carry!' The farmer waved them away, smiling.

The farm was a forest of tangerine trees. As they walked further in, Hyeyong's sunglasses kept getting knocked askew by the low branches.

'I'll take them off,' she said, slipping them into her pocket. Seokyeong, who had the viewfinder to his eye, stopped walking. Jebi also unthinkingly lowered the reflector.

Hyeyong's eyelids were almost entirely closed, her lashes dark and thick like a doll's.

'Yong-ah, there are tangerines over here!' Hyeyong's dad said, holding her wrist. 'Go on, touch it. It's in front of you. Do you think you can cut it down?'

'Of course!' Hyeyong caught the branch in her left hand before tapping on the fruit with the scissors. Carefully, she snipped it from its stem. Her dad caught the fruit and put it in Hyeyong's hands.

Hyeyong looked at Jebi, or rather, faced her. 'Eonnie, did you get a shock?'

'A little.' Jebi let out an awkward laugh, which she instantly regretted.

'That's ok. But you're not going to be weird the whole day, right?'

'Oh, of course not.' Her face was hot.

Hyeyong walked towards her, her arms stretched out in front. When she accidentally brushed Jebi's stomach, she stepped back with an 'Oops.' She held out the fruit. 'It has an interesting texture. Different from the ones we eat at home,' she said.

Jebi took it. The fruit was warm from the girl's hand.

'I heard it's okay to eat them right away.'

Jebi quickly put down the reflector and prised open the fruit.

'What a lovely smell!' Hyeyong was delighted.

'Want some?' Jebi held out a piece.

'No thanks, Eonnie. You can have it. I'll peel one for myself. There are lots of germs on other people's hands.'

At the sight of Hyeyong turning away, looking rather prim and self-righteous, Jebi mock-pouted. Hyeyong's parents laughed. Seokyeong, too, was chuckling.

Because she was working, Jebi quickly stuffed the whole tangerine into her mouth, bending down to retrieve the reflector.

'I love tangerines,' Hyeyong said. 'The skin is rough, but the flesh inside is so soft. And they're tart and sweet at the same time.'

Seokyeong snapped photos as the family hurried about among the trees. Soon three baskets were piled high with fruit.

For lunch, they had made reservations at a place famous for grilled cutlassfish. At the restaurant, the family was ushered into a private room.

'We'll eat over there,' Seokyeong said, indicating a table in the main dining area. Hyeyong's parents nodded.

Hyeyong was back in her sunglasses. 'Why?'

'Hmm?' Seokyeong and Jebi were surprised at the sudden question.

'Why don't you want to eat with us?'

'We always eat at a separate table so that our clients can relax and enjoy some privacy,' Jebi explained.

Hyeyong suddenly puffed out her cheeks angrily. 'No! You don't like me! You don't like my eyes!' From beneath her sunglasses, tears began rolling down her cheeks.

'Yong-ah, that's not true!' Her mother looked stricken.

The other diners were casting curious glances at the group.

'I'm sorry. She acts like a baby at times,' Hyeyong's dad apologised. 'We spoil her. I thought it'd be good for her to meet more people on holiday before she starts primary school . . .'

'If you wouldn't mind, would you join us?' Hyeyong's mum said with a smile, composed again.

Seokyeong and Jebi exchanged awkward glances and nodded.

Hyeyong went off with her dad to wash her hands and, when she returned, she was back to her lively self, sniffing the air to take in the spread of dishes on the table.

'Young-ah, the rice is on your left, seaweed soup to your right. There's sea urchin in the soup,' Hyeyong's mum said.

'In front is egg soup, roasted seaweed and braised tofu. The dish looks red, so it might be a little spicy,' her dad added, as he deboned a piece of fish.

Hyeyong nodded. Holding chopsticks in her right hand and a spoon in her left, she tucked in hungrily.

Her dad placed the deboned fish on her spoon.

'Dad! That's a massive piece! My mouth's stuffed full!' Hyeyong giggled, excited, and her mum hushed her, telling her not to talk with her mouth full.

Seokyeong and Jebi ate in silence.

Hyeyong's mum had only taken a few bites before she rummaged in her bag for the Polaroids she had taken during the car ride. She then started poking holes in the photo using what looked like a pen. Jebi and Seokyeong stared. Upon closer inspection, it wasn't a pen but a needle attached to a plastic pen covering.

'Mum, are you nearly finished with the photos?' Hyeyong scraped the last bit of rice from her bowl.

'Yup, you can have the first one. Do you want me to tell you what it is?' Hyeyong's mum wriggled her shoulders and circled her wrist to relieve the strain of the precise pricking she'd been doing.

'No! Mum, don't say anything!' Hyeyong begged.

The adults at the table smiled.

Hyeyong took the photo eagerly and ran all ten fingers over it.

Seokyeong held his breath, his heart tingling.

'I know! It's Hallasan!'

'Bingo! We saw it during the ride to the farm.' Hyeyong's mum smiled widely. Jebi and Seokyeong clapped.

'Wow. So much snow? That's so cool . . . we're going there tomorrow, right?' Hyeyong touched the mountain peak in the photo.

'You bet!' her dad replied.

On the way to the horse-riding centre, Hyeyong's family had an argument. Hyeyong was insisting she wanted to ride by herself, but her parents were adamantly against it. It was too dangerous, they said.

'But two people on a horse! Isn't that cruel?' Hyeyong demanded.

'They're strong horses. Big ones,' her mum said.

For the rest of the journey, Hyeyong sulked.

The argument resolved itself in a surprising twist.

'We can't let two people ride one horse, it wouldn't be safe,' said the trainer. With a whistle hanging from his chest, he looked like a referee.

'But aren't they always doing it in movies?' Hyeyong's mum asked.

'Well, that's movies for you,' the trainer replied, as he helped Hyeyong put on a riding helmet.

Hyeyong grinned. She strained her ears in the direction of the horses, listening to the clop of their hooves, their whinnying, and clapped in delight. Holding the trainer's hand, she carefully walked up the small mounting block that had been placed next to one of the smaller mares. The trainer tucked his hands under Hyeyong's arms and lifted her onto its back.

Hyeyong straightened her back as she found her balance, keeping her lips pursed tight. She seemed to be holding back a squeal of happiness. The trainer had reminded her not to make sudden loud noises to avoid alarming the horse.

The young man, standing at the horse's head with the reins in his right hand, tugged them gently and the horse started walking.

Seokyeong snapped away, capturing the proud expressions of her parents as Hyeyong sat elegantly on horseback, her face a picture of joy.

At the end of the riding session, she followed the trainer to the stables for the next part of the experience.

Slightly nervous, she held out a carrot on the flat of her hand. A foal approached slowly – Seokyeong took a photo of its dark, gentle eyes as it stopped in front of the girl – brushed its lips against her palm and chomped on the carrot.

When she reached out cautiously and stroked the horse's nose, it didn't move away, instead standing and huffing warm breath on her. 'So soft,' she whispered.

Emboldened, she stretched out her hand a little further but accidentally brushed the foal's eyes.

With a snort, it snatched its head back.

'Sorry! I'm so sorry!' Hyeyong cried out. Flailing her arms, she tried to comfort it, but the foal skittered away, and not even a carrot could entice it back.

They all wanted to be well rested for the Hallasan climb the next day – they had agreed to meet in the lobby at seven the next morning – so when they left the stables, Seokyeong drove them straight back to the hotel. Hyeyong's dad carried her out of the car. Tired out from the day's activities, she snuggled her head into his neck.

As the SUV cruised along the asphalt road back towards Giant Octopus village, Seokyeong and Jebi remained quiet, each thinking of their own families . . . If only they had done more . . . Was there more that could be done . . .?

Late that night, Seokyeong changed into his pyjamas and draped his quilt around himself like a cape. Remembering that he had yet to lock the door, he went downstairs. In the distance, the shaft of light from the lighthouse swept past the window. Snow was falling heavily over the inky sea. As he turned the key in the lock, it occurred to him that if the snow continued overnight, Hallasan could be closed to visitors. He'd need an alternative plan.

By morning, the snow had lightened considerably. Seokyeong checked the Hallasan National Park website – no closure announcement. Just then, Jebi arrived and they busied themselves packing up the equipment they'd need for the day, loading cameras, hiking shoes with snow grips, and cup ramyeon into the boot.

At the hotel in Seogwipo, they parked the car in the basement and went up to the lobby, Seokyeong noticing the yellow braille block on the floor for the first time.

In a corner of the room was a black sofa where Hyeyong and her family sat waiting. 'But you said you wanted to go up Hallasan!' Hyeyong's dad was saying.

Hyeyong was obviously mid-tantrum. 'I don't want to go anymore! It's snowing!'

Seokyeong stopped in his tracks.

Noticing them, Hyeyong's mum stood up. 'She's afraid of the snow. Snow on the ground is fine, but falling snow . . .' Hyeyong's mum smiled tiredly. 'It's important for her to be able to hear what's going on around her. Snow muffles everything; whether it's the sound of approaching vehicles or people talking. She finds it very frustrating, and doesn't like the ground being slippery, either.'

Hyeyong's dad was looking down at his daughter crossly. 'So you're just going to give up? Where's your fighting spirit!'

Hyeyong sulked, crossing her arms. 'What do you even know?' She gave a sniff. 'You have eyes!'

A short silence descended. It was as if the group were in a bubble, separated from the rest of the people in the busy lobby. A couple in mountain-climbing attire exited the lift, chatting and laughing. A raucous group of middle-aged friends, bantering loudly, walked past the front desk. One of them stopped to ask about the weather.

'Is it going to snow all day? We're planning to head to Hallasan.'

The receptionist, a young man in his early twenties, stood up nervously. He glanced at the entrance and nodded. 'The forecast says it'll snow until nine o'clock tonight.'

'A snowstorm in Jeju? Unbelievable!' someone exclaimed.

'Yeah, it's pretty rare,' the employee said. 'Just this morning, my mum was telling me it hasn't snowed like this in a long, long time, not since she was a little girl.'

Seokyeong, hearing this, sat himself down next to Hyeyong. 'What would you like to do, then?'

Hyeyong's mum sat down on her other side. 'Yeah, you can decide.'

'Dad? Where's Dad?' Hyeyong stretched out her arms in front of her, grasping at the air.

Frustrated, her dad had turned his back to them. He appeared to be taking deep breaths in an effort to calm down.

'Dad! Are you there? Answer me!' Hyeyong cried.

Hyeyong's mum leant over and tugged at her husband's jacket, glaring at him as he turned around.

He went back to the sofa and held his daughter's hand. 'Daddy's here. Okay, tell us. What do you want to do?'

'I want to play with clay. With Daddy!' Hyeyong jumped up and grinned.

Hyeyong's dad gave an exasperated sigh. 'Clay? But we came all the way here, to Jeju!' Hyeyong flinched at the sharpness in his voice. He saw this and lowered his head in frustration. 'We do that all the time at home, sweetheart'

'Daddy . . . clay. I want to play with clay now . . .' Hyeyong wailed.

Hyeyong's mum bowed her head, embarrassed. 'We'll need some time. I'm sorry, could we call you in a few hours . . .?'

'No worries,' Seokyeong said, as Jebi nodded. The two of them watched the family follow the yellow braille blocks leading to the lift.

Holding onto her dad's arm, Hyeyong was all smiles again.

As Seokyeong and Jebi left the hotel lobby, the cold wind shocked them anew. It didn't make sense to travel back to the photo studio, so they decided to stay in Seogwipo and pass the time in a nearby café. They kept walking and found a café on a quiet street away from the main tourist district.

Stepping through the door, they found themselves in a space with an industrial vibe: exposed pipes, an unpolished concrete floor, uncemented brick walls. There were no stone walls, no dol hareubang rock statues, no tangerine trees.

Jebi felt suddenly homesick. It was as if she'd been transported back to Seoul. The window faced the dreary wall of the next building. A generic jazz song filtered through the speakers.

'What would you like?'

They perused the menu. Jebi ordered a peppermint coffee, Seokyeong an espresso.

Sitting down at a table, Jebi noticed, a short distance away, the café's cat had fixed its wary gaze on them. She thought of Bell, left alone in the photo studio. Was she bored? Was she eating properly? Maybe they should've dropped her off at to the village head's house. Inevitably, perhaps, Jebi's thoughts turned to her child. She still remembered how it had felt to hold her, to see the expressions flash across her little face, to soothe her back to sleep when she woke in the night. The child she'd never given a name to. What was she doing, and with whom? Was she laughing? Crying? Was she being cared for, or neglected . . . *No, she'll be fine*, Jebi told herself firmly.

The next moment, she felt ashamed. Ashamed that Bell had come to mind before her child.

'It's really not easy raising a kid.' Seokyeong sighed as he took out his credit card.

'Yeah,' Jebi said, nodding.

'Of course. You'd know all about it. You worked in a daycare centre, didn't you?'

'But I quit.' Jebi shrugged, touching the table absent-mindedly.

At that moment, the buzzer for their order beeped, and Seokyeong stood up to get the coffee. When he returned, he looked at Jebi. 'How are things going? The swimming lessons? Must be quite tough, I imagine.'

'Not too bad.' Jebi picked up her mug and sipped the coffee, enjoying the cool minty flavour, alongside the bitterness. *Quite unusual*, she thought.

Seokyeong frowned.

'Erm . . .' Jebi began hesitantly.

'Yeah?'

'There's something I'm curious about . . .'

Seokyeong nodded, indicating that she should continue.

Jebi glanced around furtively and then whispered, 'In your eyes, what am I lacking?'

'Are we talking about your outward appearance? Or inner self?' Seokyeong teased.

'Inner self, of course!' Jebi snorted indignantly. 'That's what Stephen Gertz was talking about that day, right? That people are defined by what they lack.'

Savouring his coffee, Seokyeong tilted his head in thought. 'Really? I remember it differently. Didn't he say not to use work, or other people, to try to make up for what you lack?'

'That's the same thing.' Jebi rolled their eyes. 'That people go to great lengths, to try to fill the emptiness. Sometimes they succeed in changing themselves, but sometimes they don't.'

'Hmm.' He emptied the espresso cup.

A wave of regret came over Jebi. She shouldn't have asked. *He's just your employer. What were you hoping he'd say?* she chided herself.

She fished out her phone and scrolled mindlessly through the entertainment news. There was a headline about a female celebrity being sued for getting into a brawl. Jebi tapped into the article.

'In my eyes, you're . . . street smart. Great at thinking on your feet,' Seokyeong said. 'As for what you lack . . . I'm not sure.'

A smile started to spread across her lips, but Jebi suppressed it and averted her gaze, dropping her phone back into her bag.

'By the way, I printed this out.' Seokyeong took out a photo the size of a credit card out of his wallet.

In the photo, Jebi was behind the counter at the studio. He had caught her with a glazed expression on her face, her eyes slightly unfocused, her mouth open.

'A present for you.'

It was so ridiculous that Jebi started laughing. 'How is this a present? I look awful!'

'Is that how you see it? I think it's cute.' Seokyeong glanced at the photo and smiled.

Jebi gave him a sidelong scowl. 'This? Cute? Do you like me or something?'

'Of course I do! With you around, so much has changed. I never would have been able to do all this by myself!'

Sighing inwardly, Jebi picked up the photo. She remembered when it had been taken. She'd just started working at the photo studio; the café was empty and Seokyeong was doing test shots. It was the morning Yoona's dad had come to ask for feedback on his new buns. Just after Jebi had asked why Seokyeong had been so harsh, he had snapped the photo.

Crossing his arms, Seokyeong leant forward. 'As for what you lack, you'd know best. Everyone does. No one else can give you the answer. And you're here, alive, breathing . . . to me, that's all that matters.'

Jebi cringed, but she was quite pleased.

Perhaps Seokyeong felt the same, as he quickly took out his phone for something to do. It rang in his hand.

'Hello? Are you nearby? We're planning to head out.'

Jebi could hear Hyeyong's mum over the speaker. And Hyeyong's chirpy voice: 'I want to eat something special! Food that we can only get here on the island!'

Seokyeong drove them to Giant Octopus village. They were heading for Yoona's Bakes so that Hyeyong could try their specialty: octopus buns.

Hajun's shop was next to the sand dunes. He'd bought an old house with a low, slanted roof and renovated it; Seokyeong had helped him with this and they had bonded over shared bakes and pastries. And in that time, Yoona had been born. The small annex behind the shopfront served as their living space, and once the kitchen and display counter had been installed, the bakery could just fit two tables.

'Welcome!' Hajun greeted them enthusiastically. Wearing a white patisserie uniform, he was arranging freshly made cakes in the display fridge. Delicious sweet and savoury aromas hung in the air like party balloons.

Hyeyong stood on tiptoe and sniffed hungrily.

Hyeyong's parents complimented the décor as they looked around, not forgetting to describe the details to their daughter.

Hajun quickly pushed the two tables together and the family sat down on the side facing the sea.

'Is this new? I don't remember seeing it.' Jebi peered at the display fridge.

'They're talking about the cakes,' Hyeyong's mum explained to the little girl.

Hajun grinned. 'Our newest items on the menu! The professor gave me the idea.' He surveyed his creations with pride.

'The professor? You mean the geologist?'

'Yup, the rock expert. She gave me some very good advice, you know, the day she broke her camera.' Hajun seemed eager to tell the story. 'She came in for iced coffee and told me her woes, so I directed her to Seokyeong's photo studio. That moment, the oven beeped, so I hurried to take out the tray of octopus buns and was putting them on the rack when she cast a glance at them, and asked what they were. I replied, "Our regional speciality," but she laughed and said, "If it were me, I'd make crêpes."'

'Crêpes? What are they?' Jebi asked.

'I know!' Hyeyong jumped up. 'They're thin pancakes. You can stack them to make a cake.'

'Wow! Aren't you smart!' Hajun flashed her a wide smile.

Pleased with herself, Hyeyong grinned and took off her sunglasses. Hajun's smile faltered for a split-second, but it was so subtle that only someone who knew him well would have caught it. He went on with the story.

'She told me, "Stacked crepes would look just like the cross section of the columnar jointing out there in the cliffs, don't you think? Of course you'd need to flip them on the side." Then she jutted out her chin just like this –' he demonstrated – 'and said cooly, "Now that would be a real a regional specialty." '

Seokyeong burst out laughing. He could totally imagine the scene.

'I felt a wave of inspiration right then. Just as I was about to write it down, she told me, "Go to the Jeju Geoparks website to look at its images of volcanic layers. That should give you some ideas. And the island also has the Seongsan Ilchulbong – the Sunrise Peak volcano – don't forget." When she left, I immediately turned on my laptop. I count my lucky stars to have met her! I did some quick sketches and experimented with the designs. I've decided to launch these two. What do you think?'

Hajun pointed at the cakes in the display fridge.

'This one reminds you of a sand dune, doesn't it? It's a twist on tigré pastry, which is usually a doughnut-shaped cake with chocolate ganache in it. I used several layers of sponge cake, cut a hole in the middle and filled it with chocolate. Then I topped it with mocha cream and shaped it like a dune. See the octopus-shaped chocolate? It symbolises our village. And this one here –' he pointed to the second cake – 'is a recreation of the island's columnar jointing. To get the basalt colour I used octopus ink and layered thick pancakes with black sesame cream. Then I flipped it on its side so that it looks like a cross-section of the rock!' He beamed at his audience. 'And look – this is where it gets really arty – I used a fork to scrape the sides and recreate the detailed patterns you can see in close-up photos. It takes me about an hour to do. And on top—'

'It's the photo studio!' Jebi cried.

'Bingo. I make it with white chocolate.'

Looking closely, Jebi could just make out the words Hakuda Photo Studio, written in tiny letters above the door of the delicate chocolate figurine.

Seokyeong grinned. 'Amazing! Is it selling well?'

'It's on sale for the very first time today. Please support my little business!' Hajun laughed affably, before waving it off as a joke. 'Things have been tough. I sell the octopus buns via a courier, and that's keeping me afloat, but only just. And most of my customers were yours first. Remember the bikers from summer? They've ordered buns. Their children, as well as the newlywed couple, posted about them on Instagram, saying how delicious they were. But it hasn't been enough. I have find a way to get our name out there.' Hajun looked out of the window at the rolling sand dunes, and further off, the cliff. When he spoke again, his tone was solemn. 'If only the village were to get more popular, like the other tourist areas in Jeju.'

Hyeyong's family ordered octopus buns with red bean filling and three glasses of warm milk. They also ordered a large slice of the cliff cake, reasoning that while Hyeyong would be able to walk on dunes outside, the columnar jointing would be much harder for her to navigate. Her parents wanted her to experience it, even if only through a pastry.

Hyeyong washed her hands thoroughly, tore off a piece of the cake – as if ripping off a column of rock – and ate. green tea powder stuck to her fingers. 'Delicious! But I like this one more.' She held up the octopus bun with red bean filling. The tiny eyes, nose and mouth were made of chocolate and attached to the round body were four thick arms.

Amid the chatter and laughter, the door creaked open and Yanghee came in holding Dongwon's hand. At the sight of the group, she paused. Just as she was about to turn back around and leave, Dongwon pulled her inside the shop.

'Dongwon has been craving the octopus buns.' Looking awkward, she fixed her eyes to the display shelves. 'I'll have three, please – one each of the fillings, octopus, red bean, and meat.'

'Great, thank you!' As Hajun went behind the counter, Yanghee headed back towards the door, as if she was planning to wait outside. Jebi stood up and put a hand on Dongwon's shoulder. 'Where are you going, Eonnie? Dongwon must be freezing.' She touched his cheek lightly. 'Oh my! He's like a snowman. Come and join us.'

'No, no, we're good.' Yanghee held onto Dongwon's arm.

'Please. It's snowing out there.' Jebi glanced at Hyeyong's family. 'Dongwon is also seven this year, right? Same as Hyeyong here. They can be friends.'

'Why should we be friends just because we're the same

age?' Hyeyong retorted. 'Eonnie, are you friends with everyone your age?'

'Um . . . no.' Jebi laughed, blushing slightly as she conceded the point.

'That's enough.' Embarrassed, Hyeyong's mum scolded her daughter gently.

Dongwon turned to his mum. 'Mum, why are her eyes like that?' His voice rang out in the small shop.

Yanghee's face reddened. 'Be quiet!'

Hyeyong stood up and put her hands on her hips. 'I have anophthalmia. I was born without eyes. Because of a genetic disorder. Or chromosomal abnormality. Is that enough information for you?'

Cowed, Dongwon hid behind his mum.

Hyeyong pursed her lips. 'Hmph. Well, I don't think we're going to be friends now . . .'

Yanghee grabbed Dongwon by his collar and dragged him out to stand in front of her. 'Stop hiding behind me and say something.'

Dongwon struggled out of his mother's grip and went to hide behind Seokyeong instead. 'I'm just asking because I'm curious . . .' He looked at Hyeyong pleadingly.

Suddenly, Seokyeong turned and tickled Dongwon's ribs. The boy clamped his arms tight and giggled as he fell into Seokyeong's embrace. It relieved the tension a little.

'Samchon. Can we ride . . . that again?'

'Dongwon! I told you not to impudent!' By the door, Yanghee snapped at her son.

Hyeyong turned to Dongwon. '*That?* What's "that"?'

'Um, the sidecar.'

'The sidecar?'

'Yeah. It's a small car fixed onto Seokyeong Samchon's motorbike. Super fun! You feel like a bird, riding in it with the wind blowing in your face. I'm sure you'd love it too.'

Hyeyong wiped her hands on a napkin and clutched her mum's arm. 'Mummy! I want to try that!'

The two families made their way to the photo studio after leaving Yoona's Bakes. Yanghee had wanted to send Dongwon alone, but being a little shy with strangers, he had fussed for his mother to join him.

'You have a lovely son,' Hyeyong's mum told Yanghee.

'And your daughter is really cute.' Yanghee watched Hyeyong climb up into the SUV on her own. 'She's so bright and energetic.'

'Not so much this morning, though.' Hyeyong's dad got into the backseat and wrapped an arm around her.

'Hey! I'm always energetic!' Hyeyong pouted.

Seokyeong parked and was about to unlock the door of the studio when, on the other side, Bell started barking and scratching at the door furiously. She was getting bigger every day, and the wooden door rattled in its frame.

Jebi turned to Hyeyong's parents. 'Do you mind dogs?'

'We love them. It's just impossible to have one in an apartment,' Hyeyong's dad replied.

Hyeyong held onto her mum's hand and tilted her head. Through the widening crack in the doorway, Bell bolted out and leapt playfully around Seokyeong's leg.

'A St Bernard! One of the best search dogs!' Hyeyong said excitedly.

Dongwon gaped. 'Wait a minute! How did you know?'

'I can tell by their barks. Although I was a little confused to begin with.' She straightened her shoulders proudly.

'That's understandable. Bell's mum is a Jeju dog, her dad is a St Bernard,' Jebi said. 'It's amazing how you can tell!'

'That's our girl!' Hyeyong's dad patted her shoulder. 'She loves listening to the encyclopaedia. She only has to hear something once to remember. We homeschool her because she has such a high IQ.'

'Goodness, darling, how you like to talk!' Hyeyong's mother put her hand on her husband's arm in gentle reproach at his boasting.

Meanwhile, Dongwon was looking at Hyeyong with a new respect.

If only she could see him right now, they'd be immediate friends, Jebi thought.

In the garden, Seokyeong took the cover off the sidecar, which he then attached securely to the motorbike.

Dongwon climbed in; Hyeyong's parents were watching carefully to check that it looked safe. Yanghee put the helmet on Dongwon and did it up. Hyeyong stood to one side, head tilted, listening to the roar of the engine.

The motorbike revved and took off, the sound growing distant as the motorbike disappeared from view.

'Darling, what do you think? Looks safe enough, I reckon.'

Hearing this, Hyeyong started jumping around, her face gleeful.

While Dongwon was out on the drive, Hyeyong's parents explored the gallery, holding their daughter by the hand and stopping in front of each image to describe it to her in detail. Meanwhile, Yanghee sat down at a table and nursed a cup of coffee, reading something on her phone. Jebi cast a glance at her screen – it was all in English.

She went back to the kitchen and double checked that they had everything they needed for the viewing party later.

'I want to go round again, please, please . . .?' They heard Dongwon cajoling Seokyeong as the motorbike pulled up outside the garden.

Hyeyong whipped around, losing all interest in the photo of the diver and the clownfish her parents had been describing to her. 'Mum! It's my turn now!'

Nodding, Hyeyong's dad picked her up to carry her to the sidecar and put her in.

'Hey, don't all look at me like that!' Hyeyong suddenly starting wriggling as if there were spider webs all around her. 'My whole body feels squirmy!' Surprised, everyone glanced at one another. They had indeed all been watching Hyeyong.

'We aren't looking because it's you. We watched Dongwon too. We just want to make sure you young ones are safe.' Hyeyong's mum replied.

Taking the helmet from Yanghee, she helped her daughter strap it on while her husband fastened the seatbelt. Meanwhile, Jebi was busy taking photos.

'Ahh! It's a rollercoaster!' Hyeyong screamed as the motorbike cruised down the hill.

After crossing the bumpy cement ground, the motorbike and the sidecar started along the coast road. Seokyeong accelerated just a little and Hyeyong's bobbed hair began dancing in the wind. In the side mirror, he glanced at her face. Her mouth wide open, she had raised her arms, stretching them out above her, wiggling her fingers as if trying to touch the sky. Her expressions were all caught on the camera attached to the sidecar.

'How do you feel?' Seokyeong shouted.

'I don't know! I can't describe it!'

For a while, he kept going straight, enjoying the wind and the sounds of the waves. But then, worried she might catch a cold, he decided to turn back.

As the motorbike pulled in at the studio, Hyeyong gave a sniff.

Seeing her tears, her parents were shocked. 'What happened? Were you scared?' Hyeyong's mum asked urgently.

Hyeyong kept quiet.

'Amazing, right?' Dongwon cut in.

Hyeyong suddenly grinned and nodded.

'How did you feel? Like a bird?'

Hyeyong shook her head. 'Like an egg – fragile. It was exciting, but a bit scary too. If only I could see, I wouldn't feel so scared . . .' Hyeyong got out of the sidecar with the help of her dad.

'But that's what makes it fun, right? That it's scary.' Dongwon cocked his head in confusion.

Hyeyong hiccupped and wiped away the last of her tears. And as if she had suddenly thought of something, she grabbed her dad's hand. 'I want to go to Hallasan!'

Her dad's face lit up, but the next second, his smile faltered. He checked the time.

'It's too late. Even if we left now, we wouldn't have time to get up all the way to Baengnokdam Crater lake.'

'Do we have to go all the way up there?'

'Well, I guess not.'

'Then we can still go, right?' She turned to Dongwon. 'Hey, want to come too?'

'Sure! Mum, can I?' Dongwon looked at Yanghee eagerly.

Yanghee gave him a stern look and shook her head. 'It's dangerous. It's not a mountain for children.'

Yanghee's words had been in standard Korean, and Jebi realised that her reply wasn't just for her son to hear. Sure enough, Yanghee now turned to Hyeyong's parents. 'May I ask if you have climbed Hallasan before?'

They shook their heads, looking confused at the sudden question.

'Then do you climb regularly?'

Hyeyong's dad scratched his head. 'We used to, sometimes, before we got married.'

'We used to head to the mountains on our dates,' Hyeyong's mum added.

The look Yanghee shot Seokyeong spoke volumes. *Why did you even think of taking these folks to the crater lake?*

Seokyeong looked like he wanted to say something in his defence, but he kept quiet. Dongwon had his arms wrapped around Seokyeong's waist.

'In that case, you should go to Wollabong instead,' Yanghee said, her tone firm.

Hyeyong turned around. 'Wollabong? Ajumma, what does the name mean?'

'*Wol* as in moon, and *ra* referring to a line – basically, it means the mountain peak where the moon rises. It's a smaller mountain, two hundred metres above sea level,' Yanghee explained.

'What a pretty name! Dad, let's go!' Hyeyong pleaded.

Wollabong was capped with snow; it looked like a rice bowl had been turned upside down on its peak. Getting out of the car at the foot of the mountain, the group slowly made their way up, along the narrow path. In the sun, the snow was melting.

Hyeyong's mum clapped in delight. 'We're so lucky that the snow has stopped.'

'We'll lead the way,' Yanghee said, pushing Dongwon in front of her.

Seokyeong made to follow, walking backwards up the slope and pointing his camera at Hyeyong and her parents. Hyeyong's mum made a waving gesture. 'Please don't worry about taking photos here. It's too dangerous.'

'If you slip, we're all going to get hurt,' added Hyeyong's dad, looking serious.

'It's fine. We prepared for the Hallasan climb,' Seokyeong said, as he took out a modified selfie stick. It had a mirror next to where the camera would be fitted. 'This way, I'll be able to take photos while still looking ahead. I've practised with Jebi.'

And so they set off. Dongwon and Yanghee led the way, followed by Seokyeong, and Hyeyong and her parents. Jebi was right at the back, keeping an eye on everyone. In case of any accidents, she had medical supplies and bottled water in her backpack. If someone slipped, she would catch them, and if someone got hurt, she was ready to dress their wounds.

It had been a long time since she'd felt such responsibility on her shoulders, but she didn't dislike it. This was nothing like the stressful environment at the daycare centre. Spending time with a happy family was turning out to be nowhere near as bad as she had feared.

Her thoughts turned to the child she'd parted with three years before. Back then, the responsibility had been too heavy, too sharp, too loud, too intense. In the end, she had given up. And, for a long time, thinking about it made her feel as though she'd committed a crime that could never be put right. But today, as she hiked up the mountain, her thoughts went in a different direction. *I gave birth to a very healthy child.*

Jebi took in deep breaths of the cold mountain air. In front of her, Hyeyong was walking between her parents when she suddenly stumbled. Ahead, the distance between Hyeyong's and Yanghee's families was widening. It had been a mistake to think that a smaller mountain would be easy. The rocks were sharp and jagged.

Perhaps also aware of the increasing lag, Seokyeong folded his selfie stick, hung his camera around his neck and retraced his steps, stopping next to Hyeyong. 'Want me to carry you?'

The moment Seokyeong's hand touched Hyeyong's, she flung it away, hard. Everyone froze.

'No!' she screamed, breathing heavily.

Her dad apologised. 'I'm sorry, her hands are sensitive.'

'It's because she sees the world through touch,' her mum added. 'We might feel similarly if someone touched our eyes.'

Seokyeong stepped back. 'I see, don't worry. I understand.'

'Just a little bit further, and the path opens out and gets easier – there are rubber-link mats and wooden stairs,' Yanghee shouted from above.

'Thank god we didn't climb Hallasan. This trail is tiring enough.' Hyeyong's dad shook his head and wiped the sweat from his forehead.

'Well, I'm not tired at all,' Hyeyong shouted. She pursed her lips and forged ahead. Her dad quickened his steps to stay ahead of her.

'Mum, should I help?' Dongwon took off his jumper and tied it around his waist.

Yanghee smiled and ruffled her son's hair. 'Go on. But ask her first. She might not want help.'

'Got it.'

Dongwon let go of his mother's hand and climbed down.

Hyeyong was doing her best to keep up with her dad.

'Take your time. The mountain is very pretty.' Dongwon hovered around her, scampering up and down the steep track like a puppy.

Hyeyong turned her head in the direction of the sound. 'Really? What do you see?'

'Hmm . . . there are pine trees all around us, with white snow sitting on their branches. The pines are like bristles on a toothbrush. Oh, a small squirrel just ran past. It was super fast!'

The corners of her mouth lifted. 'That's strange. I heard there aren't squirrels in Jeju.'

'Who said so? I saw one just now.'

'I read it on the Internet.'

Dongwon shrugged. 'Well, I saw one. It was plump, with pretty patterns on its fur, and its tail was long and bushy.'

'But . . . don't squirrels hibernate in winter? The encyclopaedia says so.'

'Some squirrels do, maybe. But what I saw was a squirrel. I'm not lying.' Dongwon bent down and scooped up some snow. 'Do you want to walk up with me? I know this place very well.'

Hyeyong nodded.

'Want to hold my hand?' Dongwon offered.

'No. You hold my arm.' Hyeyong held out her right arm. Dongwon took it and began walking, half a step ahead of her. Right ahead, the narrow path became wide enough for two people.

Yanghee hung back and positioned herself behind the two children. Hyeyong's parents noticed this and nodded in thanks, Yanghee shot a brief smile back at them.

Panting, Jebi caught up, passing them and going up to Seokyeong, who was now leading. 'Now it's your turn to go behind. And let's swap bags too.' She pushed her heavy backpack into Seokyeong's arms.

When she pulled Seokyeong's bag off his shoulders, she realised that it was even heavier than hers. But it was too late to change her mind.

'Jebi . . . You don't have to . . .' Seokyeong stole a glance at Yanghee who was walking towards them.

Jebi pushed him. 'Just go.'

For several moments, Seokyeong just stood there, unsure what to do as, one by one, the group walked past him.

Yanghee came up last. 'Go on. I'll be alright at the back,' she said.

'No, I should be the one at the . . . at the back.' Seokyeong stumbled over his words.

'Please. I don't like having you right behind me . . .' Yanghee turned away, not looking at him.

From the height they had reached, the stretch of sea and the village below looked small.

'Okay, then.' Seokyeong walked on. He took a few shots of Hyeyong and her family up ahead, then he paused and turned back.

'Focus on your work, please.' Yanghee's tone was unfriendly.

'Okay.' A few steps later, he turned around again.

'You have something to say? If so, say it.'

'No. I'm just worried,' Seokyeong mumbled.

'I was born here. I grew up climbing the mountain. I can do it with my eyes closed. What's there to worry about?'

'Well, it's snowing.'

Yanghee didn't respond. After a few minutes' silence, out of the blue, she asked 'Aren't you angry with me?'

'Of course not. Why would I be?' Seokyeong hurried forward. That Yanghee was having a conversation with him was enough to make his heart burst with joy.

'That day on the coast . . . Jebi almost died. Because of me.'

'Well . . . yeah, back then, I was pretty angry.' Seokyeong's voice was quiet. 'But everyone makes mistakes. And Jebi is fine.'

Seokyeong turned and stood directly in front of Yanghee. The others would be too far ahead to hear their conversation, almost at Wollabong peak.

'I . . . I like you, Yanghee-ssi.'

Yanghee narrowed her eyes. 'Why?'

'Just because. I've liked you from the first time I saw you.'

'I hate that phrase. *Just because?* That's what people say when they don't know how they truly feel, or when they aren't serious about things.'

Yanghee pushed Seokyeong aside to step past him. Or rather, she tried – but Seokyeong reached out a large hand and took hers. Losing her balance, she fell against him. They were surrounded by the steam of each other's breath.

Seokyeong's voice was quiet. 'Yanghee-ssi, I like your brown eyes. I like your smile. I like your voice. And the way you dive into the water . . .'

'Enough!' Yanghee shook off his hand and stalked ahead.

But Seokyeong would not be put off. 'I only know how to take photographs . . . I'm no good with words. Give me a camera and some good lighting and I'll take a shot of you that brings out your very best angle. But talking, that's a whole lot harder . . . I'm sorry that I'm so lacking. But I'm telling you . . . I really like you. I mean it from the bottom of my heart.'

Yanghee looked up at the peak. Dongwon was jumping up and down and waving at her. She stood on tiptoes and waved back.

When Seokyeong and Yanghee reached the peak, Hyeyong's family and Dongwon were posing for photos. In the last few months, Jebi had grown comfortable giving the clients directions and she knew what made a good composition. She had chosen to take the photos against the backdrop of the wide sea and the sky.

Seokyeong scrolled through them and grinned. 'You're getting pretty good, eh?'

Jebi put her nose in the air. 'They're only basic shots.'

Dongwon came running towards them. 'Samchon! Can I take some pictures, too?'

'Sure. Remember what I taught you? How about you take a solo shot of Hyeyong?'

'Me? Just by myself?' Hyeyong's face flushed red.

After making sure that she was standing in a safe spot on the mountaintop, Hyeyong's parents stepped aside, smiling.

Dongwon crossed his arms and looked around for a good backdrop. 'It'd be nice to have the Sanbangsan Mountain behind you.' Dongwon held Hyeyong's shoulders and turned her.

'Sanbangsan? I've heard of it. It's a lava dome,' Hyeyong said.

'A lava dome?' Dongwon cocked his head.

Immediately, Jebi thought of the geologist they had met earlier in the year. It would have been great to have her with them.

'Yes, in the shape of an inverted bell,' Hyeyong explained.

'This one doesn't look much like a bell, though . . .' Dongwon closed an eye and stared through the viewfinder.

'Really? Then what does it look like?'

'Um . . . like a turtle, or rather its shell? Or maybe a hat.'

'A hat?'

'Yeah, a sun hat with a wide brim.'

'So it really doesn't look like a bell?' Hyeyong asked again. She sounded a little disappointed, although Jebi wasn't sure if anyone had noticed.

'Yeah, a bell would be taller. Sanbangsan spreads out too much at the bottom.' Dongwon pressed the shutter.

Seokyeong looked over the boy's shoulder. 'Good photo,' he said.

'I . . . want . . . too,' Hyeyong mumbled.

Hyeyong's mum bent forward. 'What did you say, sweetheart?'

'I want to take a photo, too.'

In that moment, all eyes were on Hyeyong. To avoid hurting her feelings, her parents had never handed her a camera before, hoping that letting her touch the pinpricked polaroids would be enough.

Seokyeong and Jebi exchanged a glance. Was there a way to teach her? Jebi's mind was a blank.

'But . . . how can you do it?' Horrified, Yanghee moved to cover her son's mouth.

'Mum, what's wrong? I'm just asking—'

'That's enough!'

Yanghee looked towards Hyeyong's parents and bobbed her head in apology. She knew she should apologise to Hyeyong too, but she didn't quite know what to say.

Hyeyong clenched her small fists and started sobbing. 'What makes you think you'll always be able to see? Forever?' Her thin shoulders heaved. 'You could get the same illness as me! Or who knows! You might fall and get injured! A branch could poke you in the eye! Or a pencil!'

At her outburst, Dongwon started crying too. He turned and buried his face in Yanghee's stomach. 'Mum, I only asked because I was curious . . .'

Yanghee comforted her son. 'I know, it's okay.'

But Hyeyong was getting more and more worked up. 'Curiosity isn't an excuse to ask whatever you want! I've already forgiven you once at the bakery!'

'Sweetheart . . .'

Hyeyong's parents tried to calm her, but she wouldn't be consoled, continuing to yell in Dongwon's direction. 'Fine! Then I'll ask something I'm curious about too! Why didn't you come here with your dad? Where's your dad right now?'

A silence descended; only the wind's howling could be heard. Yanghee lowered her head and pulled her son tighter into her embrace. Dongwon was sobbing but trying not to make any sound.

'Lee Hyeyong, if you're going to be like this, we're going straight back to the hotel.' Hyeyong's dad warned. 'I've told you it's not nice to hurt others, even if you're upset.'

'Whatever! I don't want to be nice anyway,' Hyeyong retorted.

'Lee Hyeyong!'

Hyeyong's dad turned towards Yanghee. 'I'm sorry. She was out of line. Dongwon-ah, I'm so sorry. She'll be punished.'

At that, Dongwon's sobs only got louder.

Embarrassed, Hyeyong's dad shot Seokyeong a helpless look.

Spotting Jebi behind a tree, capturing all this on camera, Seokyeong flashed her a look of alarm. She lowered the camera and mouthed, *You said to take photos of everything.*

Yanghee gave Dongwon a comforting pat on the back. 'There are times you should just keep your thoughts in your head, my love. Even if you're curious. Questions can be hurtful. Do you understand?'

Dongwon nodded.

'Don't you have something to say to your friend?'

Dongwon wiped away his tears and peeked out at Hyeyong, before turning to face her. 'I'm sorry.'

Hyeyong, too, was brushing away her tears with the back of her hand. 'Okay.'

'That's it?' Hyeyong's mum poked her side.

Hyeyong scuffed the ground with the toe of her trainers. 'Me too. I'm sorry too.'

Only then did Seokyeong let out a silent sigh of relief.

'How about I teach you to take photos? Seokyeong Samchon showed me how,' Dongwon offered.

'Okay,' Hyeyong replied.

The reconciliation came about as fast as the sudden upset. Dongwon led Hyeyong to the tripod and Seokyeong hurried over to help them adjust the height.

'Okay, put your eye here. Then you can see the scenery,' Dongwon said.

Hyeyong shook her head. 'But I can't see.'

'Oh.' Flustered, Dongwon glanced back at his mum for help. She shrugged. He thought for a moment and then an idea came to him. Standing behind Hyeyong, he took her hands gently and raised them to shoulder height, holding them a half metre or so apart.

Hyeyong didn't resist.

Jebi was surprised. Was this the same child who had complained that people's hands were full of germs?

'You can see from here –' he touched one hand – 'to here –' he touched her other hand – 'through the view-finder,' Dongwon explained.

'How much is here to here?'

279

Dongwon scratched his head. 'Hmm . . . from one end of our village to the other. About a thousand, no, ten thousand steps? Then there's the sea.'

'I still don't get it,' Hyeyong said. 'A thousand and ten thousand steps are so different. I measured the distance of my own step not long ago – it's forty-six centimetres. A thousand steps would be four thousand six hundred metres, and ten thousand steps would be four point six kilometres. So which is it?'

Dongwon looked at his mother again. Yanghee was busy tapping on her phone. A moment later, she smiled and turned the screen to him. 'Oh! It's two kilometres. My mum estimated the distance with the map on her phone.'

Hyeyong's lips moved slightly and her eyelids fluttered. 'Four thousand two hundred and forty-eight steps, if I round up to the nearest step.' She smiled. 'Can we see your house from here?'

'Yup, it's on the left there. The one with the grey roof.'

'Alright, I'll take the photo now.'

'Go for it.' Dongwon took her finger and placed it on the shutter button. 'Press here. You'll hear a click when you take the photo.'

'Can you see the moon today?'

Dongwon looked up. 'Yes, there's a half-moon. It looks like a sweet – a half-eaten milk candy.'

Hyeyong laughed. 'I want it to be in the photo. Since this place is called Wollabong.'

She stepped aside and, putting his eye to the viewfinder, Dongwon adjusted the position and angle of the camera slightly. 'Done. You can press the shutter now.'

Dongwon guided her back to the camera.

Click.

Hyeyong turned to her parents, her face radiant.

They were holding each other's hands as they looked down at her. From behind, Jebi snapped a photo.

'Are there any other photos you'd like to take?' Dongwon asked.

'You. You're my first friend and I want to have a photo of you.'

A flush crept up Dongwon's cheeks.

Yanghee smiled and looked at her son. 'You have lots of friends, don't you?'

'Um, yeah, I used to, when we lived in Seoul.' He hung his head. 'But now . . . no. Seokyeong Samchon is my only friend.'

Yanghee's smile crumbled.

'Can I touch your face first? I want to know what you look like before I take the picture.'

'Um, ok, just give me a second, please!' Dongwon ran to the woods. He squatted down, grabbed a fistful of snow and rubbed his cheeks. He wiped off the moisture hastily with his sleeves and returned to stand in front of Hyeyong. 'Okay, I'm ready.'

Hyeyong carefully reached out and touched his face. From his hair, her hand trailed over his forehead, the bridge of his nose, his cheeks, lips, chin.

Dongwon's face flushed but he held perfectly still.

Hyeyong hesitated. 'Your eyes. Can I touch them too?'

'Oh? Alright.' Dongwon closed his eyes.

Cautiously, Hyeyong stretched out her hand. Her fingers brushed over his brows before landing gently on the curve of his eyelids. His eyeballs beneath the lids moved a little.

'They're warm. I wish I had eyes too . . .' Hyeyong whispered.

Behind, someone was sniffing. Hyeyong turned around. 'Dad, are you crying?'

'No no, it's just cold up here, so I have a bit of a runny nose.' Hyeyong's dad kept his voice cheery.

'Here, have this.' Hyeyong untied her scarf and held it out. Hyeyong's mum pushed her husband forward. He bent down in front of his daughter. After reaching out to check he was close enough, Hyeyong wrapped the scarf around his neck. Then she touched his cheek. 'Dad, you lied. Again,' she murmured.

'Sorry.'

With both hands, she wiped away his tears.

At the observation deck on Wollabong's peak, three wooden benches placed side by side overlooked an unspoilt view of Giant Octopus village and the cobalt-blue sea.

Seokyeong and Jebi ushered everyone to take a seat before passing out the instant noodles. Because they'd had to slow down during the hike to accommodate the kids, it had taken them longer than expected to reach the peak.

It had been Jebi's idea. 'Michelin-quality instant noodles on the mountain! The perfect dish to pair with cold fresh air and wide-open landscape!'

Thinking that Hyeyong might not be able to eat spicy

food, Jebi had ordered udon instant noodles online. She'd bought two boxes, which was lucky because it meant they had more than enough for Yanghee and Dongwon.

As if opening an unexpected present, everyone hummed happily as they ripped off the plastic packaging, opened the lid halfway and poured in the soup powder. Seokyeong and Jebi each took out a large flask from their bags and went around pouring hot water into the cups. They'd only eaten cake and bread for lunch, and stomachs were rumbling.

Everyone sat in silence – looking around almost reverently – as they waited for the noodles to be ready. But as soon as the food was ready to eat, they forgot all about the beauty of the surrounding mountains and the sea, and dug in hungrily, slurping down noodles and drinking the soup. Suddenly, Hyeyong's mum chuckled, and everyone joined in the laughter. The kids too had a great appetite. After finishing their own noodles, they clamoured for additional mouthfuls from their mothers. Jebi snapped some more photos.

Having made sure they'd not left any litter, the expedition slowly began its descent.

'Going down is much harder!' Hyeyong complained, her thin legs wobbling.

But Jebi and Seokyeong were in buoyant mood, their backpacks so much lighter.

Back at the photo studio, the group sat down for a rest, the tangerine tea that Jebi had brewed filling the room with a sweet aroma.

While their guests massaged their tired limbs, Seokyeong and Jebi went to the kitchen to prepare for the viewing party. They kept their hands busy, ignoring their fatigue.

They had bought and prepared all the ingredients the day before, so all that was left to do was the cooking. Jebi glanced at the wall clock. It was half past five. Though they'd had instant noodles on the mountaintop, she guessed that the kids might still be hungry.

Taking out a single tortilla from the fridge, she spread it with tomato sauce and added top shell meat, bacon and lots of grated cheese on top. The smell of the pizza in the oven wafted through the gallery.

Hyeyong's dad was watching the news on his phone. Because it was New Year's Day, the newscaster was reporting on the large crowds that had gone to catch the first sunrise of the year. Footage of the heavy traffic on the motorway towards Donghae played before the scene cut to rows of excited faces: everyone closing their eyes to make a wish as the fiery ball rose.

Then it was back to the newscaster, who spoke in a serious tone. 'Breaking news. In 1982, a nine-year-old girl, Kim Seonghee, went missing. Though her family combed the entire country looking for her, she never returned home. However, in the past week, a new lead emerged in this cold case: a negative that captured a crucial scene was mailed anonymously to the victim's father. With this information, the police were able to recover Kim's remains. Preliminary investigations have revealed that the detective on the case had hidden her body in a cover-up attempt. The news is sending shockwaves across the country.'

'Crazy bastard!' Hyeyong's dad spat out, his face was contorted with anger.

In the kitchen, Jebi almost cut her finger. She quickly put down the knife and came round the counter to look over his shoulder at his phone.

The newsreader continued: 'The following is an interview with Kim's father.' A different voice echoed out of the phone's tiny speaker: 'What do you mean those people can't be punished? Just because it's over the statute of limitations! No one even listened to me when I insisted that my daughter would never have left home! Oh god, she was only nine!'

On screen, a thin, old man with a thick head of white hair slumped to the floor, weeping. The news reader took over again: 'Commenting on the case, the chief of the National Police Agency said, "I express my deepest condolences to the victim's family. We will do our best to uncover the truth . . ."'

The footage cut next to a different man, also elderly. Dressed in a suit, he was walking briskly, his face pixelated.

Jebi turned to glance at the frame hanging on the wall.

In the news report, the old detective held up his hands to shield his face from the cameras, and with a jerk, the footage came to an abrupt end.

'Shameful!' Hyeyong's dad was incensed. Next to him, his wife made a noise of disapproval and took the phone from his hand.

'Why are you so upset, darling?'

Hyeyong's dad began a tirade. 'Isn't it obvious? When things like that are going on in this country, how can anyone raise a child without worry! How can anyone be trusted? If I were that father, I'd never forgive that worthless detective for what he did. Never. Damn those TV stations! What an awful story to begin the year with.'

Jebi slipped silently back into the kitchen.

'The child is returning home for the first time in forty years. The family will finally get some answers. Isn't it right for that news to be broadcast on New Year's Day?' Hyeyong's mum countered.

Seokyeong was expertly preparing a whole cabbage kimchi.

'So you posted the negative?' Jebi whispered urgently.

'Didn't you tell me to?'

Red kimchi liquid spilled down the sides of the wooden cutting board.

'I thought you said you weren't going to?'

'I didn't say that . . . I was just hesitating.' He put the kimchi into a frying pan and turned on the induction stove, adding a swirl of cooking oil and sprinkling in some sugar before continuing: 'After sending Stephen off, I started reflecting on a lot of things. Like where do I go next, and why?' The kimchi began to sizzle, its strong, tart smell rising up from the pan.

Jebi waited for him to continue.

'Sometimes bad things happen and there's not a single shred of evidence left behind. But Stephen . . . He's dedicated his life to recording evidence. He's that kind of person.'

'Indeed. He's doing important work,' Jebi said, nodding. 'Criminals should be punished.'

Seokyeong's hands paused. 'He thought the same . . .'

'Stephen?' Jebi asked, as she took the pizza out from the oven.

'No, the old detective. He said he believed that some mistakes, some crimes, can never be forgiven, no matter how many good deeds you do.' Seokyeong glanced at Jebi. 'It looks like you agree.'

Jebi had frozen, still holding the pizza.

Seokyeong dished out the stir-fried kimchi onto a plate and sprinkled sesame seeds on it. Tired of waiting, Dongwon and Hyeyong came up stealthily behind Jebi and reached for their pizza. Taking greedy bites, they giggled, the sauce staining their lips.

When the food was ready, everyone gathered at the table. Hyeyong's family sat facing the window looking out to sea, Yanghee and Dongwon sat opposite, while Jebi sat at the head of the table. Seokyeong filled a bowl with rice and stew and went to his workroom to eat and put together the slideshow at the same time.

The table was set with bowls of rice and pumpkin leaves and sea urchin roe stew. In the middle were sharing dishes. Two large sea breams that Seokyeong had grilled with sesame oil on the rooftop now sizzled on the hotplate. There was stir-fried kimchi with tofu and fried chive pancakes with top shell meat served with a soy sauce dip and sesame seeds sprinkled on top. For the kids, Seokyeong had also prepared fried eggs and roasted seaweed sheets.

'Everything smells delicious!' Hyeyong moved left and right excitedly as she sniffed the table of food.

'A drink would hit the spot right now.' Hyeyong's dad smacked his lips.

'We've prepared something special.' Jebi set a bottle on the table. 'This is swindari, a fermented rice drink. It tastes like a makgeolli but is free of alcohol, so kids can have it too. It's a traditional drink in Jeju.' Jebi filled everyone's glasses.

'Oh, I've never tried something like it!' Hyeyong's mum exclaimed happily.

'I wouldn't say no to some real alcohol mind you—' Hyeyong's dad's grousing stopped mid-sentence. Hyeyong's mum must've pinched his thigh. 'Alright, let's do a toast!' he said, only slightly grudgingly. Here's to Hyeyong and Dongwon's friendship!'

'Cheers!' everyone chorused. The kids gulped down the swindari and mimicked the throaty sounds adults make when they take a drink – *Kyaaa!* And with their clumsy chopstick skills, they each reached out for a pancake.

After dinner, Jebi washed the dishes while Seokyeong set up the slideshow. With the chairs rearranged into a row, everyone sat facing the screen, waiting eagerly for it to start. Seokyeong put on some upbeat pop music and the first photo of Jeju airport appeared on the screen.

The family of three in matching black puffer jackets were in sharp focus, against a sea of blurry tourists. Seeing Hyeyong grinning in her red heart sunglasses, everyone clapped in delight. The real-life Hyeyong looked confused, so her mum whispered a description of the photo into her ear.

The next photos were taken on the ride to the tangerine farm: a side profile of Hyeyong's dad with an arm around his daughter's shoulders as they chatted happily; a close-up of her mum's hand as she took a Polaroid picture of the landscape. At the farm, Hyeyong scrunched up her nose in concentration as she snipped a stem . . . And then Hyeyong was on horseback, smiling proudly down at her parents.

Through the viewfinder of her Sony RX0, Jebi noticed that Yanghee's smile was faltering, and there was something like envy in her eyes as she held Dongwon on her lap.

In the next photo, Hyeyong was tearing off a piece of the cliff cake with her bare hands – it looked like the aftermath of a natural disaster. This was followed by a photo of her small hand clutching an octopus bun, and then a group photo taken outside the bakery, Hajun waving goodbye to them through the glass.

Yanghee's smile brightened again at the sight of Dongwon's face in the corner of the photo.

Next came a photo of Dongwon and Hyeyong giving Bell a belly rub. Then a series of photos of Hyeyong climbing into the sidecar, her parents lovingly helping her with the helmet and seatbelt. Hyeyong with mouth wide open and hands outstretched, the wind blowing her hair backwards. Taken with a fish-eye lens camera attached to the sidecar, the shot magnified her nose. It was cute and hilarious at the same time, and everyone roared with laughter.

The photos on the mountain taken with the selfie stick weren't great in terms of composition, but that didn't matter – they were action shots. One photo captured the moment when Hyeyong had been skipping in the snow and slipped. In the next, her mum was trying to help her up but had ended up falling to the ground too.

Hyeyong's mum, who'd been describing each photo to her daughter as they flashed past, fell quiet.

'What's happening? Tell me! What's in this one?' Hyeyong urged.

'Oh, it's . . .' Her parents cast disapproving glances at Seokyeong, angry that he had included this photo, but he pretended not to see. Instead, he stood there with his arms crossed, waiting for them to describe the scene to their daughter.

Dongwon jumped in. 'It's your mum.'

'My mum?'

'She was trying to help you up, but she fell. There is a scratch on her hand and some blood.'

Alarmed, Hyeyong felt for her mum's hands. When her fingers found the wound, her shoulders slumped.

'Mummy's fine.' Hyeyong's mum stroked her hair and tried to reassure her.

'I'm not.'

'What's wrong? Whatever it is, I'm sorry.'

'I'm the one who should be sorry! You fell because you were helping me!'

Seokyeong pressed the remote control then, and moved on to the next photo.

On top of Wollabong, the snow on the pine trees was melting, the water droplets glistening like jewels. Below the trees, Dongwon and Hyeyong were holding hands, and Seokyeong and Yanghee could be seen in the distance too.

Next was Hyeyong's solo shot with Sanbangsan behind.

'Hey! Look!' Dongwon jumped up from his seat. 'I took this one!' He turned to his mother with a proud grin.

Yanghee smiled and rubbed his shoulder.

'Mum, I want that photo,' Hyeyong said. 'I want to know if a lava dome really does look like a turtle shell.'

'Of course, we'll get it for you.'

In the next image, Hyeyong's parents, looking flustered, were trying to comfort their child. Hyeyong was screaming. Her wide-opened mouth was a black hole and Dongwon was crying in his mum's embrace.

Embarrassed, Dongwon averted his gaze.

Why did I just stand there? Why did I not comfort Dongwon? Seokyeong stared at the photo. He'd imagined so many times how, as a father, he might react to different situations, he'd even written a three-page entry in his diary detailing how he'd respond if his kid was fighting with another kid; but when it had actually happened in front of him, he had just stood there helplessly and watched things unfold. Looking at the photo, he felt he had let himself down.

'Why did you take such photos?' Hyeyong's dad sounded angry, confused.

'Because in the future, you will be grateful for these memories,' Jebi explained.

He shook his head. 'I don't see how.'

'If there are only happy photos, the emotion is lost,' Seokyeong added. 'When there are photos like this one in between, the pictures in which the kids are smiling become even more precious. Wait and see. After a year, or maybe ten years later, you'll be glad to have this photo.'

Hyeyong's mum nodded. She seemed to understand.

Next came Hyeyong's photo of the landscape. Behind Giant Octopus village, the sea stretched out to the horizon. In the sky hung a pale, almost translucent moon.

Everyone's eyes were fixed on the screen. A peculiar feeling welled up in Jebi's heart. Was it surprise or awe?

'It doesn't look like our village,' Dongwon said.

'Why? Is there something wrong with the photo I took?' Hyeyong looked around, her face anxious, her fists clenched.

'No, It's great. It's like a village from a fairytale.'

Hyeyong grinned.

The next photo to appear on the screen was a close-up of Dongwon. 'Oh my goodness! My face is huge!'

Hyeyong chuckled. 'Mum, this photo too, please.'

Her mum smiled and stroked her hair.

Yanghee gazed at her son.

After the slideshow was over, Dongwon and Hyeyong began running around in the gallery. Seokyeong knew it wasn't easy for children their age to sit still for a long time, and he moved the tables and chairs to the garden so that the kids could have enough space to play, without the danger of knocking into sharp corners.

He printed the photos for Hyeyong's mum before going to get a soft rug, laying it on the floor so that the adults could sit down comfortably.

Jebi brought over another bottle of swindari and joined them as Hyeyong's mum placed the photo of her daughter taken against the backdrop of Sanbangsan on a tray and started poking holes in it with the needle, tracing the outline of the shapes.

'That's an interesting needle,' Yanghee commented, as she lifted her glass to her lips.

Hyeyong's mum held it out. 'It's a braille stylus. I use it on photos so that Hyeyong can touch them.'

'You're a wonderful mother.'

'No, anyone can do it. You'd be able to, too.' She smiled. And when she spoke again, her voice was soft. 'My daughter . . . she's a miracle She was conceived after two miscarriages.'

Yanghee, surprised, shot a glance at the kids. They were playing a game of Marco Polo in the empty gallery. Dongwon was 'it' and, with his eyes closed, he was following Hyeyong's voice, trying to tag her.

Hyeyong's mum continued. 'When I was carrying Hyeyong, I was very anxious. Even a little fatigue would get me paranoid. One day, I noticed some spots of blood and went to the hospital. The doctor did an ultrasound and found some internal bleeding. I was told it was a sign of miscarriage. A few weeks passed, in which each day felt like a year, but Hyeyong pulled through. At my next ultrasound, I saw her for the first time, in the blurry black and white image. The doctor said she was holding her knees and turning, as if irritated by the ultrasound probe! I will never forget how I felt in that moment.' Hyeyong's mum cast Yanghee a glance. *I'm sure you know what I mean.*

Smiling, Yanghee nodded back at her.

'Sometimes people ask me if I knew about her condition when she was in my womb.'

Hyeyong's dad looked stricken. He picked up his phone and started scrolling unseeingly, as if hoping to shut out the conversation.

Yanghee, Seokyeong and Jebi held their breath.

Hyeyong's mum put down the stylus and turned to them. 'I did. During the eighth month of my pregnancy, I went for a check-up and the doctor told me that my child had no eyes.' She sighed. 'I'm just your average person. I'm not a saint. Of course, I struggled. But . . . think about it. Is having no eyes a reason to take away someone's life, just as it's about to begin. Imagine being that baby. I wouldn't want to die that way. I thought it was so unfair. So, I saved her, the way I'd save myself. And watching her grow up . . . She's so precious. We've had many, many happy times together.'

Yanghee nodded decisively.

'But it mustn't have been easy. Just look at what you have to do with the photos . . .'

'Oh, this? When we're at home, I use the sewing machine.' Hyeyong's mum smiled. 'It can be done with or without thread. It does get quite fiddly sometimes.'

Everyone looked on, waiting for her to explain. Hyeyong's dad had put down his phone.

'When there are too many things in the photo,' she said, 'if I outline everything, it ends up a mess. That's why I like simple photos. For the complicated ones, I have to choose what to focus on and it's hard . . . it's as if I'm limiting her world.'

Jebi felt a wave of sadness wash over her. She thought of her baby; the look of concentration on her little face when she had first breastfed, her cute nose, her lips stretching widely when she smiled. And the two tiny teeth . . .

I couldn't raise her, even though she was a healthy child!

Her heart felt like it was tearing apart. It was the same pain she felt the day she had left her child in the orphanage. Jebi turned her face away from the others, cursing herself . . .

Suddenly, there was a loud noise from behind her. Seokyeong and the other adults looked up. Hyeyong had tripped while playing with Bell and Dongwon.

Dongwon pointed at the counter. 'She hit her head on the corner here!'

'You should've been more careful!' Yanghee scolded her son.

'We were . . .!' Dongwon protested, upset.

'Are you okay, Young-ah?' Hyeyong's dad had rushed forward and was now hugging her tightly. His face was pale.

'I'm fine. Ajumma, it's not Dongwon's fault.' She yawned.

'Time for bed. Let's head back to the hotel,' Hyeyong's mum said.

Hyeyong tried to squirm out of her dad's arms. 'No! I want to stay and play with Dongwon!'

'Me too! I want to keep playing,' Dongwon said, looking pleadingly at his mum.

'If you wanted . . . you could all stay the night here,' Seokyeong suggested.

'Here?' Hyeyong's mum repeated, blankly.

'Yes. It'd be like being at one of those school camps, with everyone sleeping side by side in the classrooms.'

'Oh yeah, we did that too!' Hyeyong's dad chimed in.

'But . . . we didn't bring a change of clothes.' Hyeyong's mum hesitated, looking at her husband.

'The kids are having so much fun. We can all skip our showers just for one night. What could go wrong?'

Seokyeong and Jebi went upstairs and brought down more soft rugs and blankets. The kids had a fierce but short-lived pillow fight before, exhausted, they fell asleep.

Looking at the sleeping kids, Hyeyong's mum said, 'Well, we might as well sleep here too.'

'No, I should be going . . .' Yanghee shook her head. She'd already given in by allowing Dongwon to spend the night there.

However, Hyeyong's mum took her hands. 'Think about it. When Dongwon wakes up tomorrow, he'll be so disappointed to find you're not here. It will spoil this special treat you've given him. But if he sees you when he wakes up, think how pleased he'll be. He'll treasure the memory for a long, long time.'

Yanghee hesitated for a moment before nodding.

Yanghee took a blanket, rolled it up into a pillow and found a space next to Jebi. Seokyeong turned off the lights with the remote control and settled down next to Hyeyong's dad, who was lying beside his daughter.

They all lay in a row, yawning. It had been a tiring day but somehow it was hard to fall asleep, everyone locked in their own thoughts as they stared through the window at the stars.

'You two are great parents,' Seokyeong said a little while later, into the darkness.

'Don't say that.' Hyeyong's dad turned abruptly to face the other way. 'It's like you're saying our daughter's condition is some appallingly awful thing!'

Seokyeong sat bolt upright. 'No, I don't mean it that way!'

Hyeyong's dad sighed and looked at his sleeping child. Hyeyong's chest was rising and falling in a regular rhythm. 'I know. Sorry – I'm overreacting.' He sighed. 'I haven't always been a good father. To be honest . . . I tried to escape once.'

His voice was so low that Seokyeong had to strain to hear him.

'I just couldn't understand why it had to be my child, of all people,' the man continued. 'I was devastated. When she was six, I left home for an entire month, trying to drown my sorrows with alcohol. One day, my wife called. She told me that Hyeyong had been assessed at school and found to be a child prodigy . . .' Everyone waited with bated breath for him to continue. 'When I returned home, my wife didn't say anything. At first, I thought she understood, that she'd forgiven me. But now I know that's not the case.'

297

Seokyeong, Jebi and Yanghee lay still, glancing discreetly at Hyeyong's mum.

'Why are you bringing this up here?' she asked her husband coldly.

'I guess I'm drunk on swindari,' he said, turning to face her.

After an uncomfortable silence, she spoke. 'You think we're good parents . . . but honestly, what we do isn't that amazing. We are sighted people; it's easy for us. But if Hyeyong becomes a mum one day . . .'

Jebi tried to imagine what her own life might be like, twenty, thirty years in the future, and shivered. Hyeyong's mum continued: 'What if we're no longer around for her by then? I keep thinking about it. If she becomes a mother, she'll have a much harder time than we ever did. But I've realised that the only thing I can do for her is to raise her to be a strong person, someone who doesn't give up.' She shrugged, then tilted her head towards her husband. 'I'm not sure what he thinks.'

Hyeyong's dad sniffed. 'Me? I just hope she'll be happy. I'm okay not having grandchildren.'

'This isn't about grandchildren!' Hyeyong's mum whispered sharply. 'It's about our daughter. I want her to experience the same happiness I have, watching her grow up. I hope one day she'll start a loving family of her own and live well,' she said, choking back tears.

In the dark, Yanghee put an arm across her eyes and sniffed. In fact, Seokyeong was the only one who wasn't crying.

Hyeyong's mum addressed her husband again. 'Thank

you for coming back to us . . . I'm grateful that I have you.
Your love for Hyeyong is a huge support to me . . . I guess
what I'm trying to say is . . . Some people might say that
some things can't be forgiven, or that once love and trust
are lost they're lost forever . . . but I think it's not as
straightforward as that.'

'Oh, darling!' His voice choked with emotion,
Hyeyong's dad tried to reach over the sleeping kids to
hug his wife.

She quickly pushed him away. 'Omo! What're you
doing! Go to sleep!'

In the dark, everyone burst out in quiet laughter amid
the tears. Soon, Hyeyong's dad was snoring softly.

As he listened to the children's breathing, Seokyeong
closed his eyes. His heart was heavy. Why had he ever
thought he would make a good father? Doubt had seeped
in, and he was afraid. Where had his former confidence
come from? Was it because things had always been easy
with Dongwon. Because he could tell that even when he
didn't know what to do at times, or made mistakes, things
would turn out fine for Dongwon?

Seokyeong tossed and turned, unable to sleep. What if
he were Hyeyong's dad, raising a child who couldn't see.
What kind of world would he be thrown into? He couldn't
imagine it at all. He'd been convinced that being a father
would bring him nothing but happiness . . .

His thoughts drifted to his own father, who'd died at a
young age. What had being a father meant to him? He
couldn't have been proud of his son, or he wouldn't have
chosen to leave the way he had.

He turned onto his other side and curled up his big body, like a little boy again.

Suddenly, the beam of light from the lighthouse swept past the framed photographs on the wall, and the customers' faces and smiles flashed. Seokyeong remembered every encounter.

He no longer had a father, but Seokyeong knew he wasn't alone. He was surrounded by people at the photo studio, and that wasn't going to change.

The adults stirred awake to the muffled sounds of the kids playing. It was just starting to get light.

Hyeyong and Dongwon were going up and down the stairs as quietly as possible, their foreheads wet with perspiration, yet they couldn't stifle their giggles. Bell had also joined in the game, chasing them with her tongue lolling.

Jebi got up and tied her messy bed hair into a bun. Even before brushing her teeth, she went to get the camera and took a few snaps of the kids.

Hyeyong's mum and Yanghee took turns to freshen up in the upstairs bathroom while the men brushed their teeth in the toilet.

Everyone prepared breakfast together. In that moment, there was no division between employer, employee and customer as they moved about in the kitchen – they'd become one big family, a family who'd gone through bad times as well as good in the few days they'd spend together. There wasn't much in the fridge, but they whipped up dishes from whatever they could find, amid much chatter and laughter.

After breakfast, they gathered at the garden and with the Hakuda Photo Studio as the backdrop, they took one last group photo.

Later, Seokyeong dropped Yanghee and her son off at their house. Yanghee got down from the SUV and bade goodbye to Hyeyong's parents as Dongwon looked at Hyeyong with sad puppy eyes. 'Bye. Come back soon.'

'Okay, and you come to Seoul, too.'

'Mum, can I go?' Dongwon looked up at Yanghee. He was grinning before he'd even heard her answer.

'Okay, I'll think about it.'

The front door of the grey-roofed house opened. 'Granny!' Dongwon ran into her embrace.

Hyeyong remained in her seat, looking forlorn.

On the way to the airport, Hyeyong's parents described everything they went past. Jebi, who was listening in, nodded occasionally.

It had been six months since she'd started working at the photo studio. The Jeju landscape that she'd been so in awe of was now part of her daily life. Three seasons had passed since she'd first arrived in Jeju.

Jebi remembered being knocked into the sea by that man on the last day of her holiday. Her phone ruined, looking for help, she had stumbled upon Hakuda Photo Studio. There, she had ended up helping with baby Yoona's one hundredth day celebratory photoshoot, then ridden pillion on Seokyeong's bike to the coast, where she met Yanghee. And because of that, she'd missed her flight.

What if I'd gone back to Seoul?

She tried to imagine what might have happened.

I suppose I'd have survived somehow . . . Meeting other people along the way.

But would she have been happy? Somehow, she didn't think so. *Not as happy as I am here.*

At the airport, Hyeyong was carrying her own little backpack. Seokyeong continued snapping photos as they checked in. Then, it was time to say goodbye.

'This is . . . something extra from us.' Jebi reached into her shoulder bag and took out a small parcel.

Hyeyong's dad took it, looking curious.

'We put some video clips onto a USB drive. So that Hyeyong can listen to them.'

Hyeyong's dad looked at the gift for a moment, before giving it to his daughter. Hyeyong held it in her hands and felt it all over. 'Hakuda Photo Studio?' She raised her head. 'Eonnie, you know how to do braille?'

'Ah, no.'

'Oh! So this is why you asked?' Hyeyong's mum chuckled. Turning to Hyeyong, she explained, 'Jebi Eonnie asked me how to write the photo studio's name in braille, so I did it for her.'

Nodding, Hyeyong slipped the gift into her pocket and put on her red sunglasses.

'Eonnie . . . what does "hakuda" mean?'

' "Hakuda" in Jeju dialect means "I'll do it",' Seokyeong chimed in. 'At Hakuda Photo Studio, we do our best to create beautiful photos every time.'

'I see.' Hyeyong nodded.

Taking her hand, Hyeyong's dad led her towards the gate. Hyeyong could be heard singing 'Hakuda, hakuda!', while skipping happily. Hyeyong's mum watched them go before turning back to Jebi and Seokyeong. She looked like she wanted to say something.

Just like the first day we met. When she told us about Hyeyong's condition. Jebi waited anxiously.

'Thank you for everything,' she said.

'Not at all, we're grateful too,' Seokyeong replied.

'I don't know if meeting our family, and seeing our struggles, has affected the both of you in any way. When you two are not even married yet . . .' Hyeyong's mum bowed her head as if she had committed some crime.

'Not at all.'

'Please don't say that.'

Suddenly, Jebi was angry. Why was Hyeyong's mum apologising, when she'd done nothing wrong? Was it being a mother that made her put everyone else's feelings before her own? But Jebi kept quiet, told herself she was overreacting. Maybe Hyeyong's mum had always been like this.

'I just want to say this . . . I don't have regrets. None at all.' Hyeyong's mum looked up and smiled. She reached out for their hands and stacked one on top of the other. 'I hope you, too, will get to start your own lovely family. Both of you.'

With that, Hyeyong's mum went to join her husband and child.

As people streamed past them, Seokyeong and Jebi stood in the middle of the terminal, exchanged a glance and broke into giggles.

They were still smiling as they got into the SUV, happy because they had met happy people.

Before, they had both been miserable, full of anger, thinking everyone in the world was the same; that, in life, there things that could never be forgiven. But at the Hakuda Photo Studio, they had come to learn that life could be filled with moments of real happiness. And as for children . . . the more love you showered on them, the more loving and lovable they became.

Seokyeong drove out of the car park but then stopped the car by the side of the road and rolled down the window.

Hyeyong and her parents had wanted every moment of their time in Jeju recorded. So he pointed the camera upwards and snapped a photo of their plane as it ascended into the blue of the sky.

12

The Giant Octopus Festival

It was a Wednesday morning and Jebi was having a lie-in when she felt something cold on her face. She cracked her eyes open.

The moment she sat upright, a red, wriggling centipede landed on her quilt. Scrabbling away from it, she got out of bed and quickly checked her face in front of the mirror. *All good.* She opened the drawer. Holding the green tape, she scanned the ceiling and the walls. *Gotcha.* Next to the window was a small hole.

'It doesn't matter how many times I block up the holes, they always find another way in. Such tenacity.'

She tore off a section of tape, slapped it across the hole and made a mental note to herself to putty the wall after breakfast. With a shake of her quilt, she scooped up the centipede and flung it into the vegetable patch.

'Cursed creatures. Did they get inside again?' Mokpo Granny, who was outside filling a basket with broccoli, frowned. With a hoe, she quickly cut the wriggling creature in two and buried it in the soil. 'This one's still small,' she muttered under her breath.

Jebi took the basket to the kitchen. When she had first moved in, the vegetable patch had been full of lettuce and chives, but Mokpo Granny had switched to growing broccoli last autumn when she discovered Jebi's love for blanched broccoli served with a red chilli pepper paste and vinegar dip.

After a late breakfast – for Granny it was an early lunch – they headed out together. In the garden, they each hoisted over their shoulders a big basket tied with rope and filled with a year's worth of harvested dried Ceylon moss seaweed and abalone shells.

Though Mokpo Granny was in her eighties, she walked with a straight back. Jebi never had to slow down for her.

Along the thirty-minute route to the Haenyeos' Association, they were joined by several more haenyeos carrying baskets or nets on their backs. Jebi admired the rapeseed that, with the arrival of February, was in full bloom around the village.

'Mokpo Samchon, seen any seaweed near the shore?' A sanggun haenyeo called out gruffly. She looked to be in her fifties, with pronounced cheekbones and sharp eyes beneath permed hair. Slung over her shoulder was a golden fishing net.

'Nope. Maybe because the waters are getting warmer. How about further out?'

'None there, either. It's worrying.'

Winter was ending and come March the closed season for seaweed harvesting would be over. But the haenyeos had begun to notice that the seaweed was barely growing this year. Their livelihoods depended on the weather; when the waves were too choppy, it was impossible to dive. But no matter how good the weather was, if the marine life wasn't reproducing, diving would become a waste of their time and energy.

'We'd better pray hard during the festival and prepare generous food offerings,' the haenyeo fretted.

The moment Jebi stepped into the hall, an overpowering smell of seaweed greeted her. More than twenty haenyeos from the village had gathered and it looked like everything was ready.

The doors to each of the three rooms were wide open. Thinking that the women inside reminded her of octopuses in caves, Jebi followed Mokpo Granny into one of the rooms., The haenyeos moved to make space for them.

'Alright, everyone knows what to do right? Let's get started!' the president barked.

There was a flurry of movement as everyone got to work. In each room, one person was in charge of folding thick hanji paper, dyed a dark brown with persimmon juice. The top of the folded paper was securely tied and the bottom fanned out to the side to make a pouch-like shape, and the next person in line would tuck Ceylon moss inside. All year, the haenyeos had been keeping aside lower-quality bunches of moss from what they harvested, for this purpose. The next step was to sew up the sides of the pouch with half-dried seaweed. The seaweed, torn to make a thin thread that could go through the eye of a long, thick needle, was surprisingly strong.

Jebi's job was to sew abalone shells onto the sausage-like pouches; someone else had already punctured two holes in each of the shells. Carefully, she sewed the shell onto the pouch.

The team in the main room was doing the same, but on a much bigger scale. Into a pouch the size of a large, folded bed sheet, they stuffed several baskets' worth of Ceylon moss before sewing up the sides. To prevent it from bursting at the seams, while at the same time making sure that the sides could close, several haenyeos worked on it at once, with one of them at the top pulling the paper into position, and two others at the bottom quickly stitching up the ends. Meanwhile, the haenyeos in each of the smaller rooms were joining six or seven pouches together to form a long, arm-like structure.

Two hours later, they had finally finished the jumul offering — a giant octopus the size of a car. Strands of seaweed had been twisted into ropes and attached to the octopus like backpack straps.

Me? Carry that? I'll be crushed! Jebi kept this thought to herself with difficulty.

The haenyeos gathered in the main room and stood in front of the jumul. All of them sank into a deep bow, pressing their palms together as they murmured a prayer. At a stern look from the haenyeos, Jebi hastily lowered her head too.

Over at the photo studio, Seokyeong was having a relaxing day for the first time in a long while. He brewed coffee for himself, humming a tune under his breath as he refreshed the gallery's collection. The custom-made horizontal frame he'd ordered for the panoramic shot of the cliffs had arrived that morning. Next to it was a photo of the trachyte, the black lines of the fossil against the grey of the stone looking like an abstract artwork. On the wall by the stairs, he hung a photo of Hyeyong's family, and beside it, one of Hyeyong screaming and Dongwon crying. Below that, he put a sticker: *Photo by Yeon Jebi.*

Seokyeong smiled. Just then, his phone rang. It was an unknown number. He hesitated for a beat before answering.

'Is this Mr Lee Seokyeong?' A woman spoke in a clipped, dry tone.

'Yes, it is. Who's speaking, please?'

'This is Kim Yeri, the editor of *OUR magazine*. We'd like to invite you to contribute some photos for our April issue.'

Seokyeong gaped. *OUR?* As in *the OUR?* How had the editor from such a prestigious magazine got his number? Stunned, he momentarily forgot that he was still on the line.

'Hello?' said Kim Yeri.

'Yes, I'm here,' he replied. His heart was pounding. 'May I know the theme for the feature, please?'

'It's "Wild". I saw your work on Instagram. Great stuff. The big, hideous octopus sitting on top of that young model's head.'

'Oh, Jebi . . .' He brushed his hair back. 'Got it. When do you need the photos?'

'By the end of this month.' Suddenly the voice over the phone pulled away. 'This is too tacky. What did Chanel say?' Then, coming through clearly again, the woman said: 'But no guarantee that we'll run them. We'll have to see the photos first.'

'Just photos?' Seokyeong asked. He turned towards the window and stared out at the sea. Bell was wandering around the gallery, sniffing at corners.

'Yes, with simple captions. But if the photos are good, we may turn it into an interview, in which case we'll send questions.'

'Got it,' he said, and the line went dead.

It was the first of February in the lunar calendar – the twentieth day of the month in the Gregorian calendar – the day of the Giant Octopus Festival.

At the crack of dawn, the president and the executive committee of the Haenyeos' Association arrived at Mokpo Granny's home, bringing with them the chosen one's costume. Jebi was surprised to see that it was in fact just a worn-out mulsojungi – a traditional one-piece body suit made of a yellow cotton fabric. Worn by haenyeos in the past before rubber wetsuits became popular, it resembled a tank-top with a single strap across the shoulder and shorts below.

Jebi stared at the slit that ran down the side of the costume, making it easier to pull on and off. It would expose her flanks and thighs. When was the last time she'd weighed herself? She pictured her flesh bursting out between the seams.

'That's it? But it's freezing outside . . .' Jebi mustered the courage to address the president.

The haenyeo glared and hushed her with a hiss. Everyone pursed their lips tight, signalling with pointed looks for her to change into the costume immediately. Bewildered, she suddenly remembered that Mokpo Granny had told her in passing the night before that engaging in conversation before the festival was thought to bring bad luck.

Seeing no way out, Jebi took off the tracksuit she was wearing and slipped a leg into the costume. Immediately, the president smacked her hard on the back.

'Ouch! Why did you hit me!'

The haenyeo thumped her chest in frustration and pulled down Jebi's bra strap.

'Take this off? No way! Absolutely not!'

Flinging aside the mulsojungi, she hugged herself, horrified. The rest of the women glared at her impatiently, jabbing fingers at the wall clock and making the diving signal for *Hurry up*. Just then, the windows rattled: outside, the wind was rising.

Oh god. Why should I have to wear only that thin fabric in this weather? And carry the giant mulkkureok into the sea? This is too much! Defiance welled up in her.

Exasperated, the president rummaged in Jebi's closet, yanked out her long puffer jacket and shook it in front of her face, gesturing that she could wear it over the mulsojungi to the water.

'Walking down the beach is not the problem.' Jebi was beyond caring about not speaking. 'I have to get into the water, don't I? It's going to be absolutely freezing – how am I supposed to survive wearing just this? Without my underwear too,' she wailed.

But her protests fell on deaf ears. The haenyeos remained resolute. Not wanting to waste any more time, they jammed a frilled cotton bonnet onto her head. It fit over her ears and neck snugly, leaving only her eyes, nose and lips visible. Someone tied the strap under her chin.

Still, Jebi refused to take off her underwear. Holding out the mulsojungi, the president stared Jebi down, her eyes bulging. Time was ticking. Suddenly, the door opened, and Mokpo Granny came in. Her hair was neatly combed back, and she was dressed in a beautiful garot, a hanbok-style dress worn by the local women on the island.

'Granny! Help me!' Jebi cried out.

Mokpo Granny nodded, seeming to understand the situation at once. Without saying anything, she put her palms together. Looking Jebi in the eye, she went down on her knees and performed a deep bow, her forehead touching the ground.

'Granny! What are you doing!' Shocked, Jebi immediately stooped to help her up.

'There's nothing to be embarrassed about,' Granny said to Jebi.

The president and the committee members, shocked, gestured with their fingers on their lips for Mokpo Granny to keep quiet.

'Granny! You shouldn't speak! It's bad luck . . .' Jebi whispered.

Mokpo Granny shook her head. 'For many, many generations . . . haenyeos have worked hard to put food on the table for their families. In Jeju, men are scarce; so many are lost at sea. Married or not, all Jeju women have to work, and for those with children things are even harder.'

Mokpo Granny took the mulsojungi from the president.

'It was only in the seventies that we switched to rubber wetsuits. When I first arrived on the island, I had to wear a mulsojungi too. Do you know why there's a slit at the side? It's so that even when the belly swells with a child, we'll still fit into it. Even in the dead of winter, even when we are soon to give birth, we continue to dive. That's what a mulsojungi is – a mother's clothes. We don't wear underwear so that when we come back to shore, we're ready to breastfeed the baby we left napping nearby.'

'Granny, I understand now . . . Hush. I don't want you to suffer bad luck . . .' Jebi lowered her head. Tears splashed onto the fabric she clutched in her hands.

The haenyeos left the room and, slowly, Jebi took off her underwear and put on the mulsojungi. She looked into the mirror and put a hand on her stomach. Her baby was gone – she had failed as a mother. Picking up her phone, she scrolled to the photo that she had stared at countless times. The same round eyes she had, and the flat nose, the protruding forehead inherited from the baby's father . . . her precious little one.

She'd only given her daughter a nickname, as if fearing that naming her properly would make it impossible to let her go. 'Mummy is going into the sea today, little Chestnut' Jebi whispered. 'In this village, Mummy is the chosen one. I'll be carrying the giant octopus into the water. If I succeed, it will stop bad things from happening. My baby,

I'll be praying for you to grow up well, to never fall sick . . . I'm so sorry that this is the only thing I can do for you.'

When Jebi arrived at the coast in fur-lined boots and a long puffer jacket over the mulsojungi, the villagers were setting up the offering tables. The winds were strong and the waves high, so they took extra care to make sure that the food they'd prepared with effort wouldn't be blown away. It was an impressive sight to see the tables stretching out along the coast. Besides the common offerings like apples, pears and omegi rice cakes, each household also put out specialties unique to their family: bottles of gosorisul liquor, castella cakes and sides of meat had been laid out. On several tables were plates of freshly caught abalones and still-moving sea urchins. The villagers stood in front of their tables and prayed fervently for a year of safety and a bountiful harvest.

Seokyeong, wearing a sweater with Stephen Gertz grinning from it, had just finished arranging the offerings on their allotted table. He'd prepared them with Jebi yesterday: tortillas topped with bacon and top shell meat, whole chicken soup, grilled pork belly, clam ramyeon, coffee roasted with tangerine peel, and tangerine tea. It was a generous spread, but the table that attracted the most attention belonged to Yoona's family.

Arranged on large plates was an assortment of delicacies, including slices of the sand dune cake, the cliff cake and the distinctive octopus buns. A huge, beautifully decorated cake stood on a stand at the centre of the table. Blue and white cream represented the sea and the sky, and floating on the water were orange tewaks made of icing, along with several chocolate figurine haenyeos returning to shore.

After the prayer ceremony, many of the villagers whipped out their phones to take pictures of the magnificent cake as they wandered down the row of tables. Hajun pushed his shoulders back proudly. Standing beside him, Heeun looked excited. In her arms, her nine-month-old daughter pointed a tiny finger at the cake and crowed, 'Daddy, kayyy!'

'Have the cakes been selling well?' Seokyeong asked.

Hajun grinned. 'Yes, thanks to you.'

Seokyeong's photo of the cliff cake had gone viral on Instagram. Placing the sliced cake on a table outdoors, he'd taken a shot of it at a clever angle so that it looked as though the cake's columnar joints were emerging from the sea, with the real-life cliffs visible in the background.

'I hope that we'll be invited to the "choosing" ceremony this year,' Hajun said, looking nervous.

'I would think so. Everyone in the village loves your bakes,' Seokyeong said, taking several more photos of the table.

Stealing a glance at the camera screen, Hajun nodded. 'I'm going to do my best. To work hard and earn the villagers' trust. For us outsiders who want to put down roots here . . . it's the only way.'

'It'll work out. There's also Yoona.'

'Oh yeah. Everyone loves our baby girl. People always stop for a chat now if they see us . . .'

Seokyeong snapped a quick picture of Yoona's smile.

Behind him, a noise like a thunderclap suddenly cut through the air. Seokyeong turned to see a group of performers clad in colourful shaman costumes hitting gongs, bass drums and smaller, double-headed janggu drums. On a mat adorned with the traditional obangsaek colours of blue, red, white, black and yellow, the ten musicians were sitting in a circle. Men in red durumagi, the Korean traditional overcoat, waved bamboo branches as they performed a dance ritual. Soon, a ringing voice announced the start of the festival.

'Daewang Mulkkureok maeul, Giant Octopus village, the mulkkureok festival begins!' It was an unusual cry, almost song-like, the last syllables dragging and reverberating in the air.

On hearing it, the villagers gathered; arms raised, they danced to the upbeat music.

Then the door to the haenyeos' changing room opened and the divers emerged. Everyone was in a long coat or a puffer jacket that reached down to their ankles, with bare calves underneath; they were all wearing a mulsojungi. Somewhere in the middle was Yanghee, with Jebi appearing at the very back of the group.

Seokyeong waved but neither of them saw him.

'Amazing, right?'

A voice sounded next to his ear, and he jumped. 'Oh, Professor, what are you doing here?'

The geologist waved her new camera proudly. 'Here to take some videos for my YouTube channel.'

'What kind of videos? You're doing it by yourself?'

'Yeah, I started a channel all about geology and the fun ways to engage with it in our day-to-day lives. I'm starting off with video content, but I hope to compile everything into a book at some point.'

'It sounds brilliant. Where did you get the idea?'

The geologist shrugged, keeping her eyes on the dancers. 'Thanks to you. And to Jebi-ssi. And maybe thanks to myself too.' She held up the camera and tried out a few different angles. 'That day at the photo studio, when Stephen Gertz arrived – I was struck by the way you so clearly looked up to him. It was the same as the way Jebi-ssi treats you. I . . . felt as though I was looking at myself. And what Stephen said about me . . . wasn't wrong. Thinking back, I chose to major in geology because my professor was the first adult I'd ever met whom I could respect.'

Pointing her camera out over the water, she shot a few seconds of footage before continuing. 'I told Stephen I research lava flows because I'm attracted to the intensity of heat, but when I got home that night, I realised that wasn't true. What captivates me isn't the heat, but what emerges from it, the traces and landforms that heat leaves behind. I want to make a mark somehow, too. And who knows, maybe I will. And then, if I meet the professor by chance again, he might be the one looking up to me.' A faint smile appeared on her face.

Seokyeong nodded, thinking of Stephen. Last week, he had received an email from him. Attached had been a couple of photos of Ukrainian kids smiling brightly, against a backdrop of bombed-out buildings. In the message, Stephen said he missed Jeju very much.

Korea used to be a battlefield but now it's a peaceful and safe country. May peace return to these children too one day. I believe the day will come.

Staring at the words on the screen, Seokyeong's hands had started trembling, imagining the photos, darker ones, that he knew Stephen must have taken but decided not to show him.

I should send him a photo from today, Seokyeong thought, as he checked the images on the camera screen. His wide-angle lens had captured the sky and the sea, the spectators, Hajun, the geologist and Jebi.

A question suddenly popped into his head, and he stepped towards the geologist, who had begun to walk away. 'Sorry, but what has this festival got to do with geology?'

Chewing the honey rice cake that an elderly man at the next table had just offered her, the geologist pointed at one of the percussionists, still sitting on their mat under a large tree.

'Do you know what that instrument is?'

'I think I've read about it in a book. I can't remember the name, though. Pyeon-something?'

'A pyeongyeong. It's made of sixteen L-shaped stones hung on a wooden frame.'

'Oh, okay . . .?'

'Listen carefully. The drums, the gongs . . . they're making a beautiful sound, but it's not quite the traditional music we know. What we're hearing is gentler, don't you think?'

'Hmm, now that you mention it, something does seem to be missing.' Seokyeong scratched his head. 'Ah, the kkwaenggwari gong?'

The geologist nodded, smiling. 'That's right! Because the clanging would disturb the mulkkureoks, they don't use the kkwaenggwari during the festival. The village head told me that. That's where a pyeongyeong comes in. The instrument is made from pumice stone and produces a distinctive sound, clear but also soft. Pumice is a type of volcanic rock that forms when lava cools very quickly during an eruption.'

Just then, one of the musicians took up a gaktoe, a wooden stick with a cow horn attached on its end and hit one of the L-shaped stones. A beautiful, clean note reverberated around them, leaving Seokyeong feeling as though all the dust on his heart was being washed away.

The geologist held up her camera, filming the performance while narrating in a bright voice: 'Do you know how pyeongyeongs are made? The pumice is shaped with a whetstone; the different sizes to produce different notes. While this requires clever craftsmanship, once made, the pitch of the instrument is not affected by temperature or humidity, making it one that other instruments can tune from.

Just then, a villager came to offer a juicy segment of tangerine to the geologist. Over the course of the winter, she'd become a familiar face to the local people: the discovery of the rare giant octopus fossil had made a splash in the academic world and on the news too. A public TV station had sent a camera crew to the cliffs to

319

photograph the fossil. And while Hakuda Photo Studio didn't feature in the footage, Seokyeong's sharply focused image of the fossil had been widely circulated, along with, of course, a credit line for Hakuda Photo Studio.

The news piece had not been a long one, still the number of tourists to the village had increased significantly. Already, a few locals were preparing to open guesthouses. The haenyeos, too, had hatched a plan to open a restaurant and earn extra income that way. The village was abuzz with excitement.

And so, the geologist had become much-loved in the village, for having made the place not only a tourist destination but also an important heritage site.

'O, chosen one, it is time!' a shaman, dressed head to toe in red, cried out. Two drums were hit at the same time, the deep base note carrying in the air. The atmosphere was suddenly tense.

The haenyeos had moved the carefully constructed mulkkureok from their hall to the changing room on the beach the previous day, and now they carried it outside. Having taken off their warm coats, the sea wind bit their bare skin as they marched forward.

At the head of the procession was Jebi. Hands gripping the seaweed ropes draped over her shoulders, she took one measured step at a time. The spectators quietly followed behind. Seokyeong blended into the crowd with his camera.

As the procession approached the shore, the drums quieted, while the bright chiming of the pyeongyeong continued to undulate across the dunes. Carefully, the haenyeos put down the mulkkureok. Adjusting the straps on her shoulders, Jebi kneeled. The villagers crowded around her and started slipping small offerings through the gaps in the giant octopus's stitching: boiled pork lard, chicken meat, segments of tangerine and even folded notes. When this was done, and the villagers had all stepped back and put their palms together in prayer, Jebi stood up. As she did so, there was a sharp tearing sound, followed by a ripple of anxious murmurs. Checking her straps again, Jebi saw with relief that only one of them had been partially torn by the weight of the octopus, and it seemed to be holding.

The sanggun haenyeos quickly unclasped the lead belts around their waists and strapped them around Jebi's. Her back hunched now, her legs wobbling, she doggedly moved forward.

On his camera, Seokyeong captured the scene of the mulkkureok resting on the sand. Jebi was hidden behind its bulk, making it look as if the creature was crawling back to the water under its own steam. Judging by its size, it must have weighed way more than ten kilograms. Seokyeong watched Jebi bearing the weight without complaint and was impressed.

Slowly, the octopus returned to the sea. The drums started again. Dressed in their mulsojungi, the haenyeos faced the waves and sang. Their voices were low, gruff, and slightly offbeat. The villagers joined in at the chorus.

Easterly wind, northerly wind, the dark waters
Mulkkureok, mulkkureok, the giant mulkkureok
Go, go, return to the sea.

Mulkkureok, mulkku-u-reok, the giant mulkku-u-reok
Mulkkureok, mulkku-u-reok, the giant mulkku-u-reok.

Abalones, sea urchins, seaweed, conches
May the seeds be sowed in abundance
Rough seas, smooth silky waters
Let no haenyeos' lives be lost, wed or single.

Peace, peace, may peace come to the village
Peace, peace, may peace bless us always.

With this song reverberating in her ears, Jebi pushed off from the sand and began to swim. The icy cold of the water made her hands and feet ache, but it didn't matter, as long as she could hear the voices of the haenyeos on the beach. As the seconds passed though, the sound grew more distant, and the weight of the mulkkureok dug deeper into her bones.

Jebi tried to straighten her shoulders, kicking her legs out strongly. As she swam further out, fighting against the current, memories unspooled in her mind.

The day she arrived at the village, she'd slipped her hand into the mouth of the jangseung, closed her eyes and made a wish. *May my little Chestnut grow up healthy and happy.*

Taking a deep breath, Jebi plunged her head into the water, pulling the mulkkureok down with her.

Underwater, the landscape was eerie yet beautiful. She followed the steep, slippery coastal rocks past the sand bar and slowly made her descent. Fronds of bright purple coral danced before her eyes. A school of blue-striped angelfish glided past. Ahead of her was the cave where she had to deposit the mulkkureok. Once she reached it, the sanggun haenyeos would take over, settling the giant octopus at its mouth.

Though she'd been practising for months, Jebi was very afraid. The cold attacked her on all sides, and she was starting to feel dizzy from lack of air. The water around her was dark, silent, and she feared that something might glide out at her from nowhere.

Jebi kicked hard, her fins propelling her downwards. She was careful not to upset the balance of the weight between her shoulders. But the hanji, now saturated with water, tore, and Ceylon moss came bursting through the ripped seams. In the dark ocean, it looked like tufts of human hair.

No! Nothing can go wrong. I won't let anything bad happen to Chestnut!

As if the mulkkureok were a baby on her back, Jebi reached behind her with both hands and exerted all her strength to hold it together. Her lungs were tight, her shoulders aching, her hips stiff and sore . . . It was like returning to the days of caring for her newborn.

Unable to take it anymore, she released the breath she'd been holding and bubbles frothed from her mouth. She thought doing so would relieve the pain in her chest, but it only made her feel dizzier.

She shook her head, trying to focus. Her fingertips and toes were tingling. Craning her neck, she saw the water surface glistening above her. *Brightness . . . warmth.*

Jebi wriggled her shoulders, the voice in her head telling her to abandon the mulkkureok and surface for air growing more insistent. But at that moment, something happened.

In front of the cave, something glittered. What looked like yellow, red and white lights were bobbing in the dark water. Then she understood. They were mulkkureoks, octopuses waiting to greet the chosen one. They hadn't forgotten that this day was the day the villagers promised to deliver a gift to them each year.

Jebi clenched her teeth and kicked down again. The closer she got to the ocean floor, the harder her head throbbed. When she finally stopped in front of the cave, her vision was blurring. The octopuses kicked up sand as they swarmed around her, attaching themselves to the offering.

Relieved, the tension left Jebi's body – and she swallowed a mouthful of salt water. As her body grew limp, she felt someone pull the straps from her shoulders. Two, four, then six hands stripped her of the lead belts around her waist.

Warm and strong, the haenyeos were propping her up, pushing her to the surface and, finally, her head broke through the choppy waves. Several hands smacked her on her back as Jebi spat out water and took a first gasping breath.

Hot tears spilled into the sea and, as she cried, Jebi let out a long sumbisori.

Moments later, a distant sound reached her ears. The crowd on the shore was cheering. All these months, she'd considered the mulkkureok festival nothing but a superstition. But now, Jebi understood why the villagers had kept the tradition year after year.

No one else can live our lives for us, but life is also about helping one another.

When Jebi reached the shore, she was completely spent. The elderly haenyeos quickly dried her with towels. Tiny capillaries all over her body had ruptured, colouring her skin purple and red, like an octopus. Seokyeong, beaming, was clicking away with his camera. An old fisherman pried open her mouth and fed her warm liquor as the women wrapped her body with a frayed, mottled robe.

'This is the bokcharim, the lucky gown. It's sewn using strips torn from the traditional garments the haenyeos have worn in the past year,' said Mokpo Granny.

When the sanggun haenyeos' emerged from the water, the villagers quickly did the same for them, giving them pieces of rice cake and sips of warm liquor, and massaging their frozen limbs.

Jebi wanted to know what the women had done with the mulkkureok after freeing her from it, but the ladies remained tight-lipped.

One day, I'll find out. One day, when I've stayed in the village long enough.

Dinner was back at Mokpo Granny's house. Seokyeong and Bell joined them to sit in the warm kitchen and eat the leftover food from the festival. It was a long-time tradition that the offerings were shared among the families.

Mokpo prepared a delicious stew with boiled pork slices and seasoned pumpkin leaves, as well as bibimbap with sea urchin roe and abalone. For dessert, they had slices of the sand-dune cake from Yoona's Bakes.

'Granny, I didn't think you liked sweet stuff,' Jebi spoke teasingly in Jeju dialect. Her skin was still blotchy, as though covered in tattoos.

'Of course. Cakes are mood-lifters,' she replied. 'The first thing my late husband ever bought me was cream bread.'

'Oooh, were you on a date? Where was it?' Jebi lit up at the prospect of hearing Granny's love story.

'In Mokpo, of course. I only came to Jeju later. And . . . well . . . if I'd known that life would be so hard after he died young, I wouldn't have married him and settled down here.'

Mokpo Granny let out a long sigh and Jebi listened quietly as she recounted how the villagers had given the cold shoulder to the young lady who married into the village.

Suddenly, she thought of something. 'Granny . . . you knew Yanghee Eonnie's grandmother, right? How did she die? She was a sanggun haenyeo, one of the best, wasn't she?'

Mokpo Granny cast a glance at Seokyeong and bit her lip. Silently, she got up from her chair and cleared the plates. Jebi thought that was the end of the conversation, but while washing the dishes, she spoke.

'She went beyond her breath – ate mulsum, that's what we call it here. She had three young children, one of whom was still breastfeeding. Life was very tough for her. She needed the money so she insisted on heading into the sea that day, even though the sky was dark and the waves treacherous. I went with her. But being a new haenyeo, I stayed in the shallow waters. And later when I returned to shore, they told me she had drowned in the sea.' Mokpo Granny's hands paused as she stared vacantly ahead. 'I've never told anyone this. I don't want to sully her honour.'

In the long silence that followed, the three of them were motionless, lost in their thoughts.

'After your husband passed away, why did you choose to stay here? Why not join your children in the city?' Seokyeong asked.

'What a question! This is my home.' Mokpo Granny glared at him as if he'd said something stupid. 'Once I got married, I became a koendang here. Same with you, chosen one.'

'What? Me?'

'Of course! The mulkkureok picked you – you are part of the village now. You never have to worry again about not having a place here.'

April arrived, along with bright sunshine. Hearing a motorbike draw up, Bell dashed out of the studio. It was a Thursday morning and Seokyeong and Jebi had left the door wide open, as they dusted the shelves and wiped the tables.

327

Putting down their dishcloths, they followed Bell outside. The puppy was barking, her tail arched like a crescent moon, at a lanky mailman as he put down the kickstand of his motorbike. The man playfully woofed back at her and handed them their mail – a copy of the magazine *OUR*.

Seokyeong and Jebi quickly finished their tasks and washed their hands. They sat down at the window overlooking the sea and flipped open the magazine. Running their eyes down the contents page, with its edgy graphic design, they found what they were looking for. *WILD: The Women of Jeju*. Taking note of the page number, the two of them both tried to flip through the magazine at the same time.

'Stop! It's going to tear!'

'That's why I said let me do it!' Jebi replied.

Finally, they found the page.

'Wow!' Jebi gave a cry of surprise.

Grinning, Seokyeong leant forward to look closer. 'It looks even cooler in the magazine than it does up there.' Jebi said, pointing at the gallery wall. Where the old detective's portrait had hung was a new photo from the festival – the same one in the magazine – taken when Jebi had just returned from sending off the mulkkureok. She was lying on the sand dunes, the tiny capillaries broken under her skin tattooing her body like red ink. In contrast, the cotton mulsojungi she wore was a bright white. Through the slit in the costume, her ribs and the swell of her hip could be seen. The caption read: *Mulkkureok Festival in the Giant Octopus Village, Jeju*. It was accompanied by a short paragraph on why Seokyeong had opened the Hakuda Photo Studio.

'We're going to be very busy this summer,' Seokyeong said, looking excited.

'Yeah, we get multiple enquiries a day even now – July is almost full.' Jebi paused, then continued innocently: 'You know, summer vacations are impossible in this job, so don't you think that employees should be rewarded for their work with some kind of a bonus?'

Seokyeong chuckled. 'Hah! Very well. I'm sure something can be arranged.' He gave an exaggerated nod of assent.

Though the studio was busier than ever, Seokyeong still took the time to teach Jebi photography. Their lessons covered a range of topics, from the various types of cameras and lenses, to setting up lighting, and the best way to achieve good composition. He taught Jebi how to edit photos.

'Photography, especially digital photography, should be approached with imagination. Because it's always possible to edit the image. Whenever you take a photo, you should be thinking about creative ways you might be able to edit it.'

They were in the garden, and using Bell as a model.

Jebi tilted her head a fraction. 'That's not at all what I expected you to say.'

Seokyeong pointed at Bell. 'Now you know, so try again.'

'Hey, hey, stop moving,' Jebi grumbled, running after the puppy, the viewfinder to her eye.

'Actually . . . it applies relationships, too.' Seokyeong crossed his arms. 'It helps to know from the start how far you'd be willing to go for someone.'

Jebi turned around. 'Oh, you must be talking about Yanghee Eonnie?'

'Eh?'

Jebi snapped a photo of Seokyeong looking aghast.

'Hey, you didn't give me any warning!'

'I learnt from the best!' Jebi giggled as she checked the photo. 'Sajangnim, your eyes always light up when you're talking about photography.'

Seokyeong shrugged. Meanwhile, Bell, tired of modelling, had sat down for a good scratch. From his pocket, Seokyeong took out a piece of beef jerky and threw it towards her. She sprang up, caught it in mid-air and then licked her nose with her long pink tongue.

'In basketball, some players throw their fist in the air right after the ball leaves their hand. Because they know from that moment that they're going to score. It's similar for photographers. Even before you press the shutter, you know if a photo is going to be great. That feeling is amazing. Jebi-ya, do you know this word – yeolhwa?'

'No.'

'Yeolhwa means white-hot fire. Sometimes when I take photos, I can feel an intense heat inside me, as though my heart is in flames. How about you, Jebi?'

'What do you mean?' Jebi scuffed the ground with her shoe, looking a little sulky.

'Have you ever felt that passionate about something?'

*

It was evening and Jebi lay in bed, her phone in her hand. It'd been an hour since she had first looked up the number on her contact list, hovering her thumb over the call button before exiting the screen, only to repeat the process again.

She glanced at the small photo taped next to her window – the one that had been published in the magazine.

'The worst that can happen is that you're told no,' she muttered to herself.

Jebi sat up, clutching her T-shirt anxiously. With a shaking hand, she tapped the call button, feeling her heart lodged in her throat.

After a short connecting tone, someone answered. 'Jebi-ssi! How have you been?'

The friendly voice gave Jebi a little more courage.

'Yes, I'm good . . . Is she well?' Jebi fumbled, switching the phone to her other ear.

'I visited her just last week. We always check in at least once, seeing as how there have been a few cases . . . Oh, nothing that you should be worried about, Jebi-ssi,' said the person with an awkward laugh.

Not knowing what to say, Jebi, too, forced a laugh.

'It's great you called. I was going to reach out to you. The mother said it'd be okay for you to visit her. They've made up their mind to do an open adoption.'

'An open adoption?' Jebi's heart quivered. Immediately, she fretted that Chestnut would be teased by her friends in the future.

The voice on the line continued brightly. 'She wants the child to know her birth mother. You're the person who gave her life, after all. She'd like you to meet the child.'

Jebi kept quiet. Her face burned in shame. *Her adoptive mum has a bigger heart than me.*

With such parents, she had no doubt that Chestnut would grow up happy and resilient.

'Oh, and they've given her a name. It's Sarang – love.'

Sarang . . . Jebi repeated the name silently to herself. A little cheesy, but it wasn't bad.

'Anyway, is there something you wanted to talk to me about?'

'Oh.' Jebi swallowed hard. 'I . . . I was wondering if you could send me a photo. I don't want to overstep, but she must've grown quite a bit since . . .'

'Of course! She's much bigger now! She's potty-trained, and you should see the way she runs around. What a bright and chatty child! With a good appetite and the loveliest laugh. I'll ask Sarang's mother for one.'

Jebi drew a sharp breath. Before she even realised it, tears were running down her cheeks. *Sarang's mother* – the two words clawed a deep gash in her heart.

'I'm sorry Jebi-ssi, I didn't mean . . .'

'No, it's okay, Director. Don't apologise,' Jebi quickly said.

'You are both her mother, and always will be,' the orphanage director added kindly. 'There's no need to worry. And remember to live your life well.'

'Thank you.' With that, she hung up.

My baby is with her real mum now.

Pulling the quilt over her, Jebi bawled into her pillow. And in that moment she resolved to live an honest, upright, brave life, so that her child would never be ashamed of her.

Mulling over her next steps, it was only much later that she finally drifted off to sleep.

The following morning, the first thing Jebi did was to take a shower. Sitting in her room in a towel, she checked her balance in her banking app. Then she downloaded an investment app and put half of her savings into a portfolio of travel agencies.

If ever Sarang needs money, I want to be the person who can help her.

And then, opening a browser, she read up on different types of surfboards and their prices.

A month later, her board arrived via international courier. From then on, Jebi went to the sea every Wednesday, on her day off. After warming up, she'd try out the tips she learnt on YouTube, ignoring the haenyeos' laughter whenever they saw Jebi attempting to stand on the board.

'You need to go deep if you want to earn any money! What's the point of bobbing about on the surface?'

After helping the haenyeos lift their heavy nets, Seokyeong sat by the sea with Yanghee, sipping hot roasted barley tea.

'Mokpo Samchon told me that haenyeos are hungriest when they've just surfaced after a dive,' he said, as he tried to feed her a homemade rice ball with top shell marinated in soy sauce.

'I-I can eat it by myself.'

Conscious of the other haenyeos chatting not far off, she fended him off, before taking a rice ball from the dorisak lunch box between them and popped it into her mouth. To prevent stomach pain during their dives, haenyeos usually skipped two meals in a row on days when they went out to the sea, so they were always famished when they returned to shore. The fragrant taste of the warm rice ball spread over her tongue, and she closed her eyes to savour it. And because she hadn't had a sip of water since daybreak, the roasted barley tea seemed sweeter than anything she'd ever tasted.

'Are you going to come here every day?' Yanghee asked, keeping her face turned away from him. She didn't want Seokyeong to see her swollen cheeks and the deep goggle marks around her eyes.

'If you'll let me.' He uncapped the thermal flask and refilled her empty cup.

'You're doing this because you want to be koendang, someone tied to the village, right?'

Seokyeong's hand paused in mid-air.

Without waiting for an answer, she continued. 'Then you're making a mistake . . . people can get divorced, you know.'

Lowering the flask, Seokyeong took a deep breath, and said, 'It's true that I approached you because I want to be koendang.'

Yanghee gave a hollow laugh, her suspicions proven correct. She combed her wet hair back with her fingers and got up. Water droplets rolled down her wetsuit.

But before she could take a step, Seokyeong grabbed her hand and looked up at her. 'But I only want to be your koendang.'

Yanghee flung his hand away. 'I've already had one failed marriage, and I have no wish for a second. And this time round, I really have nowhere else to go.'

'You are not going to fail,' Seokyeong said, firmly.

Yanghee shook her head. 'That's something only those who have never failed would say.'

Seokyeong got up. In the shallow waters, Jebi was floundering on her surfboard. He'd seen her try to catch a wave, step on the board and slip off the next moment at least a hundred times. Almost automatically he held up the camera he'd left hanging around his neck and pressed the shutter several times in quick succession. 'In the evolution from film to digital photography, one key change is that people have started to care less about failure. On a digital camera, you can take as many shots as you want, see how they turn out, and delete the unsatisfactory ones on the spot. I started learning photography around the time digital photography was getting popular. I remember taking many, many photos at one particular shoot, and then finding when I loaded them onto a computer back at home that there was not a single one I was happy with.' He looked at Yanghee to make sure she was listening. 'I thought at the time that the whole shoot was a failure. But a few years passed, and when I happened to look at the photos again, suddenly, they didn't seem half so bad. The messy composition, the overexposure, gave them a freshness, a beauty. I remember thinking, "Oh, I was actually pretty decent back then too. I'll never be able to recreate shots like these."'

'I hate this – you'll never convince me to romanticise failure.'

Seokyeong let out a soft sigh. 'I could avoid failure by never touching a camera at all. But could I call myself a photographer then?'

With his eye to the viewfinder once more, Seokyeong snapped another few shots of Jebi.

'Hey! Stop it! Can't you just wait until I can stand on the board!' Jebi yelled up the beach at him, her voice cracking from exhaustion.

The tension dissolved and Yanghee felt a tickle of laughter well up in her. She tried her best to suppress it, but it was impossible. Turning away from Seokyeong, she laughed and laughed until she had to wipe away the tears. Then she turned back, cupped her hands around her mouth and shouted to Jebi.

'Why? Learning? Surfing?'

'Instinct!' Jebi shouted back. 'This summer! Customers will come! To take surfing photos!'

Lying on the board, she waited for the next wave. Like a skirt billowing in the wind, the wave began to swell. Not wanting to mistime it, Jebi paddled hard and, at just the right moment, she pushed herself up so that she was standing on the board. Her legs wobbled but this time, she didn't fall.

For a few seconds, she rode the wave.

One day, that customer will come.

Jebi gritted her teeth. When that day arrived, she'd teach them how to surf. How to swim, how to dive, how to read the waves.

She looked up at the sky. Amid fluffy clouds, the sun shone brightly. And then, out of nowhere, a great gust of wind blew in and a new wave surged. Jebi found her balance on the board. 'Ahhh!' she cried out, as the wave carried her up into the air.

Author's Note

I was nine when I moved to Jeju Island, and I lived there until I was eleven.

The language, the environment, everything was unfamiliar. I remember feeling very scared. But I soon made friends. I started picking up the dialect and joining my new friends playing in the sea. We picked top shells and foraged for barnacles along the basalt coast. In the afternoon, the ajusshis would come to the coast to pick up their haenyeo wives after they had finished their work for the day. They'd hoist their tewaks, with the heavy nets filled with an assortment of conches and abalones, onto their tractors or motorbikes and return home . . .

I still remember my neighbours. The people of Jeju were always busy, working out at sea, on the farms and at home. Yet everyone was friendly and shared their time (and snacks) generously with us neighbourhood kids. When I think back to those times, the Jeju that comes to mind is always sunny and warm. The shimmering waters, the fluffy clouds above the horizon, the breathtaking landscape.

Hakuda Photo Studio is my love letter to the island, the home I love and miss very much. The Giant Octopus village is a fictional village, but I have referenced real places and sights in Jeju. I hope that this book will offer some comfort from the daily grind, and encourage people to reflect on their lives and create new memories. Welcoming readers to the village feels as though I'm inviting guests over to a house I've built. I imagine people stepping into Hakuda Photo Studio to look at the framed photos in the gallery, taking a walk around the village, and snapping photos of the beautiful sand dunes by the coast.

Dear reader, thank you for picking up this book. I hope it brings you joy, and that your days are filled with peace and good health.

Acknowledgements

Writing novels and publishing them has taught me a lot about the nature of stories. This book is the result of so many people's time, care and creativity. I want to thank everyone who helped to bring it into existence.

To Kim Sunsik, CEO of Dasan Books, who gave me the opportunity to publish my second novel. To Lim Kyungseop, for your excellent and incisive planning and editorial insights. Thanks to you, working on the book was a joy. To Lee Hyeonmi, thank you for the beautiful cover illustration, and for helping me with the Jeju dialect when it was on the tip of my tongue. Thank you to Song Yoonhyoung and everyone at Dasan Books.

And to my husband, who read and gave me feedback each time I finished a scene. You're a pillar of support to me. And Hai, my beautiful daughter, I love you!

Her Taeyeon, 2022

Note: The following research paper was an excellent reference for Chapter 10: 'Geology and Volcanic Activities of Wollabong-Gunsan, the Oldest Twin Volcanoes in Jeju Island', Koh, Gi Won et al., *Journal of the Geological Society of Korea* (2021), 57(2), 141–64.